A Gang of Outsiders

A Gang of Outsiders

Stories

Bobby Williams

atmosphere press

"If you wanted to do something absolutely honest, something true, it always turned out to be a thing that had to be done alone."

-Richard Yates

Contents

Public Access

"Okay my dear Fitz, just onnnne more . . . *good*. Now, let's see how this peach number works for ya." And so, Louie Gloria snapped a final photo before removing the mauve smoking jacket with blood-red seams from his headless, legless mannequin friend—thus stripping Fitz bare, down to his ivory, Davidian midsection. Louie hangs the smoker on a coat rack previously positioned next to Fitz in the front yard. A relatively mild winter in Upstate New York gives the impression of late March in early February, snow has commenced its yearly concession to the yard's ugly, muddy underbelly that sticks in gobs to the bottoms of Louie's white tennis shoes as he circles the mannequin. Similar surrounding homes are seen easily between empty tree limbs alight in the impotent sun—no skiing, no swimming.

Louie Gloria, marketing magician, *ad man* extraordinaire, sees not seasonal purgatory but an opportunity to make a quick buck: he is fully aware that the time for acceptable jacketed indoor cigar smoking is about up; he's also heard whispers that radiant seamstry will fall out of favor next season and give way to a smoother seamless look more metaphorically aligned with the culture of jacketed indoor smoking.

The peach polo now modeled by Fitz was originally

purchased for Louie Gloria's son, Rock Starr Gloria, who noted, "This color is *so* fuckin' gay, Louie," then balled and backhandedly threw the peach number at the kitchen garbage can. Louie had long since been distressed by Rock Starr's use of homophobic slurs and so confronted the associate head of the local golden-banistered boys' school.

"They're all boys. It's kind of their *thing* . . . you know? Anyway, at Rock Starr's age the responsibility for that kind of . . . *thing* . . . falls on the parents, or . . . *parent*, in your case."

"What about all that 'honesty, tolerance, and integrity'?" Louie said to the associate head of school.

"Hmmm, I'm seeing a pattern here," the associate head sips coffee, "the line you are referring to, surely from our online brochure, talks about our *educators* leading by *example*. We cannot force students to *follow* that example."

"So it's just bullshit?"

"Is this about your wife, Mister Gloria?"

"Do you feel gay, Fitz?" Louie asks the mannequin who certainly seems a happy peach. As predicted by Gloria, the shirt radiates enticing spring fruits when pit against the dreary background. To purchase this color of polo in early February demonstrates optimistic commitment to an early spring no matter the rodent forecast. Louie flips the shirt's collar down with great care, irons out some wrinkles in the abs region with the moisture in his palms, takes two steps back and begins photographing the mannequin in this second outfit—like after the jacketed cigar, a tennis match is in order.

Louis shoots directly from the front at eye-level (if Fitz

had eyes, that is, or even a head to put them in) three pics—click-click-click, just like that, quickly and clearly practiced, maybe like a surgeon, or at the very least like a man who'd sold a few *other* outfits online. Louie squats down and takes three more pictures from an upward facing angle to give the impression of powerful manliness, counteracting the allegedly effeminate color. Satisfied, Louie circles around to the back of Fitz, shooting the side aspect on his way, and from the back he repeats the standing-squatting picture process.

Louie approaches Fitz again, flips the collar up now, and whispers, "You can never tell what people might be into," at the vacant area above the mannequin's shoulders, now occupied by the odd collar. He photographs this more pompous version of Fitz at a much closer distance to suit the likely punctilious nature of a man who'd prefer his collar this way.

"YO LEWAAAYYYYY!"

Louie's younger neighbors Michael and Linda Coleman release their Saint Bernard onto Louie's muddy lawn and follow up the front walk. They always look like they'd just finished a deep bottle of red by the fire, handholding on some super expensive carpet and all that. These are people that say they communicate without words, or, you know, 'We always know *exactly* what the other is thinking,' but if you were to ever witness this telepathic interaction it'd look more like two people about to say the kindest things while making love. Michael fumbles through the muck, clutching at the ass of his fluttering fairy dust smile of a wife—Apollo and Daphne, with dog.

"C'mon how much, how much?" Michael asks, pointing at Fitz's peach polo.

"For you, twenty-five. I paid fifty for it," replies Louie.

"Do I have to wear the collar up?" Asks Michael, shaking Louie's hand.

"Hello, Linda," says Louie, quickly forgetting Michael.

"Hi, Louie," answers Linda, her smile aware of its place in neighborhood lure. Her summer runs are the rural equivalent of seventies appointment television. It is no coincidence that the men of *Timber Creek* do their gardening and lawn work Sundays at 8:15am . . . 8:17am . . . 8:21am et cetera, respectively. She returns every drooling stare with that smile and wave. Linda is not quite self-absorbed enough to realize they're all checking out her ass.

"What's up for tonight, Lou? Comin' to this Cabin Fever thing or what?"

"I'm not sure—Rock and I are supposed to work on the derby car."

"*Shit* man, the big race, is it that time of year again already?"

"Oh yeah."

"What'd you guys get last year?"

"Second."

"Not bad, you're doing better then?"

"We're not worse."

"It must be hard without Grace around," offers Linda.

"*Jesus*, Linda, he doesn't want to talk about that."

"It's fine, Mike. She's supposed to at least come up for a visit this summer, said she might even check in at the race in a few weeks. It was always kind of, uhhh, tradition, ya know? Dinner afterwards . . . get some cocktails . . ." Gloria's voice and gaze drift toward the boring sky, color of spent ash.

"That's great," Mike and Linda answer in unison—they say it in a way that can't hide the latent doubtful nature of the statement—in a way that speaks more to pride in their own domestic bliss and makes Gloria aware of his not being 'great' at all—in a way that really asks, 'dear *God* what must that be like,' and answers 'thank *God* that's not us.' Now all three release eye contact and betray the hidden longing to end these neighborly pleasantries. Louie's gaze settles unfortunately on Fitz, who has no gaze to accommodate him. The Saint Bernard eats snow at the base of the mannequin, then takes a step and lifts his giant leg to pee on the iron rod that extends from the base of Fitz's torso into the muddy snow.

"Basho!" Linda shouts, running after him. She laughs while yelling, "Bad boy," at the poor pup and the cute chase provides an opportune exit for Mike who takes off down the walk toward his own home across the street, encouraging the dog, "Basho! Come on buddy. Yo, Lou, maybe we'll see you later on tonight?"

Louie waves goodbye to his neighbors, smiling as all three sprint like hellfire from his lawn. He yanks the peach-poloed mannequin Fitz out of the earth and brings him into the house, reminding him on the way, "Yes, Fitz, you never can tell what someone might be into."

Cabin Fever Dance At The Historical Women's Club, 725 Madison Avenue.

Saturday February 4th 8-11 with a free hour-long dance demo with Herschel Allen from 7-8. Tickets will be sold at the door: $12 for HWC members and $15 for the public, singles welcome. Come have some fun and dance away those winter blues!

Louie Gloria sh-sh...sh-sh-shimmies his toweled body from the master bath into the bedroom, strokes at his salt and pepper mustache while singing along, "YOU COULD HAVE A *STEAM* TRAIN, IF YOU'D JUST. . . LAY . . . DOWN . . . YOUR TRACKS." He enjoyed two cocktails while eating dinner in front of the television where he tested his brainpower against the night's *Jeopardy!* contestants:

"*This* irksome sensory experience has recently been linked to pain."

"What is, *an itch*," answered Louie.

He enjoys the program so much these days that he sports a mustache in homage to its host, who by the way he faintly resembles, though Louie is wider and less pampered looking, a rugged Trebek, a guy who'd seen long nights transition into early mornings where he'd wrestle the rising sun without ever shutting his eyes, a man alone, grizzled and dark, occupying pub corners. And now like so many other youngish retirees stuck Upstate, Louie Gloria often pictures himself playing guitar, writing a book, or dominating *Jeopardy!* "So...Louie," the host approaches him last, at the far end of the tri-podium arrangement, "our returning champion." Louie bows slightly in respect to the host as he scans the audience for the proud, smiling faces of his family, "I see here that you invented the split screen paper towel absorption comparison test." The crowd chuckles, delighted by this mid-segment tidbit, "Yes Alex, that's correct," he imagines a modest response when asked to quickly explain the history of this transcendent bit of visual stimuli, "I'm just a former ad man who happened to spill a beer one day and run out of one paper towel brand in the middle of wiping, and finished cleaning with what was clearly a vastly superior brand of towel—I thought, people need to see this." A casual laugh from the host, "*Wonderful,*" and more respectful nodding from the challengers complete his fantasy before returning to finish the Jeopardy round.

Louie trims his mustache just under the nose with a shiny straightedge razor. He stretches his top lip way down over his teeth as he stares into the mirror. With the razor-sharp mustache, slicked back hair, and tuxedo, Gloria looks like a guy you'd expect to see smoking a lot of cigars, like a guy you just know was the coolest in the seventies but didn't necessarily peak there—it always seems appropriate for him to be casually leaning against something.

The Historical Women's Club of Albany, New York is a three-floored Victorian that would look more appropriate in Georgia. It's pretty clear someone's been keeping an eye on the shrubbery, some of which actually appears in bloom. Flowers explode from lingering snow like fruity pebbles in a white bowl. Above the flower patch, a white front porch demands yellow lemonade and wicker rocking chairs with flakey lacquer paint to be rocked to the rhythm of a gorgeous soprano songbird whose voice flies from the gramophone that rests on the wide front railing.

Louie Gloria leans against a great white supporting column puffing the cigar he'd started on the solitary ride over. His right foot is crossed over the left, he tells all the passing ladies "Evening," just before they enter the Victorian. He pretends not to notice or care when they take a second look back at the refined man.

Just before seven, Louie goes inside to check the free dance demo with Herschel Allen. Herschel Allen's kiddy tux shines with the gloss of a recently renewed rental, a thirty-year-old man attending his first prom, desperate for his first hand job. He doesn't seem nervous, exactly, more anxious, ready to dance, desperate to dance; sweat pours over patches of adult acne that pop from his pale eggshell skin—he pulls and pulls at the bottom of his black vest while waiting for people to take one of a hundred surrounding folding chairs positioned at the absolute edge of the ballroom.

As the demo begins, it's instantly clear that Herschel Allen has given little or no consideration to the age of his audience. It's not that his moves are too sexy or age-inappropriate by way of being lascivious, but that they are grotesquely athletic. The terrific bending and spinning contortions torture the aging onlookers as Allen glides his demo partner across the floor. A dipping motion that seems to be Herschel Allen's signature maneuver punctuates each set of steps and likely takes years of yoga training to achieve. He dips the partner up and down and up and down with the frequency and rapidity of an elementary school seesaw at high noon, "Just like this," he keeps saying in between breaths/dips, "See," more breathing/dipping, "You see . . . now just take your partner like this," his awkwardness results in an utter inability to teach that manifests for the hour as less of a demo and more of a cruel exercise that illuminates the mortality of his audience.

The historical women are nonetheless impressed; "Oohs" and "Aahs" echo throughout the gaping ballroom and pair nicely with the sound Allen's swooshing steps make with the dance floor. A chorus of bobbing heads nod to each of Herschel's dips, the wood paneling and chandelier light cultivate a cruise ship aura adrift after fried buffet—all that spinning, all that lolling about, vomit or worse on the horizon.

"Come *ON* now," Herschel waves his right hand, dipping his partner with the left, "you try," he breathes, imploring all onto the floor.

Louie Gloria heads instead to the bar for a cocktail. He turns to observe the dance floor but instead locks eyes with a woman in leopard print. She'd been stalking him.

"I've missed you, Louie," Martha Vineyard whispers, "Vodka Martini, shaken with a twist," she tells the bartender.

"Hello Martha, how are you," Louie hugs her, kisses both cheeks and concentrates on the way her breasts press against him. Martha's body doesn't curve so much as it protrudes. Louie has always admired her breasts and the fact that she's confident enough to show them off—full and round and soft like her painted lips. She obsesses over her eyelashes, always flicking and miniature combing with that stick that leaves them black and stiff and not really all that much longer. These lashes strike a dark and Halloweenish contrast to her neon orange hair that contributes to her radiant sexuality.

"I asked Linda *Coleman* if you'd be here, if she'd even *seen* you, she told me you weren't coming . . ."

"Yeah well you . . ."

"Said something about a rally car and Rock Starr, I didn't know *what* the hell she was saying. I *love* that tux on you."

"That's because you're not a good listener Martha, and thanks," Louie says, smiling.

"Yes, well, I've always preferred to be listened to."

"So I've heard."

"You should have listened to me about Grace, Louie," says Martha, ignoring the joke. A dense thud sounds from the dance floor. Followed by nervous laughter and many people saying, "She's okay."

"They're all trying to do his dance," mentions Louie.

"Don't try to change the fucking subject on me; you're *always* changing the subject."

"I was just mentioning . . ."

"Where is she?"

"Who?"

"Don't *fuck* with me Louie, where'd she go?"

"I don't really know. I got a letter from a lawyer in Miami."

"What are you gonna do? I know some really good people in New York."

"I just need to talk to her . . ."

"She's not coming back Louie."

"Well . . ."

"Look at me, Louie," Martha jabbed her thick, red fingernails into his cheeks, turning his face to hers, "she's *never* coming back, she didn't want a kid with you, like I said . . . she's not out *finding* herself—she's a loser, Louie."

"She's beautiful."

"I'm beautiful."

"Yes you are."

"Why don't you let me move in and help you with Rock Starr?"

"I don't need help with him," Louie laughs.

"Where's he now?"

"Studying with his friends."

"And you *believe* that?"

"I've been getting on him about his schoolwork."

"Bull-*shit*, he's out doing whatever he wants Louie, you *let* him do whatever he wants—it's like you and Grace think he's this angel just because he's so damn handsome. I'll tell you, he's an entitled brat who thinks he's had a hard life. For Chrissake Lou, you let him pick his own name."

"That was Grace's idea."

"And we all know what a dumb bitch she is, don't we?"

"Jesus, Martha."

"Let me come over tonight, Louie. I miss you," Martha plays with the tip of Louie's bowtie and says "Please," blinking the crusty eyelashes at him, pushing the breasts and lips into his face, "I've been feeling this *itch*. I *think* about you Louie—Don't you ever feel that itch?"

"You know, Martha, an itch is related to pain."

Monthly Breakfast Buffet and Omelet Station 45 N. Mohawk Street Cohoes-Waterford Elks Lodge 1317.

Sunday February 5th 9am to Noon. Come to The Elks in your Sunday best and eat bacon with your neighbors. Hagar Andersen will cook omelets to your liking all morning. Elks care, Elks share.

"What about the guns?"

"What guns?"

"All your *guns* Louie, we're going hunting, aren't we?"

"Why would we be going hunting, Rock?"

"The *Elks* club . . ." applies finger antlers to head, "is a hunting club, isn't it?"

Louie laughs, "It's just a spot where guys from the neighborhood get together and talk about improving the community."

"That sounds puh-*ritty* gay," he pauses, "but you, like, have to kill stuff to get into the club, right?"

"You have to be twenty-one and believe in God to join."

"So, we're just gonna eat and that's it?"

"We can go to the store and grab some stuff to start painting the car afterward if you want? It's about done . . . was saving the final touches for you."

Rock Starr releases an 'hmph' noise from his nose and goes back to pushing the radio buttons in Louie's car—one three and five the same station, two four and six dedicated to one other station, "What the fuck, Louie?"

"Hey."

"They're all the same. There's only two stations."

"Well, there are *many* stations, but I . . ."

"This one is AM, it's fucking talk."

"Music to my ears," Louie turns up the radio. The sun burns through the windshield and onto his face but is unable to penetrate his mirrored aviator shades that coolly conceal a nagging Catholic hangover. The worn-out landscape peels across Louie's lenses while he drives— gutter-gray side streets fester with new weeds that reach at the car for attention. The squat, three-story buildings that hide neighborhood residents are wilting, like the weeds, they can be seen swaying in the breeze, they are cracked, chipped, cruddy, dusty, yucky, rundown, haggard and cold, with whole runs of siding missing and A/C units inexplicably jutting out from murky windows housed inside shit windowsills. Cherry Pie people in Sunday sweatpants stare up at the sky, maybe they're waiting for the sun to rise to its position at pulpit. They peck-peck, peck-peck their way along concrete sidewalks past muffler repair shops, Wendy's, a misplaced jewelry store—great sweeping gusts of chilly, pickled smoke billow from the Burger King's chimney. The loafer's coats are thin and raggedy, stained dark and ill-suited in the bitter morning air; they blow stale breath into praying hands, put them back into their pockets.

Louie made this same drive exactly one year ago. The whole damn town sticks in place like a memory buried in the recesses of one's mind, waiting around to be foraged by some other chance happening. He's part of it now, one of the stuck. He and Grace left the busy city to come to this world of stagnant lingering, of waiting for nothing in particular, the next day, the next season, "the sun to take its place at pulpit," but who even knows what that is? Or when that might be? He felt Grace's parents lived like two mannequins in a front window watching and waiting for Louie to bring their daughter back to watch them die, "They didn't really show affection, and we didn't have much money—but we always *survived*," Grace said of them. Surviving had been a given to Louie Gloria: what a bullshit saying, nothing he could ever admire. He knew immediately that they'd come to the wrong place. Her parents and the rest of the wearisome town woke up each day wanting to survive. He couldn't get over it. With each sun they prayed for one magical instant that might make their life worth living—and then the story of that one moment would serve to define their entire time. Grace was that special thing for a lot of people and most of all Louie, but he wanted, and had, even more than just her—a full and meaningful life made more so by her presence. Her parents stilted without her around, just waiting, they moved about seeking the lowest common denominator of goals, the dream of dying a natural death.

Louie asked himself why, Louie *had* been asking why for weeks and now (many) months—why he came and why he now stayed. The feeling he had watching her round feet walk the morning carpet to bring him a cup of coffee—that peace and tranquility and stability she said they'd find here, the land of pools and driveways and cars, cars to go everywhere with little or no traffic, waving to neighbors who also have pools and know your name and what your children want to be when they grow up and have stone countertops and know the name of the wood their floors are made from and also walk *their* dog at the same set of shaded trails and talk about that good wallpaper guy and specific cabinetry during a break by a stream where the dogs lap up the clean water—her legs in those shorts, no edges but all flowing curves, smooth valleys of splendid flesh like polished porcelain—his delicate Grace, a bubbling torrent of sweetness.

The move to stability brought boredom instead—eating and drinking and eating and sleeping and eating at the same three places. Freezing cold winters, numb leftovers from the in-law's funeral. All their friends running here and there with their kids, too tired to ever go out on a Wednesday. 'Why don't you have kids,' they'd always ask. We met too late— "Oh," they'd reply with the same downcast eyes seen for generations by those perceived by others as unfortunate.

And so they got a kid, a family of their own—a real family with a son. But months and months of credit/background checks do not substitute for passionate, purposeful lovemaking. Pictures of preteens stapled to an application do not provide the same shared experience as hand-held glimpses at life on an ultrasound and while it may have felt like a miracle when they finally went to pick up Grace's "favorite one" from a nondescript brick building three towns away, the action was in truth just another errand that did not involve real tears or a nursing infant or all those folks smiling in their hospital scrubs. And somewhere during the constant effort to bring the mean and spoiled boy happiness they'd forgotten their own. Her feet now pounded the carpet, no giggles, dusty carpets, slumped shoulders. She stopped whispering her little non-secrets, '*Hey...Louie*, do you want me to get up and make you scrambled eggs,' or something silly like that. She'd say it like the fate of the world depended on no one else hearing the statement but Louie, like she was making the sweetest drug deal on earth. In many ways these things were drugs to Louie and so he started having withdrawals. The lighthearted observation "You're drinking," shifted to the identifying character flaw, "Your drinking." He was stuck, a shivering junkie alone in this stagnant corner.

"Louie . . ."

". . ."

"YO, Louie, you alive?"

"Yeah buddy?"

"You think they're gonna have jalapeños?"

"You *love* jalapeños."

"So do you."

"Yes, I do too," said Louie, "they're on *fucking* fiiiiiyerrrrr, yeah."

"HEY, I thought we weren't gonna say fuck anymore."

"We're trying."

The Benevolent and Protective Order of Elks (Cohoes-Waterford) Lodge is set back one hundred yards from the main drag and sits on top of a hill overlooking the Hudson River. That's not to say it's some majestic architectural highpoint; it is a *lodge*, it's a wart that should be steamrolled yet lingers for reasons related to Native American virtue. Back when shipping mattered, this Cohoes-Waterford region served as a major port, ask anyone wandering around about the Eerie Canal, they'll tell ya. The empty docks and yards are still crowded with rusty, decayed equipment that makes a good playground by day and safe haven for junkies howling at the moon.

Elk members and visitors are greeted by a white sign with big black letters "Cohoes-Waterford ELKS BPOE 1317" that stands threateningly in its plainness. The parking lot is too large—it's like a big, black concrete football field that makes the club itself look like a concession stand. In the days of the port, they needed that much space. Back then the fifteen cars here for the breakfast buffet would have been hammered stragglers from the roaring evening before instead of this disappointing turnout for a lame morning activity. An elk head attached to a central green awning sizes up all entrants from a position of power.

Louie and Rock Starr pause in the foyer by a small table with a shiny silverware set for one: white cloth napkin, empty wine glass, empty water glass, bare plate, vacant seat. This table honors the POW/MIA Elks. Above the table is another elk head looking down at the arrangement, appropriately stern. Rock Starr is silent and uncomfortable; he stands with his hands clasped in front like he's arrived at an impromptu wake. The air in the foyer is thick, and while it doesn't *smell* exactly, it definitely feels polluted by bodies.

Louie leads Rock through the barroom. The bar serves seven seats that point at a centrally located television. An orbit of twelve glossy card tables with green lamps cling to the gravity of the central bar. Just like the foyer, these tables are unoccupied, relics in a museum. Louie is overcome by the undeniable presence of an era gone by each time he moves through the room. He's haunted by echoes of shouting and laughter from all the late-night card games. Louie sits with a herd of suited Elks who cockily show flushes and sweep great sums of ale-soaked cash to their bellies, heaving at fat cigars lit by the burning fires of industry smoke that rise like an army of specters from the moonlit shipping yards along the Hudson. A record player behind the bar sings sweetly to the smoke as it weaves between the wispy hairs flailing from their stately, bald heads—*these* men are proud to be here at the Elks, here in Cohoes-Waterford. They'll walk home with those smoldering cigars jammed into the corner of their half-cocked smiles, heroically wobbling, footprints of the American dream fading with every step.

Sunlight from the dining room reaches through a door at the back of the bar and with it wafts of breakfast buffet (with omelet station) that beckons Louie and Rock Starr, salivating. A few men turn to nod at Louie as he enters. Lou and Rock grab two plates and head directly for the buffet. Louie goes first and is careful to leave a semicircular area at the top half of his plate free to accept an impending omelet. He peers to the very end of the buffet to confirm Hagar Andersen has taken his post. And yes indeed, he has. Louie is also glad to notice that Hagar is wearing a very tall white cap.

"You see that," he says to Rock Starr, as he tongs massive portions of bacon and sausage onto his plate.

"What?" Rock Starr asks, barely listening, tonging some sausage of his own.

"Mister Andersen there is wearing a toque blanche."

"What?"

"He's wearing a *toque* Rock, means he's probably an actual chef, not some asshole on loan from the Burger King."

"I like the Burger King."

"You're not even listening," the two continue with the tonging—pancakes, waffle, bits of fruit, looking down as they talk like cheating students trying to avoid detection.

"I just wanna *eat*."

"Ahck," says Louie, "people just can't appreciate the

gifts they're given," his voice trails off at the end, he tongs a piece of ham and cheese quiche so violently that it splits in half. The pieces crumble back onto the heated platter, lying abstractly atop the otherwise intact quiche. Louie leaves the tongs on the table and moves toward Hagar Andersen, "Hello, *Chef*," he says. Andersen grips a spatula, lifeless eyes await details of the next omelet. From his powdery skin and see-through irises, Louie predicts the chef is hiding albino blonde hair. The toque mushes folds of forehead over his eyebrows—Andersen is clearly trying to hide those eyes, the only visible bits of the chef that *should* be so white are instead blood red.

The word, "Ya," burps from between Andersen's lips.

"How ya doin' there chef?" Louie asks with a sympathetic and understanding wink.

The chef chuckles at the wink but lurches forward and makes an alarming noise like, "*Urrumph*," which forces Louie backward because it seems that Chef Andersen might vomit. But instead the chef rights himself and asks, "What, uhh would you having, want in the omelet?"

"I'll let you do your thing *chef*, I respect the craft . . . all that I ask is that you use three eggs and include jalapeños in some way."

"I don't have jalapeños," he tells Louie.

"Hmmuhhh-what?" Louie asks.

"No jalapeños, guy."

"Guy?" Louie asks.

Louie inches closer to Andersen, so close his feet tuck beneath the white tablecloth. His belt presses the table itself and even right above the pungent omelet station he can sniff the shit stench of cheap vodka seeping from Hagar's chalky pores. "Listen you alcoholic piece of shit,"

Louie begins, "me and my kid want some *smoking . . . hot . . .* jalapeños in our omelets and you're gonna give 'em to us."

"Sir," Andersen begins, now realizing this is a serious man he's dealing with, "I can fry up some bell peppers with garlic, onion, and cayenne pepper for you. It'll be hot, spicy, I can make it hot, but I can't have jalapeños because the seeds, they get everywhere, into other omelets, you know?"

"I can appreciate that."

"No jalapeños?" Rock Starr interjects. Andersen looks like he's going to cry, like he had way bigger culinary life plans and that all of those plans are washing away in these exact tears of realization—but to be fair, it could just be the onion he's slicing.

"He's gonna make something special for us Rock, calm down."

"This is fucking *bullshit.*"

Andersen stares down at his spatula and remembers how close he was to buying jalapeños at the market this morning. He's crying, it's now clear to Louie.

"All I wanted was some fucking jalapeño om—" Louie jerks Rock Starr away from the table by his elbow and relates the likely depressing details concerning the life of Chef Hagar Andersen; who serves morning meals to people who think fifteen dollars is an obscenely expensive entrée, who doesn't live with his parents but borrows rent money from them, who thinks more about masturbation than prospective meals, who would never want any girl to see the state of his furniture and who is surely spending this Sunday at the jalapeñoless omelet station of the Cohoes-Waterford Elks. Louie convinces Rock Starr to settle for the bell pepper/cayenne blend.

At the table they both know it's not the same.

"Still good," Louie says to Rock Starr's muted face before becoming distracted by a pregnant mom wheeling a fancy, navy-blue stroller across the room. She wheels up to a table that already has one stroller parked next to it. A different pregnant woman gets up from behind a stacked plate to greet her. The men responsible for all this bountiful life shake hands and smile. Neither man has a mustache or any facial hair to speak of at all. They've got on a matching uniform of gray crewneck sweatshirt and denim pants that recall the word dungarees. It is also unlikely that either of them ever wears sunglasses for style. They just sit there plain-faced and let their bloated man-bellies boast a certain pride in the power of sperm.

The ladies pose for phone-pictures together, their lively lady-bellies hang over stroller handles. They make kissing faces and point their hips forth for the men's phone-cameras. Now they move in front of the buffet procession, plugging up the whole damn works for this phone photoshoot. Louie is upset by the phone-photographers' inability to take advantage of the room's natural lighting. The women stand there with happy hands cupping stomachs in front of the tables of food with the light shining onto their backs. The light makes it easy to see millions of kitty hairs poking electrically from the lady on the left's inappropriate Christmas sweater. The guys look through their phones at the women now standing back to back to show the proud protrusions in profile. They turn their heads to face the camera as a traffic jam of hungry citizens begins to pile up—they're standing in front of the bacon and the pancakes and the waffles and the sausage and part of the fruit and so it is impossible for those in limbo to simply go around. Finally they unite the two bellies; the jam of folks believes this pose to be a clear finale, and the belief is reinforced by the satisfaction this pose gives the women, whose laughter probably reaches all the way back into the barroom and disturbs the ghosts trying to concentrate on their card game. It certainly disturbs Louie—not just the laughing and crap photography. People in line yawn and stretch in anticipation of a clearing, but instead, puzzlingly, the ladies turn around and point their derrières at the phone-cameras. They bend down even further than you're imagining and stay like that longer than you would believe; it's as if they're airing out for the entire world to see, no one can make heads or tails of it. Distressed citizens contemplate starvation. The men continue push-push-push-pushing their phones like toddlers do at mom's nose until the women finally turn around to (surprise!) display one plate brimming with bacon and the other stacked with sausage. They rest the plates on the bellies and laugh with such ebullience that those waiting for bacon and sausage are terrified of a double spill. Louie contemplates potential titles for this last picture and settles on, "Meat," or "Cannibal's Last Meal." He puts his sunglasses back on and wryly smiles at Rock Starr, who is examining the elk heads.

"Are you *sure* you guys aren't out hunting all the time?"

"We don't shoot them our-*selves*. The elk is an American symbol, one of our largest native land mammals. . . . it beat out the buffalo by a vote of eight to seven in the late nineteenth century to become the image of the order."

"I bet you know even more shit about it than that."

"They shed their antlers every year."

"What's that got to do with believing in God?"

"In eastern Asia, the velvet from elk antlers is said to have spiritual force."

"Do you even believe in God, Louie?"

Louie lowers his shades so slowly, gravely, he peers above the frames and tells his adopted son, "There is only one way to find out."

"Mom just believes."

"Mom?"

Adoptive Parent Support Group at the Albany High School Gymnasium, 700 Washington Avenue.

Friday February 9th with adoption-competent therapist Harrison Abbott from six in the evening until the healing is complete.

The gym is gigantic with spectacular lighting. Eight black folding chairs with leather padding form a circle at absolute center court and the feeling of vacancy, of open space and great emptiness, doesn't go unnoticed.

"Christ, it smells like *nothing* in here," Louie Gloria moans to the woman sitting next to him. Her purse is on her lap and her hands are on the purse. Her lips are pursed and her legs are crossed tightly below. The ceiling has exposed beams that are dull and alien in their cleanliness. The hoops and nets do not move; they've not been used for days—the Albany team is playing a tournament out of town. The fragile eight-person group feels fortunate that the accordion-style stands are empty.

Harrison Abbot begins the long walk from gym entrance to center court. He is dressed in all black except for his socks, which are white, and cotton. The spectacular lighting makes his black shoes shine spectacularly. This pleases him; he smiles down at his own feet walking along—the slight heels and hard-toe region combine to create a military "click-click . . . click-click . . . click-click," sound as he continues the walk to center court. The sound's echo is so feeble as filler for the cavernous court that Mister Abbott starts humming. His humming is like someone trying to obscure embarrassing noises coming from a public bathroom stall or make a petty book theft look like browsing or soften a silence made uncomfortable by a conversation that's ended abruptly—it is rhythmless, "Hmm Hmm Hmmmmmmm," a man going about his business with clear disinterest, this Abbot.

The kind woman next to Louie says, "Hello, Harrison," as the adoption-competent therapist (ACT) enters the circle. He does not stop humming even to answer her, just opens a manila folder and places it atop his own tightly crossed legs, "Good eve-uh-*niiing* class," he says without looking up.

"We're a group," replies Louie.

"Oh, right," remarks Harrison, "so last week we talked about *traditions* . . . starting rituals and traditions to help *normalize* and *stabilize* family life," he finally looks up at the group, "does anyone want to share their progress?"

"Uhhmmm, well, yeah, we started a family storybook about two weeks ago," says the woman next to Louie, lifting her freckled hand slightly from the purse.

"That's fan-*tastic*, Stephanie!"

Stephanie smiles, her head and neck recoil demurely from group attention. In the next black, padded folding chair Louie Gloria can see that her dimples are freckled and cute—she reminds him of an apple orchard. It is possible that she smells like one. He fakes a stuffy nose and asks, "What did you write?"

"Well, first, like Harrison told us, me and my husband wrote the stories of our own childhood and followed through to our decision to adopt. Jeff . . . my *husband*, didn't really finish writing his, said it was stupid, but I told him I didn't think so, but then he wouldn't, so I wrote the rest for him—we've been together since high school, so I knew it all anyway. We showed it to Jackson. It had a picture of us three on the cover and everything, we let him read it."

"Mmmmand how did he like that?" asked Abbott.

"Well, he's only six right now so we're not sure he really understood it, but I think he liked the picture at least."

"That's very nice, did you invite Jackson to write his own story?"

"Well, uh, we *invited* him . . . but he just drew some pictures and put a few letters down. He's really just learning to write and stuff, he's only in first grade."

"That's great, and do you feel the exercise has helped establish some comfort between the three of you?"

"What the hell," Louie begins to mumble.

"Maybe a little. I mean, we're pretty comfortable. Remember I told you we have an open adoption?"

"Yesss, yes-yes-yes," says Harrison, waving his hands, bowing his head.

"Jesus Christ," Louie mentions. Everyone turns to him.

"Ex-*cuse* me, Mister Gloria?"

"You're not even listening to her. Jackson is *six . . . years . . . old*, did you hear that? He doesn't even know what *dis*-comfort would be. And anyway, what happens when they outgrow the tradition or ritual you've spent all this time creating?"

"Is this a problem you're currently facing, Mister Gloria?"

"Louie."

"Louie."

"Yes, it is."

"Do you want to share with the cl—group?"

"You know me and the kid have always built and run soap box derby cars in the race right, for like four or five years now?" Louie looks down at his fingers.

"Yesss yes-yes-yes," the others nod their heads. Louie looks up again to meet the group's collective gaze.

"Well this year things have been a lot different."

"How so?"

Louie's heavy head sinks down again as he tries to calm himself. His eyes focus on the spotless gym floor where hundreds of feet have run and left no trace at all. Somebody comes and cleans the floor every single day. A few basketballs are at rest twenty feet from center court. They are orange, round, full.

"You all know my wife Grace moved to Florida."

"She left you, Louie," says Harrison Abbott. "Remember to stay in Honest Adoption Language."

"Jesus Christ, what the fuck *is* it with you, man?"

"Leave him out of it."

"Oh *God*, everyone says that. You're like some automated response system."

"What's that supposed to mean, Mister Gloria?"

"It means you talk about life like the answers are in a textbook. Rituals and storybooks and *honest* adoption language or *positive* adoption language, that's bullshit, it's just . . . it's not real life."

"These are proven methods, which you've made great use of in the past, Mister Gloria. You seem very emotional right now. I think you should share what's bothering you."

"Emotional?" Louie asks. Finally looking up again he addresses the entire group, "what's more surprising . . . my emotions, or Abbott's utter lack of any emotion whatsoever?"

No one answers. This is quite a break from the normal, tempered discussion concerning the unique challenges of adoption. The gymnasium's emptiness expands with Louie Gloria's impassioned prompt—fans hum electrically from hidden recesses, the nearly silent moonbeam lights above punish the group with a blazing fake radiance—there is nowhere to hide. An octet desperate to be on the lamb from life is instead imprisoned by reality. Up to this point it'd been clear that the group met for information, not answers, "Is it more surprising that I'm *pissed* off about my wife leaving me, or that this asexual, childless, *fucker* . . . is teaching us how to raise kids we didn't even make?" Louie's voice rockets into the rafters then reverberates back to the court, striking each set of ears at least twice. "Honestly Abbot, have you ever fucked *anyone*? Guy or girl, whatever, doesn't matter. Just tell us you have at least *some* real-life experience." A few group members adjust pieces of their clothing and look up at the heavy rafters, others rub their tongues along the inside of their cheeks. One guy giggles a little.

"That's none of your business, Mister Gloria."

"So you've never been laid before?"

"This is *highly* inappropriate, Mister Gloria."

Louie drops his head again, stool-sunk like a fighter unable to answer the bell, "I'm sorry Abbot, just, so . . . all right, what happens when they start traditions of their own?"

"Traditions of their own?" repeats Abbott, joining the gym echo.

"Yeah, you know, like my son calling everything gay."

"That's hardly a tradition."

"And writing letters back and forth with my wife who left me."

"They write letters?"

"Don't you listen? Letters, yes, they're writing fucking *letters*."

"Mister Gloria, *please*."

"I know, okay, I know, it's fine, I'm sorry," finally Louie tells his shoes, "I had to open one."

"What did it say?" the group is silent, entranced.

"Oh, you wanna know what it said? Shouldn't you be telling me that violates the adoptee's trust or some sh— something like that?"

"I think you know you violated his trust, Mister Gloria."

"What about the fact that he didn't tell me about the letters?"

"It's healthy that he communicates with both his adoptive parents."

"No it isn't."

"It's a natural reaction. You shouldn't be jealous, you should support the relationship."

"Again, you don't know what you're talking about."
"Do you want to share, Mister Gloria?"

My shining Starr,

You look so, so, so, big in the picture! You really are becoming a handsome <u>man</u>. I don't know what to do either, but you should at least help with the car and run the race with your Father—sorry, I know you hate when I call him that. He really does love you, Rocky. He used to get so excited watching you ride down the hill in those silly soap box cars, you couldn't wipe the smile off his face for days. Just think, if it weren't for Louie we never would have met, so despite what you think-you do owe him something.

Hope to see you soon,
Grace

"I don't really think sharing would help."
"It's up to you."
"There's nothing in your textbook that could help me."
"Maybe the group can help, Mister Gloria, that's what we're here for." The group nods at Louie in warm affirmation of this statement. Stephanie can see the veins popping from his neck and sense the sickening tension plaguing her neighbor. She wants to tell Louie that everything will work out, be fine, come around—or whatever other cliché jovial folks use to comfort the struggling. But she's too honest. It's going to take time to soften the razor-sharp corners of Gloria's eyes, her commitment to the group is strong. She *needs* to help this man and so she whispers, "It's probably just a phase," into Louie's ear. She moves the freckled hand toward his

shoulder but places it instead just above his knee. Louie answers her, "Yeah probably," his quiet voice no longer echoes. Stephanie's hand has the unintended effect of driving Louie away. He tells the group he needs to clear his head and that he's sorry for leaving early, before the healing is complete and all.

On his way out, Louie picks up one of the orange basketballs and dribbles it to fill the silence. The dimples sooth his palms and fingertips. He can smell the leather. The bouncing ball rings through the gym like cannons being fired from a valley as he bounces it harder (*harder . . . harder*) and harder (*harder. . . harder*) and harder. The group members stare at Louie's back, they long for his exit more with each successive step. No one wants to say a word about the bouncing ball. It's as if he's bouncing it off their heads. They hope the basketball will help him in a way they couldn't.

Fifth Annual Capital Region Soap Box Derby at the Empire Plaza.

Race Director Hailey Albright is pleased to announce the running of The Fifth Annual Capital Region Soap Box Derby. Competition starts at 8am Sunday February 25th with the Stock Car division (ages 7-13). Super Stock (ages 9-17) will begin by 10am and overlap with the start of the Masters division (ages 10-17) around Noon. Races will be contested down Madison Avenue from Lark Street to Eagle Street, friends and family are encouraged to attend—complimentary breakfast and refreshments will be served throughout the day.

Louie Gloria opens his eyes to find wet windows. The raindrops land and stick, gather, then give way to gravity, all sliding down at a similar speed. He pushes the white coverlets away from his half-naked body, lays there annoyed with the rain and how loud the crinkling sheets sound in the empty room. Slow moving cars slush along oily streets outside. Louie stares at the steady ceiling fan, his long, pretty, salt and pepper hair spills over the white pillows. His beard is thick and bad. He runs his hands against the overgrown face and releases all the air in his lungs at once, in an exaggerated huff—putting on a display for the mannequin Fitz whose ivory chest considers the scene. Louie turns and looks at Fitz there next to the bed, who has no gaze to accommodate him. Desperate to break the silence, words and thoughts and actions gathering too quickly in his mind, they spin south into his chest and some sneak from the crack in the corner of his mouth, "Ya fuckin' know *what*, Fitz, I'm going down there anyway."

On this date one year ago, and for the three years before that, Louie and Rock Starr would already be unpacking the derby car from the back of Lou's Jeep, watching the early races alongside psychotic mothers rooting on Stock Car kids—screaming, clapping, pogoing from the ground—gunshots signaled the start of each race and made Louie's heart flutter. It sure filled him up, their special day, Father and Son as far as anyone else knew, something to hold on to, that *one* thing. . . .

Louie pulls this year's derby car out through the basement's storm door and loads it into the back of his Jeep. He's wearing a steel gray cardigan over a peach polo tucked into his jeans. His hair is slick, he's got the aviators on even though the day is cold and misting. He used to call these glasses "race shades" on this day. When he drives, he can hear Rock Starr's helmet clunking about inside the derby car and so he turns up the radio and sings, "Some folks are born, made to wave the flag—EWWWWW that red white and blue. And when the band plays Haillll to the Chief, they point the cannon at youuuuu, Lord!" He slaps the steering wheel with both hands and checks for confirmation through the rearview mirror with the oddly positioned mannequin sitting stiffly and diagonally across the backseat. Louie is driving faster than normal. A basketball rolls back and forth on the floor beneath the empty passenger seat. The ball stubs against an object during its journey from side to side and either returns to the previous side or hops over the object depending on the sharpness of the turn and Lou's speed.

Louie finds his parking spot—reserved for the parents

of children who placed in the top three at last year's event. Twenty yards from the lot, a race in the Stock Car class starts with a BLAST. This is a one-on-one race (as are most preliminaries) and so each child has his or her head all the way down onto the derby car dash in duel effort to reduce today's considerable wind resistance. Their heads are so far down it's a wonder they even know where to go— although it is impossible to really steer the cars, they kind of just run down the thirty-five degree start ramp and glide for two hundred yards along the smooth Madison Avenue between Lark and Eagle, and so this effort to reduce wind resistance is actually a very big deal and more or less determines the winner.

The announcement for the Super Stock finals respectfully begins after the Stock Cars have coasted at least halfway down Madison, "Driving a purple cloud car, and racing for Bill's Wings and Suds . . . Hannah Algaard," Hannah's mom is standing right next to the race announcer and screams, "LET'S GO HANNAHHHHHH," into his face. He briefly looks at the mom, the droplets on his face could be spit or more mist. "And for the boys," Louie Gloria is listening but also watching the Stock Car race that is being hotly contested down Madison. He believes the car on the right, the blue winged pig, has a slight edge, "Racing for The Albany Firefighters, in his *very* own Fire truck, Hilliard Archer," Archer bows and waves to his parents, and to Hannah's mom, who mouths the words, "Cocky son of a bitch," at him, to which Archer responds with a knowing smile.

"That Archer is a real badass," Louie Gloria tells the woman in the registration tent.

"Won it four years runnin'," she responds.

"He's thirteen now, we'll see what happens next year when he moves up to Masters."

"I guess we will. You here to sign up Rock?"

"Yes, Ma'am I am."

"Where is he?"

"Out getting coffee."

"All-righty, you're in the Masters division again right? And what car's he runnin' this year, hun?"

"Yes that's right, Masters division. And he's running a flaming jalapeño."

"That sounds very hot, hunny, and *very* fast," she smiles.

"You know it," Louie smiles back.

"Okay hun, you're all set then, his heat starts in half an hour."

Gloria walks away from the tent and back to his jeep. A few more parents have gathered to cheer on Hannah Algaard. The starting gun announces another heat in the Super Stock division and another shot goes off directly after to signal the first Masters heat. The gun smoke quickly fades into the day's gray fog. Volunteers place blue tarps across the white, wooden starting ramps in between heats. Cars pull in and pull out of the drop off area. Children size up one another. They show each other new helmets with their names painted on the back, which is everyone's favorite—they're painted on the back because obviously with the ducking front dash head motion no one can see the front during the race.

Parents crowd around the Master class start ramp. This is essentially the championship division—the participants are a little older and some are even adolescents who look nervous. The sponsors are more elite in this group, well known law firms and big Italian restaurants. The cars are heavier and faster, the parents spend more time painting intricate designs, some even hire local artists. Old folks in gloves clutch at their coffees, their breath spews visibly with rumors concerning who will get caught for weighting or magnetizing their car this year.

"In today's third Masters heat, driving a Barbie Lamborghini and racing for Levy, Strauss & Koeningsberg . . . Jenna McDougal," Jenna's parents clap modestly—this is serious business. Her dad loads her car into the starting ramp and whispers some final instructions into the side of her helmet. He taps the helmet with the palm of his hand and says, "You can do this," before walking back to his wife's side. Jenna sits in her Lambo, held against gravity by one single, white, wooden block called a starting pin.

"And on this side, driving a flaming jalapeño, racing for the Brawny Paper Towel Corporation, is last year's runner-up . . . Rock Starr Gloria."

Louie walks to the starting ramp, bracing the flaming jalapeño car on his shoulder. The car bangs metallically against the helmet he is wearing that says "Starr" on the back in sparkling silver lettering. He loads the car onto the ramp, resting it against the starting pin, and gets inside. Jenna's mother says, "Rock Starr grew a *lot* this year," to her husband. "That kid is a stud," the husband says, "kind of weird that Louie isn't here helping him."

Louie is leaning a little far forward in the car, not quite at rest. He appears uncomfortable. He reaches into the back of his waistband and pulls something out that seems to be causing the discomfort. He looks through the helmet's visor at the hay bales lining the course—just a bunch of old dead sticks lumped together. American flags flap audibly around the Empire Plaza, the metal harnesses bang against the metal flagpoles, clink, clink, clink, clink . . . he can hear his own breathing inside the helmet. It stops misting, "READY?" the race announcer asks. Louie lifts the rain-splattered visor to show his face, all the hay bales and flags and tires and people and buildings come into focus like an eye adjusting to darkness. "Heyyyyy, HEYYY," Jenna's parents both yell and point. They see it's Louie inside the jalapeño, "SET?" the announcer asks. Jenna's mother runs toward the start ramp and yells, "STOP THE RACE," but no one hears, "Stop the *fucking* race," she yells again. Louie hears her, he's still laughing, the helmet makes his head itch terribly and he wonders why his son never mentioned it. Jenna's mom is frantic, she's fifteen feet from the starting area when Louie Gloria closes his eyes, points a shiny silver revolver at his smiling teeth and pulls the trigger. The starting pins are released, Jenna McDougal's screams call attention to this race as both cars roll down the starting ramp. Now a lot of other parents are running and yelling to stop the race. It takes the starter entirely too long to realize that it wasn't *his* gun that released the starting pins. Louie's heavy body blazes down Madison Avenue in the fiery jalapeño. His head rests properly on the dash but rolls back and forth with the wind and chatters up and down with the bumps of the road. Thick blood cascades onto the front of the jalapeño, causing sweet, screaming Jenna to vomit inside her helmet. Her ears feel like they're gonna explode, chunks formerly food cling to the foam padding and ooze down her bare neck, soaking the collar of her shirt. When she desperately pulls the helmet from her head the puke touches her lips again, eyelashes, some sticks in her hair as the pink helmet ricochets off the pavement toward the hay bales that line the course. People watching from the finish line notice blonde hair fluttering and fear the screaming, helmetless rider wildly wiping at her face. They finally shift their gaze to the other car—a flaming jalapeño that leaves a sickening crimson streak in its wake. They notice parents from the starting line sprinting downhill, haphazardly flinging coffees and donuts, slipping and rolling into hay bales, getting up frenzied, dizzy to stop the race. Parents by the checkered finish line all begin to buzz and point with natural wonderment. The jalapeño wins by a large margin but drifts eerily onward, beyond the finish line. The crowd turns its collective head to observe the adult arms dangling outside of the car. Louie's bloodied knuckles drag along the wet pavement and stun the astonished onlookers, yet, no one chases the jalapeño. They turn instead to screaming Jenna McDougal, who is desperate to escape her Barbie Lamborghini. It doesn't take long at all for the referee at the finish line to dismiss the legitimacy of Louie Gloria's victory.

Two hand holders walk smiling along a sun-kissed beach in Florida.

"How do ya think he's doing? I can't *believe* you didn't at least stay for the race."

"He'll be fine. I always thought that race was kind of gay anyways."

The Hanger Thief

I'm going to tell you about the first two things I ever stole, though I doubt you'll blame me for it. At the time I decided to become a thief, I was in the habit of attending various artistic outings around New York City. I'm not really an artist exactly, but certainly someone who enjoys watching others bashfully explain the genius of their own work. The other thing is I'm quite poor. It just fills me up when I get to wear a tie and drink clean, cold water and walk across those plush, violet, velvet carpets they've always got in the entryway—the ones drenched by a subtle chandelier sunset so soft I feel like kneeling down to pray. It's peaceful, everyone whispers.

"Evening, sir," the *doorman* said to me.

"How do you do?" I replied, entering the hall.

"Just fine, sir," said the cordial doorman, nodding and all.

A different employee, a coatman of sorts, came by to take my coat. It felt very posh, handing the coat off like that. I held it out for him with my fingers trembling to show that I couldn't be troubled to bear the weight of it for another moment. He kindly accepted the coat, nodding thanks as he walked toward the set of hangers. Glistening metallic hangers all in a row, perfectly spaced two inches apart from one another. An alignment of soldiers from an alien race so ideally composed that they need no alteration and should never be defeated—they don't even compete anymore. They alone are responsible for keeping resting clothes in place. They remain proudly stilted throughout time and toe the line of arrogance but never cross it. Their form and function are united in an eternal, euphoric reverie that begs and teases the ordinary and imperfect things that comprise the world around them.

The coatman selected a hanger and slid it gracefully through the vacant arms of my coat. A stunning curl of hanger head turtled from the collar, sparkling in the bright lights of the entryway, or, "the foyer," as some like to call it. The hanger body held the coat exactly in place. The coat looked comfortable and assured, as though it'd just come in from a long day's work, ready for a nap. I needed to get a closer look at some of the still naked hangers.

"My good man, which way to the lavatory?" I asked the coat checker.

"Right over there, sir," he said, pointing just passed the hangers.

I didn't want to look too suspicious, so I rooted about in the pockets of my jacket, the fake search allowing for closer inspection of the adjacent hangers. They held every type of clothing with a most rare and quiet confidence. Vests relaxed, shawls wrapped and reclined, heavier coats like mine snored obediently next to the lighter spring coats that fluttered when disturbed but never enough that one should have any fear of their falling to the ground.

In the bathroom, urinals opened their haughty mouths (probably pretty pissed about their lot in life) screaming that I should take a silver souvenir for my troubles. Who would know? And more importantly, *what* troubles? A well-made hanger is just like a urinal. A manicured man in the bathroom murmured to his urinal, "The atmosphere . . . is *abso*-lutely . . . opulent," and before I could agree, "the atmosphere is abso-*lutely* opulent," still in agreement, "the *AT*-mosphere is . . . absolutely . . . *opulent*," he'd been rehearsing the line, an interesting line to say the least. The urinal attempted to interject but could only manage a faint gurgle. The man leered at himself, showing the urinal his teeth, apparently checking his reflection in the metalwork above the urinal proper.

I left him there and made my way to the stage where the artists were about to speak. At the entryway, yet another employee said, "Enjoy your evening, sir," but I ignored him, figuring that the proper thing to do for a patron of the arts.

In the back of the main room were four large glass windows looking out on a silent SOHO street. The lack of foot traffic greatly disappointed those in attendance who were dressed desperate for notice. Luckily for them, four television cameras stationed symmetrically around the room all pointed at the small stage, front and center, break a leg. Up there on the stage, more subtle lighting blessed four comfortable-looking black chairs. Each chair came with its own water station where presumably perfect, pure water from pristine pitchers could be poured at will into spotless personal pint glasses. I couldn't find any spots at all on the glassware. It really was a fine atmosphere.

I took a seat next to an intelligent-looking woman and adjusted my tie.

"Fine atmosphere, eh?"

"Hmph," she said.

Clearly, she couldn't be troubled by my small

observations and so opened her informative guide to further the point. I did not have an informative guide so decided to fiddle around with my fingers a bit and adjust my tie once or twice more, clearing my throat without cause. I really had to find something to take my mind off those hangers. I stole a glance at her informative guide and thought that she might not know anything about the playwrights now taking the stage. Probably never even saw a show by any of them. I knew one of the writers, a small Korean with a flashy, multisyllabic name whom I'd recently seen perform a satirical monologue about a lonely subordinate sailor on a whale ship that she'd written herself. The thing that got me was how accurately the piece depicted the angst involved in the highest levels of male bonding. I immediately began to doubt the informative guide's ability to relate the feeling of watching the unbearably cute Korean girl's anxious smile while lamenting topics like when to curse, yell, insult a superior officer's wife, or commence a conversation concerning relative penis size (this topic most unavoidable on any respectable whale vessel). She even pondered the universally debated conundrum of what amount of alcohol allowed for the inception of the word "cunt" into casual speech. I firmly believed that after the show, having read her guide and watched the playwright panel, the woman would meet up with her friends, drop a few juicy quotations, and parade with pleasure her vast knowledge and love/support of "the arts."

The playwrights and moderator then received their introductions, walking across the stage one at a time. The woman folded her informative guide inside her hands, pursing her lips in artistic anticipation. I looked to the exit, hoping to see the coatman there, taking in the art, leaving the hangers unattended. No such luck. In succession, the playwrights nervously explained themselves and why they hated their lives. The audience laughed at them but not rudely. The moderator turned to the last playwright who explained himself. He explained that he watched his Uncle (who'd been raising him) get shot and die right in front of his ten-year-old face. He explained that he then had no money or food or family and was forced to act adult at a very early age. He explained that he had to attend community college before he met someone that knew someone who swore she knew someone that could bring him to Yale. The television monitors zoomed in ultimate definition upon the shifty countenances of the fellow playwrights forced to remain onstage. The atmosphere became suddenly serious, ties were adjusted all around. I asked the woman next to me, "Did they chronicle these tribulations in that informative guide?" This time she waved my question away like an annoying fly had been attempting to flutter up her skirt. Another obvious question would be why did the moderator opt to present this playwright last? What a vicious finale. The audience had felt so light, so utterly *artsy*, we were millenniums away from these real-world issues of pain and poverty. The cute Korean had just finished describing the sheer horror of leaving a nearly completed Stanford thesis to chase her drama dreams in N-Y-C. She was *so* brave. Oh, can you believe it? Oh, oh, ohhhhhhh, what courage. But now this writer/actor hijacked the entire event, fantastically trivializing her tribulations. I loved him then. He started screaming up there when it was time to perform his prepared piece. He became the first person in the whole place to get up from his seat. "AND I PUT MY HOPES AND DREAMS INTO *YOU*? WHAT DID YOU DO? YOU FUCKED IT UP . . . I WANTED TO DO THINGS, I HAD HOPES AND DREAMS OF MY OWN BUT I PUT 'EM ALL INTO YOU . . . AND WHAT YOU DO WIT' 'EM? YOU FUCKED 'EM UP, YOU FUCKED 'EM UP!" He thundered on and many more ties were adjusted. Someone said, "Oh, *my*." A few rows behind me I heard a man say, "This atmosphere . . . is *absolutely* . . . repellent." The chaotic scene finally drew the coatman out of position; I noticed him adjusting his tie against the far wall.

The writer/actor thumped his chest with his fist as he stepped to the edge of the stage. He was abusing his body. His chest took each fist and released a hollow echo like a boulder into a cave. Every sentence was punctuated by this dull, throbbing throttling. Easily visible mists of impassioned spit sprayed from his mouth and looked like devil raindrops out to extinguish the offensively subtle stage lighting. Someone needed to put this killer whale back in his tank. Gentle citizens in the front row were getting soaked, he was frothy, he wanted to rip their doughy bellies open and eat their organs for goddamn dinner. He stood directly over them and looked into all their eyes at once, "AND WHAT YOU GONNA DO NOW? AHHH MAN . . . BOY, YOU *SURELY* FUCKED UP!"

The coatman looked in a trance. He moved closer to the stage, further from the exit, every eye in the place now fixated on the stage performer. I got down on the ground and began to crawl away so as not to block the rolling cameras (action). I crawled clear across the aisle without any notice, and then crawled along the back wall by the big windows. A streetwalker noticed my crawling, noticed the performer, she pointed out these happenings to her friends who all laughed. It looked as though she said something clever as they walked away like, "What a city," or, "lots of weird artist types around here," or, "hang on, I wanna get a pic of this."

All was quiet in the foyer. The hangers hung still, unguarded—I took a few glances around and acted quickly, like a thief. Grabbed my coat and the hanger in one swipe, then dashed out the door, down the steps and into the empty street. Two civilians walked on the other side of the street. I could tell they were looking to my side of the street, though at what exactly I couldn't be sure.

I moved briskly from the scene. Not hurrying like I'd done something wrong, but instead stepping confidently with insanely assured shoulders—thus projecting an air of intense stress that would force others to assume that I'd been a bit too hot under the collar to wear the coat that actually concealed the hanger. This projection of confident shoulders carries with it several beneficial characteristic assumptions or stereotypes stemming from the common conclusion of stress via importance in the work place. I do recommend this look—walk quickly to the point of breaking a sweat, in nice clothes, on a decently cool evening. Carry your jacket over your arm and look straight ahead like you absolutely *have* to be at someplace in ten minutes or less. If someone gets even the slightest bit in your way be sure to shake your head as you speed-walk around them. If you smoke, smoke. If you have a phone put it to your ear, no matter what, even if no one is calling. Do not yawn for any reason. Do not slump. Do not tolerate pleas from any homeless that may be lying around. People will admire you and move out of your way. They may even look up the street after you and ask a friend, "Who *was* that?"

Eventually I calmed myself and put the jacket back on. I tucked the hanger under my shirt and partly down into my pants for security. This caused a slight hitch in my normally hitch-free gait. I limped down into the subway and cocked my whole face a little sideways like I'd just eaten something sour—a more fitting demeanor for someone with a hitched gait. The hanger went "ping" as I pushed through the subterranean turnstile. Someone whispered, "Is that that guy with the metal dick?"

"No," I answered, "just a hanger."

"I don't see how it could hang, being metal and all."

"It's a hanger, not a metal . . . "

CLICKCLICK-CLICKCLICK-CLICKCLICK. The concrete ground vibrated with the approaching train. Tons and tons of steel burned through the tunnel.

"What?" She asked.

"It's a hang . . . " CLICKCLICK-CLICKCLICK-CLICKCLICK, "why do you think I'm limping?"

"That *definitely* doesn't look limp to me." She said, staring at the curvy hanger head slithering about my slacks.

I wiped my forehead and forced my eyes to look stressed and even blew a plume of hot breath into a few locks near one of my eyes, "I don't have time for this," I told her.

"Well . . . if you're not *him*, then who are you?"

Of course, I had to answer, "You don't know who I am?"

Of course, she had to answer, "Sorry, I really don't," she looked embarrassed so I just shook my head and limped away at a safe distance from the platform edge.

Inside the car, there were two things of note—the first being the reek of a man who'd fallen so low it was clear he'd been unable to even wash himself for years. The stench was inescapable. He must feel that way, imprisoned in his only garments. I got so caught up thinking about how long it might take him to ruin a space this large that I almost didn't notice the fact that standing against the pole next to him was the cute Korean playwright. The playwright smiled in a way that made me realize I'd never been truly happy. I found her smile, her happiness, a little disturbing in that moment. She'd just been made to look absolutely foolish by the more talented and dramatic playwright. Now she stood next to a man who had accumulated so much filth that it was inappropriate for him to exist in shared spaces. I was sick thinking of all the things he's had to endure. What's she so happy about? It didn't take me long to find the answer—the answer was a hot man. I will say he was dashing, a large breed with slick hair and noticeably blemish-free skin. You can imagine the smell of *him*. If you can't, or don't want to—a log cabin filled with fresh roses. His eggshell sweater was all filled with muscles. The girl stared longingly at her man. Opening her eyes so wide, blinking like Bambi, lust dripped from the corners of her lips. She slipped her tiny, brownish thumb into the back belt loop of the man's jeans. Her other four fingers teased the wispy hairs hidden beneath a Calvin Klein waistband. Their eyes were locked. The fingers silently asked if he wanted her to slide down a bit further. He silently answered yes. Her fingers looked so dexterous and soft. She'd taken great care to paint the nails a subtle, yet suggestive pink. As you might expect, the muscle-bound hunk acted aloof during this whole thing, like in his life it is normal for attractive women to put their hands down his pants in public. I wondered how good they smelled as a team. These people are always up to smelling lovely for each other and looking into each other's eyes, taking pictures, posing and smiling. I knew then that I wanted to rob them of something, and so, I'd just have to follow them home.

He said something into her ear and she nodded her head. This is the kind of guy you'd always see girls nodding their heads to. He probably said, "Do you want to come over to . . . *my place*?" And off they went.

Streetlamps highlighted the rain that poured over their shared umbrella. Steam flowed steadily from the street grates and danced romantically about the elbow-locked lovers as they hurried down the street. Their umbrella was orange with white and purple circles, making it easy to follow them through the dark night. Before long, they stopped in front of a building. I felt a happiness of my own at the sight of his low-rent building—covered in graffiti, its nasty gravity attracted an orbit of loose garbage. How long were we on the train? What sick ghetto was this? It was clear that the hunk was a struggling model/actor; perhaps this whole thing was a futile effort to sex his way into one of the Korean's forthcoming shows. The bastard couldn't even find his keys. The playwright bobbed up and down uncomfortably in the rain. After a terrible amount of time they started to converse about something. Before I knew it, they were walking my way. I was only slightly nervous she'd recognize me as the guy who crawled out before the artistic event had concluded. I shifted the hanger in my pants, preparing to flee if the hunk decided to attack.

"Hey," called a voice behind me.

"Yeah?"

"Get out of the way."

"What?"

"You're blocking my entrance here."

It was only a bouncer. He bounced me so the couple could enter the pub that'd been behind me the whole time. The up-and-coming model/actor shook the bouncer's hand on his way through the door. I followed them in.

"Hey?" asked the bouncer.

"Yeah?"

"How 'bout an ID, boss."

"Your name is Boomboom?" He laughed at me.

"Clearly."

"What kind of name is that?"

"It's a lot like yours."

"I've *never* heard a name like *that* before."

"Sure you have."

"No, I've *never* heard a *dumbass* name like that before."

"Ohhhh, what's in a name?" I lamented.

"My name is John, I know a fuckin' thousand people named John."

"You know a thousand people?"

"You getting smart with me, Boomboom?"

"No."

"You better not be."

"I'm not."

"You're a weird guy, Boomboom. Don't cause any trouble in there."

I limped into the bar. I figured, after I robbed the up-

and-coming actor, the cops would begin their investigation by asking the barflies if they'd seen anyone strange hanging around the night before, "Yeah, we saw a weird guy with a limp." So, naturally, during the actual robbery I planned to act utterly without limp. That way, when the cops brought this limp info back to the playwright and actor they'd say, "No, no, this guy wasn't limping at all."

Inside the bar, a beast man was sucking booze with such energy I thought his stool might be the positive end of some new-age alcoholic energy socket. It seemed to surge infectious effervescence into his backside and then out into the patrons dancing kinetically around him. He shouted at the barmaid. He gargled his glass, laughed, spit up ice chunks that stuck to his beard, half unplugged from his stool to fart, coughed, burped, ordered drinks for everyone in the place. He did all this while redefining the word demonstrative. He ordered drinks for people who did not exist. Drinks surrounded him and he did not discriminate, he stuck his hand out and brought whatever glass he touched to his mouth. He placed that one down and pulled a different one back—pints of beer, cocktails, a few shots lingered about like pawns resigned to certain destruction. He continued to order drinks as most people breathe, instructing the poor working girl to make him a drink, damn it, "Just enough orange juice to insult the ice," he'd yell and hayuck-yuck-yuck along, slapping everyone's back. I limped up next to him and stole two of the drinks then moved to a less populated corner of the bar.

I watched the patrons continue to circle the beast in a vibrant orbit. He'd hand them a cocktail if they got too close. Jim Morrison howled from a neon jukebox in the corner. He implored them to set the night on fire from the dungeon of his lungs. They danced with dizzying precision, arms raised, shouting Morrison's words in unison, not touching each other, touching each other— holding hands and hugging, eyes closed, eyes opened, beast in the absolute center with two drinks in the air and a crazed look in his eye like he'd been born of this place, like everything happening was sustaining him, he was feeding on it.

The actor and playwright leaned coolly against the bar. The lower half of their bodies pressed together. They stared at each other for a very long time before they started kissing a wet kiss. They weren't even thinking about the unfortunate writer/actor anymore. It's like, they see a bad thing, make a brief thoughtless remark and then go on to make plans for dinner and vacation and holidays and weddings. They'd probably be doing this next to the corpse of the playwright's dead uncle.

"HEY! WHO . . . the fuck are ya doin' there?" The beast man yelled to me from his electric stool. He had a comfortable flannel shirt spread across his ice block back. He pulled a loose ponytail of rusty curls behind his balloon head, his face and grin gave the impression of a jack-o-lantern.

"Fine atmosphere," I said to him.

"AHHHHHHH, *THIS* mother *FUCKER*," he said, slapped me on the back.

His eyes were serious, green with red lashes draped over the top and set way behind his forehead.

"What about it?" He asked me.

"Oh, nothing, just saying this is a fine atmosphere."

"ANNIE! Get *THIS* mother *FUCKER* a cocktail!" He

held up his hand and threw money down on the bar. Just outside his semicircle of drinks, a collection of homeless five, ten, and twenty-dollar bills huddled together in a futile attempt to stay dry and warm.

"HEY!" He spoke whimsically. Each word seemed to take him by surprise.

"Yeah," I said, standing right next to him.

"Where'd you get *those* drinks?"

"I ordered them earlier, you didn't notice me."

"You're a slippery bastard, I know where all my drinks are, and *those* . . . are my drinks. You stole them, didn't you? You're a *thief*." He laughed, yelling and pointing at me, "THIEEEEEEEEEEF!" "THIEEEEEEEEEEF!"

He put his arms on the bar, sheltering his drinks from my alleged grasp. The bar became silent, someone cut off the Morrison.

"You think you can come in here . . . to this bar . . . where you don't know anybody . . . and start stealing drinks?" He stood up, towered over me. People took notice.

"No . . . I . . . no, I'm sorry."

He looked down at the top of my head. I could feel the force of his hard-working lungs. His massive, red paws flanked my chin. In one hand a pint of ale and a vodka soda in the other, "Welcome to O'Nolan's." In front of my face I saw his chest erupt with laughter. I looked up at him and was handed both beverages. The gentle beast even pulled a barstool, inviting me to sit.

"So, what are you doing here? I've never seen you here before," he said.

"Just in the neighborhood," I said.

"This isn't much of a destination," he told me.

"I like the atmos—"

"Don't bullshit me. You're very quiet and I know you stole my drinks. Why you standin' up? What the fuck is that in your pants?"

"Which would you like me to answer first?"

"What's in your pants."

"A hanger."

"A hanger?"

"Indeed."

"It isn't a snake?"

"Not a snake."

"A banana?"

"No, not a banana."

"Certainly not a candy cane?"

"Certainly not that."

"You haven't got a curvy, upturned cock then?"

"No, just the regular."

"Can I see it?"

"The cock or the hanger?"

"The hanger."

"Not the cock?"

"Certainly not."

"Well, the hanger then?"

"Yes, may I see it?"

"You may not."

"What do you have it for?"

"I hang my coat on it."

"Don't bullshit me."

"What else would I use it for?"

"Why did you steal my drinks?"

"I didn't think you'd mind."

"No, I don't mind."

"So, you're a thief then?"

"No, not a thief," I said.

"A doorman?" He asked.

"Not a doorman."

"Concierge?"

"Who?"

"Someone who opens doors and hangs coats."

"Certainly not that."

"Then I suppose you're standing up because of the hanger in your pants?"

"That's correct."

"Well then, it's all settled."

"I suppose," I said.

"What *is* it about the hanger then?"

"You don't know?" I asked.

"Certainly not," he said.

"Well, I can tell you . . . that a hanger is very much like any urinal you might find."

"You haven't said much," he said.

"Surely I have," I replied.

"You're a weird guy, what's your name?"

"Boomboom."

"I used to have an Uncle named Boomboom," he said and went on demolishing his mountain of cocktails.

The actor and playwright had by now fully discarded their drinks onto the bar and commenced with a lusty performance. They squeezed ripples into each other's clothing. It looked like they wanted to become one being. No one else seemed to notice or care. They went at it for another five minutes before she grabbed him by the hand and pulled him out the door. Since I'd begun following them, I couldn't recall one moment in which they weren't touching.

I followed them outside and watched them enter his building—he had the keys ready this time. Man, they went up the stairs in some rush. I pulled a hood up over my head and lit a cigarette as I moved across the street. I kept a keen eye on the building, watching to see what set of lights flickered to life. I thought all about them as I smoked, the night they shared—he must have watched her at the artistic outing, he must have been proud, and jealous, the train ride, coming down from the euphoria of her performance, their shared umbrella, drinking and kissing in the bar, I grabbed at the hanger in my pants and wondered if the troubled writer/actor was having this kind of delightful evening too. I wondered if I wanted a sexy playwright to put her hands down my pants while riding the subway. I wondered what happens if the up-and-coming actor sees someone else getting his butt touched on the subway. Tough to be sure about anything. I followed the curvature of the hanger in my pants with my hands, wondering how I should go about this. I let some smoke seep over my gums and escape through a narrow opening between my lips.

The lights went on in the actor's apartment. I walked over and climbed up his fire escape. I enjoyed climbing the metal stairs. Up I went in the wet rain. Not a single person on this planet could place me there.

Once I gained the landing I looked inside—candles everywhere. Candles on every table and surface. Candles on the counter in the kitchen. Candles next to the bed. Candles on the dresser. And I couldn't see, but I had to assume candles in the bathroom. Pink candles and red candles. Candles inside big glass jars. Candles atop trays.

Candles in multi-pronged candle holders. I'd have to call it a plethora, there isn't any other way—there indeed may have even been a myriad of candles. I wondered if she bought the candles for him or did he stock this collection himself? What day of the week does a ravishing man decide to populate his apartment with such waxy diversity? I calmed myself with the possibility that all the candles were the product of some ill-advised gift certificate.

To be fair, the candlelight painted a stunning aspect on the couple's still-touching skin. They moved through the apartment as one shadow pirouetting about the walls. What a world. He brought her into his room. He took off her pants, slowly, savoring it. They were right in front of me. She laid on her back. He crawled on top of her. She smiled and looked deep into his smooth face. He had a piece of beautiful, rich hair swinging down. He smiled and looked deep into her smooth face. She put her hands down the back of his pants again, this time way down in there.

I crept across the fire escape to the adjacent window, pushed it open and stepped inside. I stood in what appeared to be a guest bedroom. A rather nondescript shelter intended for crashing after a guest's long night of watching the touching couple or listening to the model/actor lament his lot in life. Actually, it's a lot more likely that similarly happy couples occupy this guest bed. I sat down on the bed and pulled my hood off. The hanger made sitting uncomfortable. The rain that crashed down on the roof of the apartment building likely masked my entry, "It smells really good in here," I whispered. "What a fine atmosphere."

I sat there and listened to them go at it for a few

minutes. The bed springs called out for me to save them, squeaksqueaksqueak, pleasepleaseplease, squeaksqueak-squeak. I'm telling you it really was a hot time, candles all about and everything. I made my way into the kitchen. A different cityscape of the same city hung on each of the three walls in the living room, serving to remind the up-and-coming actor where he lives.

The whole place had a theme to it: Christmas. A Christmas tree with Christmas ornaments hanging and Christmas presents underneath. Christmas placeholders and napkins on the coffee table surrounded by Christmas candles. Christmas lights shaped like icicles were clustered in groups running along the apartment walls and even on a piece of wall that jutted out to separate the kitchen from the living room. On the refrigerator were magnetic elves dancing in place and an updated comedic version of Chris Kringle, blazing his way to all the happy homes wearing sunglasses in a mustang sleigh.

Inside the refrigerator were delicious cookies, meats, white wine, good beer, cheeses, everything you'd hope for. I suddenly felt the promise of a great new year. Towels situated around the sink and stove said, "Merry Christmas!" and were exclusively green, red, or white. Someone (likely the playwright) had stenciled a message on the wall between the kitchen and living rooms, "Life is a bountiful buffet, a delicious and infinite feast. . . ." certainly an interesting statement. She even stenciled a couple of butterflies and hearts around the message for good measure.

I grabbed a good beer from the fridge and went to the bathroom—Christmas towels, Christmas candles, Christmas hand soap, pictures of the actor and playwright opening the presents of Christmas's past. They looked incredibly happy with perfect handsome smiles flanked by hot dimples, dimpled pictures. I thought it'd be a good idea to give that a shot so I smiled into the mirror. As I watched myself pee I dreamed of the three of us taking an impromptu photo together, "Us in the bathroom with the guy who robbed us. Christmas Eve, 2016!" it'd probably say on the back.

Before I sat down to open a few gifts I noticed how many other pictures were framed and scattered throughout the place, each one taken in a different sunny locale. I strolled around like a museum tourist looking at the snapshots. You could tell the actor liked to hold his breath in an effort to accentuate his abs. He always stood on the left side, the playwright appearing to his right so that the left side of her face was slightly hidden. The photographs were grouped in clusters by location. On one wall you'd find a shot of them just arriving onto their hotel balcony (taken by hotel staff probably just after carrying their bags to the room), followed by one of them on the beach, playwright standing to his right, or, "photograph left" (taken by a fellow tourist), then one of them sitting sunburned at dinner, then another beach shot *with* tans, then one of them looking sad back at the airport. The outer edge of the apartment could be used to trace their path around most of the equator—a map of their love, this travelling infatuation, a bountiful buffet indeed.

The first present I opened was a camera. This seemed like maybe something he or she already owned. I opened a pair of women's workout sneakers—pink and purple Nike's accompanied (in this same box) by a purple jumpsuit. Was he encouraging her to work out more?

Risky move. I opened a color printer, the box said, "Photo Smart Photo Printer," and on the cover of the box was a couple smiling in some sunny locale. I opened a men's belt, brown, men's business casual shoes, brown, a fine pair. Was she suggesting he get a better job and a better apartment? Then I came to a flimsy little envelope. Opened it up—gift certificate to Yankee Candle ($200). I folded it up and put it in my pocket. He already had more than enough candles in there. I did it for everyone's sake.

The lovemaking reached a crescendo in the next room and then stopped abruptly. I guess it always stops abruptly. I finished the good beer on the floor by the tree. They sat in silence, their breathing mixed with my own. Rain continued to beat down hard on the rooftop.

"Whooof," the Korean said.

"Yeah," he said, huffing.

"I love you," she said to him.

Before these feelings could be reciprocated, I grabbed a Christmas candle and casually made my way into their bedroom, like they'd be expecting me. The candle lit my face, probably a minor mistake.

"What the fuck!" She screamed at me.

They were naked. They put their hands over their respective private areas. They were really strikingly good-looking people, even naked. The girl kept trying to cover up her breasts and vagina at the same time. Squirming wildly, she attempted to put a forearm across her breasts while draping the other hand down to her vagina. She looked like a spider stuck in a wet sink. She tried turning over and balling her legs up closer to the breasts and using her hand on her ass. He looked at me. He looked mad, scared, naked.

"Who *the fuck* are you? Get outta here, please, take whatever you want, man, please. Please just leave." He told me.

"I've already taken something," I told him.

"Who the fuck arrrrrrre youuuuuuu!" the playwright screamed at the wall, her back to me, clearly unhappy.

"Okay, so then get the fuck out," the guy said.

"I want to ask you a question first."

"Get OUUUUUUUUUUUUT!" She screamed, again, still balled up.

"Calm down," I told her. She was making me feel awful.

"What do you want?" asked the man.

"I want to ask you a question."

"Ask it."

"I want you to answer honestly though, and I want you to think about the answer. Don't just say anything so I'll leave." The girl kept shifting her arms back and forth. I feel terrible saying it now but I let a giggle slip from the side of my mouth. I wanted to mention that this little plight of theirs was nothing compared to that of the writer/actor, but I could tell I didn't have a lot of time.

"Okay, just fucking ask the question."

"Okay."

"Okay."

"Are you ready?"

"Yes."

"Are you going to think about the answer and tell the truth?"

"Fucking *ask* it!"

"Okay."

"Well?"

"If you're on the subway, and you see a girl putting her hand down the back of someone's pants, how do you feel about it?"

"OH MY GODDDDDDDDD. GET THE FUUUUUUUCK OUT, YOU'RE A *FUCKING* PSYCHOOO!" the talented playwright shrieked and got up to hit me. Swinging wildly, she no longer appeared a sexual being—her violence and anger cast a *National Geographic* aspect over her nude body. The whole thing was really turning a little chaotic. I accidentally spilled the candle wax on her naked leg when she tried to punch me. She screamed again. This angered the up-and-coming actor. Instead of answering the question he charged at me, holding his breath in, puffing his nostrils out, no longer bothering to cover his private area— his abs looked pretty sturdy in the candlelight.

"Come on, just tell me, come on," I asked as they forced me back into the guest room against my will. Neither of them would answer me. I tried another question, "What about that other playwright? He's better than you. . . . He's *real*." They both stalked me, not holding each other but shooing me out the still-open window. "Come on, don't you feel bad for him? Everything he went through?" As I flung my body back out onto the fire escape she said, "Daniel was in character the entire time."

The Voice of Degeneration

It might not seem that strange to you, now, that at seven-seventeen in the morning a coffee maker just gurgles itself alive with absolutely no one around or having been around at all for twelve hours, but it really is. All these *things*, they're coming to life, no one really notices. Even if they do notice they certainly don't seem to mind. And so that's what happened—right there in Marco Salazar's metallically dull kitchen, the coffee commenced its daily dribbling at precisely seven-seventeen. Marco had told his clipboard-carrying interior designer that he wanted the kitchen to feel *and* operate like a spaceship. And so that's what happens—Marco inhabits the kitchen from time to time but really the ship just cruises. His nutritionist arrives just before the first of every month to preprogram the refrigerator's computer to communicate with the computer at the grocery store, which finally tells a team of human employees what stuff needs to be brought over and put into Marco's fridge for the next month. The nutritionist is the closest thing to a friend Marco has left, always telling him during each visit, "You're lookin' guuuuu-*ud*, are you making your shakes like I showed you? Yes? Okay good, that's really really good, *great*—and what about that salmon with bronze fennel? I fucking *know*, right? When I saw it on the screen last month I almost *shit* myself. No, oh my god, that was *duck*, Marco. I see, yeah. No, it isn't *weird*. Okay fine, we don't have to." And all this time the nutritionist jabs and jab-jab-jabs his fingers at the screen.

The rising smell of space-brewed coffee gives Marco an added punch in his pants upon waking. A massive white screen in front of his bed shows office action featuring a receptionist in something that leaps over the line for casual and lands in the strictly forbidden (as far as office attire is concerned). And hello, she bends over much further than necessary to answer the phone. Marco strokes himself and laughs, now that's a real fantasy. The fact that Marco is personally responsible for the near extinction of receptionists nationwide makes him feel powerful and he can't help thinking that this day, February 28th, is going to be oh, oh my god, oh my god, it's going to be *so* good, *so* good, oh my god, it's going to be, oh, oh, oh, ah, ah, *so* good, oh my god.

Note: The author is aware that the story begins, more or less, with the main character waking up in the morning. Please don't be alarmed or turned off or anything, silly, it's just that if he is going to die at the end, and he might, isn't it comforting to know that he had a pleasant morning? But really the point here is that although Marco Salazar is a hot young software man, and if we're being honest-*the* hottest, he still wakes up and inserts himself into improbable pornographic scenarios before having coffee and leaving for work just like everyone else.

And of course, also like everyone else, Marco Salazar admires his still-shirtless physique while pouring space-brewed coffee and flipping on the news. This physique is one thing that separates him from some of the less hot, young software men.

Local weatherman Johnny Mountain is a combed and hyper hurricane of a man whose weather forecasting technique is best described as threatening. His face lunges toward the screen, "Now, there is a *chance* of rain today," then quickly retreats to the map, "but I'm not *sure* that it will," and approaches again as though he's working up to something violent, "you should definitely bring your umbrellas to work . . . just in case." He is stern, his hands squeeze the air in front of the camera, the viewer senses that he could become unhinged by the slightest unforeseen gust of wind.

Johnny today: "I wore this white suit because that's what you can count on this morning and probably into the late evening, Long Island. That's right, it's Ice, Ice, *baby*," Johnny says, laughing, retreating, continuing, "you see what we have up here is this *thick* layer of warm, *above*-freezing air," Johnny's arms flay about the map like he's spray painting, "and down below, boy, as you can see, the surface temperature today is *frigid*, in the single digits—when *this* group of high pressure clouds arrive and eventually burst, the precipitation will pass through the warm upper region and into the frigid zone absolutely *freezing* what normally would have been your standard messy mix. I hate to say this, Long Island, I really do, but we might have a Glaze Event on our hands."

"Ice isn't white," Salazar says into his mug, sliding his other palm along his abs.

"A Glaze Event? Wow. That sounds pretty *bad*, Johnny. Back to you," says the made-up anchorwoman in a daring, lobster-red business suit.

"Bad it is Umi. Back to you."

"Do you have a fun fact for us today, Johnny, or have you canceled it due to the Glaze Event?"

"Oh, yeah, sh— sure I do. Got this one from our Money Watch team . . . last year the number of Americans who drink coffee dropped from sixty-six percent to sixty-one. Back to you, Umi," he points.

"(politely interested laughter) Well that's certainly bad news for Starbucks. Wonder what that's all about," Umi smiles at her male co-anchor.

"Fascinating," mocks the male co-anchor, reasonably jealous of Johnny's white suit, or the way his co-anchor's red ensemble mutes his otherwise spectacular February tan. "Maybe the Money Watch team should invest in *tea*," he adds.

The big bad sky is the color of arrogant disinterest. Just posing there . . . making you beg for it, ready to hurl but nothing falls yet. Marco's cigarette smoke blends in nicely as it exits through the sunroof. He's a practiced smoker, looks (and feels) cool doing it, holds the cigarette between his teeth like a happily perplexed pirate before draping his lips around it oh so gently—doubtful the cigarette would prefer to be smoked by anyone else. When he puts the cigarette out the window to ash, the motion is so elegant you'd just think *everyone* was watching.

Marco Salazar knows that The Number 2s will be picketing in his parking lot today, rain or shine, even ice. In the halls of Egostatistical, he's been referring to them as, "the cleaning crew," or, "maid ladies." The group of unemployed Hispanic receptionists would kill Marco Salazar if it would help them get their jobs back, but it's too late; they prefer instead to make his life a living hell.

The protest outside of Egostatistical started after a bitter revenge interview Salazar's former patent editor, LaMichael Carmichael, gave to *High-Tech Times*. In the interview, Carmichael recounted and really enumerated the constant (almost daily) need to remind Marco to include Two for Español while developing the software and patent for his Automated Answering System (AAS)— the technological device now credited with putting most receptionists out of work and steadily *increasing* cellphone usage minutes nationwide.

Carmichael also alleged that Salazar had made a lucrative agreement with multiple cellphone corporations in which he promised to program the AAS to ask meaningless and unanswerable questions like, "What is your account number" to drive up minutes and so further increase cell revenue. Salazar is *also* rumored to have guaranteed that with the simple push of a button, a company could ensure that all operators were busy helping other customers (this is true). Cellphone companies would then offer a kickback to businesses that kept their customers on hold the longest (unconfirmed). LaMichael Carmichael concluded the interview by asking, rhetorically, "What kind of guy thinks up twisted circular lines of automated questioning but can't remember half the country's population?"

Salazar was eventually recognized for having created the most Significant Technological Device (STD) of the new millennium at a *High-Tech Times* fundraiser event. When Marco failed to credit, thank, or even mention LaMichael Carmichael once during his acceptance speech, LMC lost it, "Surely his Technological Device wouldn't have been nearly as *significant* had I let him exclude half the damn population. And I won't even mention the sheer stupidity of his original idea. The idea that eventually became the Automated Answering Service."

And so, these newly unemployed Hispanic receptionists banded together in protest outside Egostatistical headquarters and branded themselves "The Number 2s" (some say L. Carmichael invented the name though he receives no credit from the 2s). *High-Tech* took notice of the racially charged movement and sent a journalist to the scene to see what Salazar had to say for himself. His now legendary statement, "I don't give a shit about them," got labeled insensitive, a corny fecal faux pas, a confirmation of bias. It wasn't long before the whole mess spread around the Internet. Do I need to explain what clever Internet individuals do with a story that involves a hot, young, wealthy entrepreneur, minorities and a few juicy out-of-context quotations?

They invent clever captions for unrelated pictures.

They use this symbol "#" to reinforce everything already overtly hilarious about said captions.

They "tweet" "at" everyone even remotely involved.

They cry injustice and form sentences that include phrases like 'this country' or 'the government' and 'how can something like this happen in (insert current year here).'

They influence late night television monologues.

They want to *do* something about it.

They want Salazar to apologize publicly for what he did.

They do not ever consider how many people he *does* employ.

But he doesn't even notice because he's got a company to run.

Another public figure commits a newer and/or funnier faux pas.

They move on.

They leave the Number 2s behind.

Salazar pops his trunk and The Number 2s "BOOOOOOO" at him, jerking their signs of protest up and down for his notice. Marco Salazar cannot read the signs as they are of course written in Spanish. He's got about fifteen umbrellas in his trunk and he invites the protestors to come over and take one. Their English-speaking representative yells to him, "No way man, you just want us to put these signs down."

Salazar can't stand arguing with them anymore. He'd long ago added numero dos for Español. He'd been feeding them lunch on and off for months.

It really hasn't helped that a younger and Hispanic software man developed a similar system (exactly the same) to Marco's that allowed Spanish-speaking callers the honor of pressing One for Español. The Number 2s spend a lot of time calling local Long Island businesses to find out who still uses Marco's numero dos answering service and then they picket accordingly. There is a merger/buyout being worked up by the Egostatistical legal team that should soon quell the Numero Uno rebellion.

Marco Salazar leaves about fifteen sets of Gore-Tex brand gloves with the umbrellas on the sidewalk. He looks at the poor, cold protestors on his way in and announces, "There is going to be a Glaze Event beginning any minute now—you're welcome to stand in the lobby while you wait for rides home."

"We're not going *anywhere!*" the representative replies, blue lips, teeth a-chattering. No matter how many pizzas Marco orders or gloves he hands out, The Number 2s will not understand their time was coming one way or the other. If Marco Salazar had not invented the Automated Answering System, it is a metaphysical certitude that someone else would have. Direct human communication and basic human labor are things of the past—he tries to make this as clear as possible to whomever will listen, but no one will listen.

Boss Salazar runs his fingers through his hair in the elevator. He looks up at the mirrored ceiling and it is clear that he's flicked all the just-now-falling ice balls from his gorgeous black strands. Using the small mirror on the back of his cellphone device, he checks to make sure he's got no boogers in his nose—it is important for a boss not to have boogers in their nose—you never think about it, and that's because the boss is always thinking about it. Boogers undermine a boss's authority. Tiny food particles flying from the boss's mouth while eating, or sticking just barely to their lips or chin, can have this same effect. That's why you never get to eat lunch with the boss.

The elevator doors glide open and Salazar strides booger-free into the office where the office weasel is pecking around at everyone's desk. His moronic, orange, button-front shirt is buttoned up all the way, it constricts his Adam's apple and could be the reason he is always stretching and recoiling his neck when he speaks. Boss Salazar actually has zero clue what the weasel does, a perplexing department called 'Human Resources' does all the hiring around here now. The boss has often thought about his company as developer of inhuman resources and wonders in this same vein about what then alien resources might entail—a directory of available extra-terrestrials? Too many lonely lunches.

"Yo, *BOSS*-man," shouts the weasel.

"Good morning," replies Marco, who is also unsure of the weasel's actual name.

"Yes, *morning*, grrrreat morning all right," he may as well have just gone ahead and replied with 'Sheez, I'll say,' and looked out the window. He's stretching his neck toward the Boss. A beacon signaling intended conversation from which the boss must flee, quickly. He rushes to his executive assistant's desk.

The weasel yanks at his tight, orange collar. With two fingers he pulls it the opposite direction of the momentarily outstretched neck and awkwardly lurches at the boss, who has noticed a consistent spike in weasel energy during national news events like this weather thing, or a tragic airport shooting. Anything that might elicit passionate general conversation or permit early release from work seems to get him all jazzed up.

"Did you see Johnny Mountain's 'Mountain Call' this morning," the weasel asks.

"Sure," replies Salazar.

"Ever been in a Glaze Event before?"

"Not before today, no," the boss replies, still inching closer and closer to his charming executive assistant's desk, who does get to eat with the boss from time to time and so is aware the weasel's presence is unwanted.

"You may go home now, Scott; they're closing the roads soon," she's got exceptional organizational ability and writing skills, highly motivated, a self-starter, comfortable in a fast-paced setting, able to work independently or in team environment, uses "may," when most would use "can".

"*Oh* yeeeeeahhh, is that okay with the boss?"

"Have a good one, Scott."

"You've got a conference with Legal in five, Marco."

Scott skips back to his desk, shoots his neck and announces, "I'm outta here." The few employees who have made it to work are relieved.

In the office, Marco tells his executive assistant, Kelly, that *that* kind of shit right there is why I need you.

"What does he even *do*?"

"Scott's a field tech."

"A field tech?"

"He visits local offices who are having problems with their software."

"Don't most offices have their own IT professionals?"

"Yes."

"Does our software ever break down?"

"Not really."

"So that's why he's always around and never has anything to do."

"Right."

"If we gave him his own office would he stay in there?"

"Already tried it."

"And . . ."

"Nope."

"You're good."

"I'll figure something out soon enough. We can't fire him."

"Why not?"

"Scott's Hispanic."

"Fucking Christ."

"You should just tell everyone what was on your mind, Marco. They'd understand."

"Is *anyone* even racist anymore?"

"Sure, people in the South are."

"*That's* racist!" says the boss.

Kelly laughs too. She's so pleasant to look at. One of those girls who puts ribbons in her hair Saturday afternoons and with whom you imagine a whole life with right after meeting her (they haven't had sex yet). Here's part of the reason why:

"You don't *really* have a call you know."

"I figured, heard something about a winter weather advisory on the way in and schools closing—that where all our moms are?"

"Yeah, they all sent emails."

"So . . ."

"Emma called earlier and said you should collect her stuff and leave it in the garage."

"Okay."

"She also insisted on returning the ring and car."

"Okay."

"Are you mad?"

"I don't know."

"Well, *I* think she's crazy."

Just as the Boss was about to take this suggestive bit of phrasing to the next level, a meteoric cacophony *sprack* and *cack-cack-cacked* against the office windows. The Glaze Event kicked off with the force of a great blind pigeon apocalypse and all anyone in the office could do was quietly exclaim the f-word and rotate their nervous gaze from the front door to their car keys to Marco Salazar.

And so, after Marco sent everyone home to tuck in, he

stayed to collect a few framed photographs for the impending and non-confrontational garage return. He looked into the eyes of the photographed Emma, staring and thinking—like, in a way that if the person in the picture could sneak into the room without notice and see you staring like that, she might think twice about calling off an engagement.

Salazar exited the elevator carrying his clinking cardboard box of frames. Before he walked outside, he took a moment to observe The Number 2s bracing themselves against the sharp and constant ice. They'd put their signs down and were using their forearms across their foreheads as shelter; ineffective, some had picked up and unfurled the donated umbrellas—all wore the Gore-Tex gloves. The ice that did not pelt their bodies went ricocheting cartoon-like off the parking lot pavement and some that really slanted in with the furious wind skidded along the black ice for yards. The Number 2s weren't speaking to each other because opening one's mouth had become dangerous: early ice had split a few lips, drawing blood.

When Marco reentered the lot, they acted like nothing had changed, like an adolescent busted mid-whack by Mom, they all rush to grab their signs again in the manner of the dishonestly self-assured. They *are* quick—quick enough to convince themselves Marco had not seen them on break, nearly defeated by the still infant storm. But not quick enough to be certain. Really, slow enough to admit it's likely he'd seen them. And still they bob the signs up and down in his face, taking out their ice-fed frustration on the owner and chairman of Egostatistical.

Marco addresses the group, "I am leaving the office

now and it is Friday and neither I, nor anyone else will return here until Monday or whenever this is all over." As he speaks, the chairman is party to the same blistering, icy onslaught. He speaks like he's addressing his own soldiers and not the enemy. His loosely combed black hair pairs nicely with the ice in it. As the world around him becomes all white, Marco's dark features stand out brilliantly in contrast. Not only is he immune to adversarial conditions, he thrives in them. The balls seem small and futile when they bounce off his awesome black leather jacket.

"I'm getting in my car now . . . and I'm not coming back here . . . until Monday," he speaks slowly, toeing that so fine line between offense and courtesy when addressing foreign speakers, "no one . . . at all, is going to be here again . . . until *Monday*. You can all go home now. You should all go home. Now. Okay, I'm leaving." The Number 2s make no reply. It is pretty much understood that they're going to leave and that no one is going to blame them for it, or even notice.

Salazar hops into his ride, black leather jacket against black leather seats—leather euphoria. He pushes in his personally designed and installed (1 of 1) old school cigarette car lighter and turns up the tunes as he shifts manually into reverse.

He pulls up alongside The Number 2s and rolls down his window, "De veras, regresen a sus casas y a sus familias y disfruten el fin de semana."

"Eres pura mierda," replies one Number 2.

El encendedor de cigarillos del coche suena y despierta el interés de los "Numero Dos" pero no lo suficiente, entonces el líder dice, "Jódete hijo de puta."[*]

Cars dawdle fitfully forward along the Long Island Expressway like lemmings headed to the edge, taillights lit in red alert, wipers sloshing and resloshing, thoroughly mucked slush, performative arms flung frustratingly into the air, stabbing middle fingers, yelling —total disrespect for the rules governing the HOV lane. Marco Salazar shoves his high-performance, wide-tired ride nearly up somebody's wet and icy rear-end, tiredly yelling, "Come on," more like a passive reaction than a guy who cares or actually has to be somewhere. Though in truth, Salazar did want to be somewhere, namely, anywhere but stuck next to exit 35, "Patchogue," where he grew up. He looked at the giant white word every day; sounds like a poison radish, a dimwitted, burrowing creature that should have fur but doesn't. Just to say "Patchogue," one must contort their mouth and tongue in a way that encourages drooling and there is no way to clearly enunciate something so marbled and so makes you sound dumb or low class even before the other person confirms that you are as poor as *those* clothes would indicate. Goddamn "Patchogue," the only word his mother could still properly pronounce after losing control of her entire biologically western hemisphere. "Patchogue," the sign yelled, former home of the slackened beast woman and her dull-seeming son, forced to rub her left leg nightly, hoping to reinvigorate the loose, white, hanging marshmallow muscles. And she, this beast, Misses Salaznek, blowing Marlboro or Parliament cigarette smoke into her massaging son Mark's

---

[*] *Translation: Marco tries to endear himself to The Number 2s by speaking Spanish —he fails, horribly.*

teenage face—Mark often considered this brand shift while rubbing and rubbing and rubbing her in their dreadfully earth-toned living room. He eventually concluded that the corner store clerk had great difficulty discerning if she'd said "Marlboro" or "Parliament" and as both are quality brands, it is doubtful she ever bothered to correct him. After the accident in their shitty, shitty driveway, she did not speak so much as words leaked from the corner of her perpetually down-turned mouth, drooling out from the jaw. She'd say things to Mark every night, he could hardly tell what they were, "Duneverrr fuhgit whooya-arrrr," and the like, little inspirational clichés.

Marco Salazar tries not to think about *those days* anymore. But he knows if it weren't for Patchogue, and his mother, he'd never have invented the Automated Answering System. One thing for another, I guess. He grrr *injects* the car lighter, "Ack," turns up the music. The lighter ejects. It pops and he pulls it. Puts it to the butt, sizzles. Makes that flashy ash-movement as the car is overcome with his created haze. He guides the wheel one-handedly down the exit 41 off ramp: "Old Brookville."

He used to make this trip from Patchogue to Old Brookville on Mondays in the summer with his mom. He'd roll down the window as they pulled off the exit. She'd always have hers' closed to support the weight of her leaning left side, drooling a bit down the warm sunny glass like a dog does. She spoke into the glass, to Mark, "Thave ta bes fishear . . . *ta bes*!" From his opened window he could smell . . . "Fresh air." But that's not it at all. This is an *atmosphere* we're talking about—the cool presence of freedom, freedom from worry, freedom from morning and evening flabby calf massages. The stuff sifting into their rusted car wasn't fresh air, but elegance spiked with mint cannabis and chased with Spanish Rioja. The Mothers of Old Brookville walked on tanned feet, treat morning and afternoon like separate events, just front yarding it in white pants, all day, holding hands with bonneted babes. Destination: nowhere in particular, maybe to the beach, or stop at Fred's to get *something*, smiling and waving at the sweating men perpetually raking and mowing these yards. Mark sometimes noticed that the Moms and Dads would shelter their children's ears from his mother's car; its mechanic echo did rudely pierce the otherwise perfect atmosphere, rumbling along to the fish market where Mark would have to roll his window back up.

If you don't already know, Monday is not the day to buy fish. What is left on Monday is left over from Friday, Saturday, and Sunday. Anything they can move on Monday is just a bonus. Those fish are rank. They smell like their gaping mouths and bulging eyes look, puking at the thought of themselves lying around in the sun for so long. Misses Salaznek, leaning and cane-bobbing her way into the market, didn't give two shits about the smell. She didn't read the sorry gaze of the fishmonger when she asked, "Wus-goodeer?" She tilted against the cane, waiting for his answer, not swatting the flies swarming around her cigarette smoke and briefly nesting in her dry, orange-yellow hair. Her son Mark stood back, checking to make sure no classmates were around to pass judgment. The monger also looked at Mark, who could read his gaze—it was pity, makes ya feel too small, insignificant. His mom kept leaning there, smoking with her right hand. The thin left strap of her purple and tulip dress fell from her shoulder and landed in the crease of her elbow.

"Well," the fishmonger said, averting his gaze from her contorted mouth, "the catfish fillets are good, okay, they're *okay*, in the summer."

Misses Salaznek considered this, jabbed her cigarette into her hanging mouth and pulled on it with half lips, "Dey standup toooda heat aright enuff?" she asked, not fixing the strap, not swatting flies, sun blazing directly against her face.

"Yeah, they do okay."

She turned to her son, "*Marky*, wuddya think?"

"Hey, yeah, if they're good," said Mark, trying to sound excited but wanting so badly to just exit unnoticed.

Misses Salaznek pointed her cigarette at the monger, "Baggumup, yav da bes fishear. . . . I tell erybuddy dadullissen, *da bes*!"

Marco remembered the way she smiled, pressed up against that window all the way home. Her right-sided smile made the greater by contrast. And she'd been right, correct, too—those catfish filets were tasty and, when removed from that mountain of rotting fish flesh didn't actually smell that bad.

Marco kind of chuckled at the familiar memory, thinking about the ocean of topnotch fish he'd consumed around the world since, as he watched his garage door glide open automatically and almost too quickly for comfort. The door ascended in a manner befitting a lair instead of a home, the lack of a swooshing, futuristic sound only made the motion more unsettling. Emma always hated these garage doors, "Can't we just have normal ones that move like a grandpa," she would plead, "come on, let's get the grandpa garages." But Marco Salazar exclaimed that *this* home is a testament to the power of technology. The door slid closed behind and so shut out the smacking sound made by cascading ice. Even in the garage, Marco could see his breath and feel the tightening grip of nature cast upon itself.

These are the days meteorologists dream about, major airtime for Johnny Mountain, front and center fella. The lone regional voice tasked with unveiling the intent of an angry regional god. This bitch could get national coverage. Tree branches might fall over. And land on power lines. Grocery stores turned battleground, utter lack of any fresh bread, whispers of stocking the basement among the elite. The word "crisis" started to get flung around the writers' room. The possibility of Johnny's big break includes the possibility of trickledown benefits. He needed words appropriate for chaos.

Marco opened the space fridge to discover a barren landscape. He phoned his nutritionist.

"Chew, yo man."

"Marco, what are you doing?"

"When you coming over?"

"*Whaaaaaat* I'm not going anywhere in this, Marco. You're crazy."

"Dude, come on, tomorrow's the first."

"Tomorrow is *not* the first."

"Today is the twenty-eighth, Chew. You need to program the fridge."

"It's leap year Marco, tomorrow is the twenty-ninth. Marco, fucking trees are falling down. I lost power. I think my phone's gonna die. I can't be driving around."

"The twenty-ninth? Shit. Come over here, I have power."

"I'll try to make it over tomorrow. You should really go get some food for yourself."

"I have a wine cellar, Chew."

"Marco, my phone's gonna die."

"I'll call you tomorrow."

". . ."

"Chew?"

Ah shit. Salazar flipped on the TV.

"It makes sense Long Island—the devil bestows his wrath with fire, God uses ice. I don't know what some of you did to *deserve* this," Johnny steps close to the camera, smiles, winks, retreats to the map of Long Island's sliver, now enlarged to fit where the whole entire USA used to be.

Salazar could sense the desperate local writers being pressured to uplift the storm's prestige. He sipped some stale coffee, "*Wrath* isn't *bestowed.*"

"Steer clear of the roads for the rest of the day, this Glaze Event is kicking into high-gear with gale-force winds. . . ."

"Maritime term," Marco noted.

"Beware of falling branches and downed power lines, if you still have power and heat, turn it up, the temperature will drop precipitously as the sun sets . . . towns without power . . ."

"They can't hear you buddy."

"Bellport, Blue Point, Brookhaven, Calverton . . ."

Marco makes that 'blah blah blah' motion with both his hands, chomping like a babbling meteorologist.

"Mount Sinai, Patchogue," Johnny pauses to wipe the corner of his mouth, "Port Jeff, Port Jeff Station, Rocky Point, Ronkonkoma . . ." you get the sense that there are interns scrambling to various alphabetically arranged locations holding cue cards in the way Johnny Mountain shifts slightly and pauses when he gets to a new letter.

Marco looks at his blender. He's supposed to make a shake but opts for a bottle of wine from the cellar. He's kind of annoyed Chew isn't coming over. He sends Chew a tempting text message: `Just cracked a bottle of Rioja . . . 1990. Let's party.` But the message just hangs there, not going through: the death of Chew's phone is confirmed.

"And in Nassau County . . . Baldwin, Bellmore, Bethpage . . ."

Salazar starts wandering around his house, which is actually really a mansion, most of his neighbors' mansions have names and the names usually include the word 'manor,' like Saddlewood Manor or Stone Manor or Avebury Manor for instance. He moves slowly into the vaulted living room, like hoping the longer it takes him to get there, the better chance he has of finding someone. No such luck. He jumps and is startled by the pronounced sound of crystalline trees snapping in the proverbial distance. The initial *CLAP* is so thick and unavoidably real that it rattles his spine, the bareboned echo that follows calls attention to the abnormally vacant streets just outside. This raucous splattering of timber becomes so commonplace, almost rhythmic, Salazar anticipates the phrase "Fee Fie Foe Fum," anytime now.

"Garden City, Hempstead, Hewlett . . ."

"Old Brookville."

"Oh, shit."

"Ohhhhh no, no no no no no," Marco pleaded with his empty house.

Oh yes, everything off. All Marco's humming electronics simultaneously shut down with a defeated sigh. The modern domicile in a cold coma. . . . Modern man struggles to survive.

What to do first but light so many candles? The aroma actually occupies the just unplugged mind for longer than one would care to admit. Oh wowie, I should light candles more often . . . what is *this* waxy blue gem, "Lilac Blossoms," a holdover from Mother's Day no doubt. And now "Bahama Breeze" and "Banana Nut Bread" and every Christmas candle including "Spilled Wine" and "Refrigerated Spinach" certainly no bestseller but why actually make the stuff when you can just light a candle? Once the mansion is fragrantly muddled, it becomes apparent to Marco why people always use the term 'Candlelight' instead of just 'light.' He can't really see but traces of everything once familiar, now dominated by the longest indoor shadows possible.

The unplugged mind soon returns to its default setting.

"Hello, you have reached the Long Island Power Authority, para Español oprima numero dos. For billing inquiries, press or say one. For trouble with your service, or to report an outage, press or say three."

"Three."

"I didn't get that. For billing inquiries, press or say one. For trouble with your service, or to report an outage, press or say three."

Marco presses three.

"Thanks. We are currently experiencing high call volume. All of our customer service representatives are busy at the moment. The approximate wait time to speak with a representative is forty-five minutes."

Wildly inappropriate Muzak slithers into Marco's ear and so he pushes the button that ends the phone call, defiantly gulps his wine and heads into the basement for another bottle. He's got no food, *his* phone will probably die soon, and he's in the romantic stage of a solid red wine buzz. The beam from his heavy, black flashlight forms intricate bottled shadows on the cellar walls and his mind recalls Roman times, when men *claimed* ladies and lusted after every single thing candlelit and appealing.

```
Kelly, it's like ancient Rome over here.
Hi Marco.
Come over.
Whaaaat? Are you drunk?
Whaaaat?
They shut down the expressway. Even if
I could get there, it's probably a bad
idea.
Just come on, I need your assistance. I
don't even have any food.
Where's Chew?
He said he's not coming over because
it's leap year.
You poor thing, what're ya gonna do all
night?
I guess drink and wait for the power to
come back.
Might be a while.
No way.
You want my assistance?
Yes. Please.
Start boxing up Emma's stuff. You don't
need power for that.
I might.
Call me tomorrow, my phone's gonna die.
```

And so now, finally confronted with the option of

reading by candlelight to pass the time, Marco Salazar decides instead to collect his ex-fiancées stuff. Great word, stuff, perfect for describing all that might go into a box or any number of items one leaves behind. It is, of course, also right here that you'd be expecting a catalogue of these cute little *things* going into the box so cleverly used to recall cute little memories. But I wouldn't do you like that. Are these physical manifestations of time spent what you think of when you think of memories? Do you actually believe that when Marco Salazar still thinks about Emma every single day of his life, he meditates on vague seashells or pictures from dinners and ballgames and vacations and weddings and holidays? That's all just stuff. Actual memories are no more static than those who fill them. They are stored not in a cardboard box but within the most complex human organ, and here they are eternally alive. They are not posed or captured, but accidentally retained, forcibly ingrained through significance. What Marco boxes are trinkets and artifacts that only act as signifiers for what goes on inside said organ, they cannot convey the smell or sound of her and even after they are boxed for garaged return and forgotten she will still *exist* to him as strongly and as clearly as the day they first met. He holds so tightly to that first day, cued on continuous loop, it waits backstage every night for the hacks to clear out, then, moonlit, takes center stage to tuck Marco in and hopefully guide his dreams somewhere pleasant.

It was the day he first presented what would become the Automated Answering System to a group of investors in Manhattan. He was twenty, entering his sophomore year of college and still living at home to take care of his Mom, whose condition had worsened, which is the word people use in place of the phrase 'gone completely to shit.' With his notes and computer packed by the front door he sat on the ottoman massaging the limp calf muscle—it'd been limp for five years and yet she insisted. She still cashed the smoke from her lungs into his face. She'd gotten into drinking more seriously. Mark dreaded what he'd find each night when he arrived home from school.

"Ya fugedding hooda fukyarrrrr," she'd have ashes right on her shirt, her left side unraveling further into the muddy recliner, that left arm dangled off the side so much it appeared now longer than the right.

"Enn waddaya doon tudday fuggin bigschot?" she asked him that morning, noticing her son in a suit for the first time.

"I have an interview."

"Zit aboudat musheen ya made me?"

"Yeah."

"Skippinda margit tuday den?"

"I'm gonna have to, pick me up something for when I get back though."

"Yarryarrya, jus dun fugget hooyarrr-kay," she reminded him, arm dangling.

"I won't."

By 8:15am that Monday, the Long Island Railroad car fully smelled of unflushed urine and sweat and hairspray and soggy newspapers and Redbull and coffee and residue from thick green soaps and smoke and gum. Mark tried to go over his notes but got distracted by the girl across the aisle and up one row. The ever-present male fantasy of the beautiful woman spotted alone on public transportation took hold. He couldn't turn away from the display of gentle dexterity made by her purple fingernails breaking that bagel down into bird bites. With each successive stop the conductor reminded everyone that *this* is a particularly crowded rush hour train and that they're expecting another crowd at the next station. After the conductor punched her ticket, she thanked him. Mark would later tell his buddy about the sound of her voice and take a lot of shit for it.

At the next stop the conductor came on again to announce that *this* train is particularly busy and those riding together should sit together.

And why wouldn't it be particularly busy at now 8:45 on a regular old Monday morning.

Mark looked at his notes. Just black blotches on a screen. This dexterous distraction might be his unraveling. He felt himself sweating and considered not what to say or how to sell but what some money might do in helping to rejuvenate his deteriorating mother.

And at the next stop the conductor again reminded everyone that the train was crowded and those riding together should sit together.

And Mark considered the absolute fact that *we are all riding together* and that there really is no way for those riding together to not sit together.

She started popping baby carrots into her mouth one . . . at . . . a time. Looking out the window with something on her mind Mark figured to be as interesting as her profile, cut like a sparkling starlet against the humdrum towns whizzing by. Not at all static but full of something actual and alive Mark wanted. She wore a jean jacket with the sleeves rolled up to give her various bracelets room to jangle up and down her arm. Olive skin and blonde hair, these traits provided by nature and not a salon, everything on her face rounded and soft.

Mark convinced himself that his open seat, and her open seat, and the relative proximity, were all good fortune fated and so took his shot.

"You know," he quietly croaked up to her seat.

She didn't respond, as there were a lot of voices on that train.

"*YOU* know *what*?"

She turned around, still unsure, "Me?"

"Yeah."

"*What*?"

"We're actually *all* riding together."

"What?"

"The conductor . . . he keeps saying 'if you're riding together you should sit together,' I mean, *we are all riding together* . . . ya know?"

She did laugh and she did get up.

"What's all this?" She asked, sitting down next to Mark. Confidently too, like no way she could be feeling what he felt—he kind of just stared in a trance at her two scarves that hung so colorfully they radiated with the force of fifteen. She was thin, a small little lady but with a full face, almost pudgy in its cuteness. The way she walked across the aisle and sat, you could imagine her dancing for a lifetime without a moment of embarrassment. Black sunglasses rested on her head, dimples flanked charmingly crooked teeth—eyelashes flashed and flashed. Mark always told her she was too cool for him, even after he became really cool.

"It's a presentation, for uhhhh device I'm inventing."

"Ah, you're an *inventor*," she said coolly.

"I hope so."

"What's your name?" she asked.

"Marco," he lied.

"I'm Emma," they shook, bracelets jangling.

Salazar's long ass shadow wobbled a bit down the garage steps. He put the second box of stuff on the freezing concrete floor, unsure of how much time had elapsed. He'd thought it must be like at least two hours. It'd gotten dark, good-for-nothing sun out napping somewhere in the back. The once radiant candlelight now receded into itself, swallowed almost completely by the black sky that cloaked the powerless house.

"So, what's this *device* all about?"

"It kind of allows people who can't speak to make phone calls."

"I've never really thought about what a pain in the ass that probably is."

"The first one I made was for my Mom."

"She . . ."

"She went to remove a telephone wire that'd been sticking out of our driveway. It was live when she grabbed it—she couldn't let go."

"I'm so sorry to hear that."

"Took out her whole left side. Doctor said the current ripped through her nervous system like a lighter on tissue."

Somehow, she stuck around even after that way too personal intro—though in Mark's defense it *was* topical. In the meeting, with the investors, they acknowledged a societal need for such a device but asked how it could be possible for someone to carry on a conversation with only "yes" and "no" as available responses. They were right—he'd witnessed his mother struggle to make it work—the inability to make the linguistically capable aware of the yes or no situation was a big issue:

"Hello."

"Yes."

"How may I help you sir . . . or . . . ma'am, maybe?" Operators not yet versed in the proper pronouns for conversing with computers.

"Yes."

"Ma'am . . . sir? What can I do for you?"

"No."

And so it went. The thing needed work. After the meeting, Mark was interrupted on his way to the subway, "Yo, kid," shouted LaMichael Carmichael.

"Yeah?" Carmichael approached him, put his arm around him—walked him around the corner. Pulled out a smoke and handed one to Mark who said, "I don't smoke."

"Listen," Carmichael started, "you write code or what?"

"Yeah."

"Flip that bitch around."

"What?"

"*Listen*," Carmichael repeated, "you got it backwards. What you need is the computer to be on the other side. The person calling won't have to talk at all."

"Oh, shit."

"If you can write code for what needs to be asked, like, do you need to pay a bill, or call a specific department or whatever—check movie times for god sakes, all you need then is the responder to press a button in a reply that the computer can read and move to the next option—no one ever has to talk."

"That's brilliant."

"You can write code, right?"

"Fuck yeah."

LaMichael Carmichael, 42, quit his job within a week, backed and even befriended the young code writer, and, as we know, did save him from nearly blowing the whole thing via a certain recurring omission. After the infamous STD speech, Carmichael called Marco and asked stuff like "What's gotten into you?" "What's your problem, *dude*?" "Is something *wrong*?" "Are you even listening?"

Wasn't long before Marco moved to Old Brookville and hired someone to take care of his mom. That first someone got hit, mid massage, with a right-handedly swung bottle of Jack Daniels. The second someone took great offense to her cigarette smoke, then Marco had sex with one, and another, then the rest all got sick of constantly being asked the unintelligible question, "Hooina fugz MARGO SALZRRR?"

Who indeed.

Barefoot and bored in the garage, indifferent to both his freezing feet and the cardboard boxes. The moon taunted him through the small garage windows, all calm and silent and one-eyed, hidden behind many twisted black branches that, given the ice-aided thickness, did actually appear glazed—they tentacled into aching, complex spirals, fusing with the yellow moon a delightful lunar design like a bad tattoo. The too familiar racket of ice thrashing ice no longer filled the sound void left by all that forced powering down. And for the first time, Marco felt cold.

"Hello, you have reached the Long Island Power Authority, para Español oprima numero dos. For billing inquiries, press or say one. For trouble with your service, or to report an outage, press or say three."

"Three."

"We're sorry, your response was not understood. For billing inquiries, press or say one. For trouble with your service, or to report an outage, press or say three."

"*Fuck YOU*. OPERATOR. OPERATORRRR! I need a *HUMAN*. HUMAN BEING."

He stomped back into the house.

"We're sorry, your response was not understood. For billing inquiries, press or say one. For trouble with your service, or to report an outage, press or say three."

He pushes the part of the screen on his phone programmed to represent the number three.

"We are experiencing unusually high call volume. The approximate wait time for a customer service representative is one hour and forty-five minutes."

The absurdly inappropriate, mind-numbing, sunny-psych ward, driving-to-insanity Muzak had returned for an encore, happily leaping through the phone like a clown on a daycare murder spree. There would be a Monday meeting about this on hold Muzak.

Marco noted his cell percentage like a pulse. He felt hungry; cold, drunk, barely functioning on fifteen percent power. He needed to leave; flee, like the birds and bears had done months ago. He hung up. And he dialed.

"*Welcome* to Oheka Castle, Long Island's premier hotel and estate. For directions, press one. For weddings, events, or corporate sales, press two. For group hotel sales, press three. For fine dining, press four. For mansion tours, press five. For media inquiries, press six. . . ."

"*Un*-real," Marco begged the machine.

"For the corporate office, press seven. For a hotel

reservation, press zero."

He presses zero.

"Oheka Castle, this is Suzanne."

"Yes, hello?"

"Hello, sir."

"You have *power*?"

"Yes sir, is there something I can help you with?"

"Can I get a room?"

"I'd be happy to check for you sir," she checks, punching keyboard, the spongy oral sound of her gum chewing almost too much for Salazar to handle, "hmmmm," she says, chewing. "Well, all we have left is the Olmsted Suite. . . ."

"Book it."

"Sir, I should tell you the Olmsted Suite is nearly two thousand dollars a night."

"It's *no* problem," his chuckle is relief, not conceit— maybe a hint of conceit.

"*Fantastic,* sir. The exceptional suite pays tribute to the Olmsted Brothers who designed the *reflective* and *stately* formal gardens here at Oheka Castle. You will have access to two *glorious* balconies that overlook the great lawn and the reflecting pools—course, I do apologize sir, that all that's frozen tonight."

"That's fine Su—"

"Su-*zanne.*"

"Suzanne, don't worry about the reflective pools, you saved me."

"Come check in anytime, sir. Plenty of people staying the night. Executive Chef Horatio Ettore Felice has decided to conduct an impromptu tasting for tonight's guests."

"Thanks *so* much, again, I really appreciate it."

"Can I just have your name sir?"

"I'm Marco Salazar."

"We hope to see you shortly, Mister Salazar, drive safely—I do take it you live close by? The expressway's closed."

"I do, this isn't my first trip to Oheka. My first solo trip, well, yeah."

"Very good, Mister Salazar. See you soon."

Marco Salazar sets his wine glass on the counter. He hops up his grand staircase two steps at a time, rushing to his closet for some proper dining attire. He's no longer thinking about what could have been, what was, but what *could* be going down at the Oheka Castle tonight. The Olmsted Suite, the *Olmsted* Suit, he rehearsed in the mirror—Would you like to join me . . . in the *Olmsted* Suite, he's buttoning up a checked shirt that would look like the blue tablecloth from every picnic but the material is too fine, his tailor too talented, his downcast eyes just too damn debonair, he's gonna *fuck* somebody tonight. Yeah, you know, I have a view of all the frozen ponds from my two glorious balconies. That's funny, it's cute and witty and humble, the tie might be a little much, could come off as desperate. . . . He tucked it into his overcoat on the chance other dudes were wearing them.

And also if the suite wasn't stocked with champagne, he grabbed a few bottles from the cellar, wrapped them in his overcoat, and threw them onto the passenger seat of his jumbo truck—a vehicle so large and so in charge that this Glaze Event marked the first time in its generally garaged history that the word 'needed' could even be considered appropriate. The tires still smell like rubber, flawless black paint all-polished, hungry front grill shining like a great white opening up for dinner.

Marco presses the button on the wall that opens the garage door caging the black beast. Not much is happening. Of course, he thinks, power's out. He pushes the button on the driver's side visor that opens and shuts the door. Nothing going on.

"COME ONNNNNN," he screams at the imprisonment that is his garage.

Marco smiles that, oh god, kind of terrified, unsheltered smile that acknowledges he might be totally screwed. He looks at the door, runs his fingers through his hair, adds his blazer to the pile on the passenger seat, unbuttons the sleeves on his tablecloth shirt, fuck it, he unbuttons the whole shirt and takes it off, adds it to the pile. And now in his shirt sleeves he can really feel that blistering cold sneaking through all the miniscule cracks that come with any house, even a named mansion or manor. He still takes the time to admire the definition of his goose bumpy arms—biceps, triceps, forearms, the whole works on the ready.

First from the inside, first behind the black beast, Marco bends over and pulls the manual override handle with all his might. He wants to use his hands and his arms to manually open the garage door. But sadly, the hefty door does not concede one inch.

He gathers himself, hands on hips, takes a few deep breaths, goes back down and this time with both hands squeezed into the handle he jerks and contorts his reddening face to aid the struggle. He *puuuuuulls* and releases an anthropoidal screech of pressure from deep in his guts, wine colored dabs of spittle drip onto his chin and some rocket through his teeth to the cold concrete, sharp

ripples of skin cut into his cheeks with the effort and his
eyes ooze liquid tension. He knows it's the ice. He gets up
and shoulders the door: BANG—BANG—BANG, trying to
shake it loose. He shoulders it three *more* times. The crazy
bastard elbows it and punches it on his way back down to
the handle. He yells, "FUCK *you*," at the door before
pulling again. He pulls and he shoulders at the same time,
his shiny shoes are slightly slipping and leaving signs of a
struggle on the concrete. The goose bumps have vacated
his arms that aren't yet sweating but do test the limits of
flexibility in such a chilly and unstretched atmosphere. He
continues to pull up and shoulder out, he grunts "HA-
URRRRRGGGG, MMMMMMUHHH, HUUMMMMMMM
MUHHHHH . . . ," that classic vein-popping grunt from the
tomato-faced world of the hopeless and desperate.

This is usually when someone watching would coolly
mention, "I don't think that's gonna work," from a few feet
away. And the hopelessly desperate would answer, after
three or five dramatically heavy breaths, "Well," more
breathing here, "what do *you* think we should do?"

Then they'll mention something annoyingly obvious
that, unless you're dumb, you probably checked even
before you started the wildly physical exertion, like, "Did
you check to make sure it's *unlocked*?"

The sweaty individual would then reply in the
rhetorical, "Waddaya think I am, an idiot?"

The conversation will end there and the two, or the
one (in this case) will just stare at the problem for a while,
not yet ready to admit total defeat. The ice sounds like
laughter sprinkling daintily down to join its massive and
amassing crowd of compatriots outside the garage doors.
Marco Salazar kicks at the door with his brown dining

shoes, even throws another straight right that stings his knuckles. He yells the f-word; he hadn't elongated the middle vowel like that in a while. He shoulders the door again, pathetically, he pulls at it now like a dedicated crew member—one, two, three . . . one, two, three, *huh*, *huh*, *huh*, resuscitation, unsuccessful. He considers reversing the black beast straight through that bastard door. But luckily, '*christ*,' Marco laughs, the sound of anciently thick trees toppling like dominos in the distance reminds him of the potential havoc wrought by massive collapsing structures. He thinks of the mocking front-page headline, the photo of his crushed and half-stuck truck, that most unfortunate moment when supposed freedom turns instead to unexpected end.

And now is when that still-standing fool's errand foreman will say, "Why don't you just go outside and break the ice?"

Yeah. Just break the ice.

He puts on sneakers, his leather jacket, walks out the side door. Ice descends from the sky in unnatural heavy and then lighter spurts, assaulting Marco Salazar's face like the regional weather god is salting dinner. Stiff trees line the perimeter of Marco's property, utterly black and indeed, thick with glaze. The moon brings hints of electric white definition to all the trees' frostbitten fingertips. Misshapen limbs lay perverted all over the ground, twisted, inky against the snow. Wind squalls scream in vicious howls through the branches and over the icy lawn, thrusting into Marco's ears so powerfully his brain feels in a vise. He puts his hands there, over the ears, thinking that might help things.

The ice has inches on the garage door, on all the garage

doors. Marco kicks the ice bashfully, like aw-shucks, this requires tools. The word that comes to mind is *pickax*. A tool that you can't just buy, if they even *have* it, because of the way the cashier looks at you. Unless you look like a real miner or railroad man, you'll look like a criminal up to *something*. You're forced to come up with a ridiculous excuse for the purchase like, "Never know when there might be a Glaze Event."

Instead of the necessary pickax, Marco grabs a yellow-shafted shovel, orange shovelhead/handle (plastic). This tool looks like it came with a Happy Meal. He lifts it above his head with both hands on the shaft, takes the frigid air into his lungs for a step, and then plunges the tool into the ice with the ferocity and pride of a Coliseum victor.

YEAH.

YEAH.

YEAH.

Small bits of ice splatter to the sides. The back of Marco's leather achieves its own glaze inside ten minutes. His hair stiffens with each successive skewer. He bends down to check his progress, prodding the ice with his fingers. Dented it, size of a golf ball—fresh ice fills the hole almost immediately. Marco knows it's hopeless. Tree limbs splinter and fracture around him, the freeze bites into any exposed skin, his face is like a cadaver, his fingers frozen. He is tiny in the tundra. He's not getting that Olmsted suite, no frozen reflecting pools, no impromptu tasting and certainly no sex of any kind.

He smashes the shovel into the ice repeatedly until it splits up the middle.

NO.

NO.

NO.

He's audible again but in the great space, his frustrated grunt produces hardly an echo. He Mickey Mantles the door twice, WHACK-and-WHACK, which entirely detaches shovelhead from shaft and handle. He calls the fallen shovelhead a 'fucking piece of plastic shit' and kicks it away for icy burial. The remains of the tool reveal a not-that-sharp edge of yellow plastic. The knight and his plastic lance are an epically futile pair. And that unfulfilling slash of sunny color rises against the sable sky then stabs into the ivory earth like the forlorn filter of a failed photographer, something so incredibly not artistic or meaningful that it makes you sad and so becomes a work of art.

Marco Salazar persists in the hopeless deed, he stabs and stabs and stabs and stabs, he's yelling at the ground, spit sticks to his purple and frozen lips. He wants the not-so-sharp shaft to impale his own vulnerability, to gore and release the prison of pressure gathering in his guts, to free him from whatever he's thinking 'here' means to him.

Marco's last stab is a catastrophe. His right foot slides backward as he goes for another plunge, the angry momentum sends him to the ground at breakneck speed, his hands brace for the forward fall but his right wrist snaps on impact like one of those far-off tree limbs and from close proximity the sound is disturbingly similar. The wrist's concession allows for the head to crash down next. He can't open his eyes to accost the sky. His face is pelted by jagged hellfire ice-fairies. Marco rolls to his side and eventually works his way up. He's covered in everything. He grabs the shovel with his good wrist, takes it inside and stabs it into Emma's box of stuff so it looks like, you know, he's just a good dude returning her cute plastic shovel.

Back inside, he seeks nothing but the passage of time. He needs *this* to end. He feels himself withering with each frozen moment—his cell percentage in the single digits, the hope of existing on hold long enough to reach a human voice even more impossible than freeing the garage door. He finishes the last half of an already opened bottle of Rioja with his wrist dangling and pulsating. Nothing left to do but try to sleep.

The once pornographically alive white screen in front of Marco's bed is confrontational, hauntingly pale, white, powered down, dead. The cold has even reached the top floor. The hot young software man has the coverlets pulled up to his chinny-chin-chin. He chucked his dining attire in the laundry basket and pulled on all kinds of sweatpants and sweatshirts. He stares at the ceiling, wrist throbbing, thin white curtains just hang out on the side, allowing unwanted moonlight through the windows, lifeless sheets drawn together, two anorexic models in bridal gowns waiting for just a breeze to blow them bare, the physical manifestation of sheer silence that invades Marco's mind. All the forgotten people are resurrected in the vacant space—Mother, Fiancé, Partner, Victims—abandoned, lied to, forsaken, and fucked. He feels like the center, eye of the storm, he blames the telephone instead—for crippling his mother and costing her her job and livelihood, "Misses Salaznek, putting you up in front of those kids, it is, it's, well, it's kind of like a cruel mirror," the pit-stained head of the school for autism told her. Her slackened left side couldn't put up much of a fight, "I gessurright den." Nor did she fight with her husband who deemed her unfit for marriage, "Take care of your mother," was all he told Mark as he rushed to his car, his freedom. She didn't even fight with her son when he decided to move out. She conceded to everything and everyone, even gave up her choice of cigarettes and sat alone smoking them in the empty, earth-toned house. She fought only to be *acknowledged* by her own son and for him to acknowledge his family name. The only thing she cared about, all that she asked of him or any of 'em—for her son to just remember that she exists, to remember and talk about the life that made him. She showed up unannounced at the mansion to find a mysterious and naturally cool young woman, Emma, to whom she asked, "Hooa fuggaryoo?" To which Emma answered with a question, "Well who are *you*, at my house?" and naturally, she found out. Misses Salaznek also found out that she'd been described as "dead" from day one. The two women sat there in this same silence recalibrating their opinions of mighty Marco Salazar, formerly plain old Mark Salaznek of Patchogue, NY—who while inventing the most Significant Technological Device of the new millennium also had to make sure his degenerating mother received constant care and had to fight and plead with her to accept that care. Who after working on his device and patent for double-digit hours still went back to Patchogue to massage the mushy leg and help her in and out of the shower. Who when his mother could no longer stand up in the shower he helped her in and out of the bath and was told, as her naked body dripped all over the bathroom floor, not to forget any of it—and who, when finally called upon to make a pointless speech, spoke with the sole intention of *ending*, of finishing, of moving on to something else—of getting the hell out of whatever 'here' meant for him then. He forgot to thank a few people along the way, he changed his name—then all those people lost their jobs, and so *what*, who are they? Who are you? Who *cares*? You have to choose.

I tucked Marco back in, powerless and injured, right back where he started—I did it for you. It's about you. Everything, for you. . . .

If you frequently ask others to photograph you and your smiling spouse, press one.

Don't worry about it—nothing was ever wrong. The power comes back on, the mansion warms up and Marco places the most thoughtful handwritten note on Emma's stuff. The note wins her over, it explains *everything,* and she forgives him. They hug and kiss and get married. Misses Salaznek (body rejuvenated) is a bridesmaid and moves into the guesthouse after the couple returns from the most extravagant honeymoon where they do not fuck even once but do often make love.

If you're pissed, press two.

Marco is overcome by dread. His throbbing wrist spreads and so consumes his body. He deteriorates into wine bottles, trembles at evil thoughts of what he has done *to* people in his life. He can't pull the covers up high enough. That note he writes to Emma is now also addressed to his mom and the subject matter is changed. He goes downstairs into that stainless-steel kitchen and pulls out a pistol or revolver or shotgun, whatever you choose to imagine. He puts your firearm into his mouth and pulls the trigger, spreading guts all over the space kitchen, but the guts, like stuff, just a potpourri of nonessentials that don't quite comprise what makes a life.

If a song has ever moved you to tears, press three.

Marco writes the note and it is sweet with perspective, the content matters because it is reflective and so totally honest. The power does come back on, but he does not revert back to his constructed self. He shows Emma the real Mark Salaznek, he brings his mom over, all are humbled—the time without power has changed him for the better, reminded him who he is, who he always was, forced him to think and act like a real person instead of someone defined by *things* that will never be alive, and he finds fulfillment in this—he is finally *himself*.

For the operator, press zero.

Hi, it's me, the operator. Imagine my human voice. Admit that we're both here. Listen, all that ice, it's just gonna melt. No matter who you are, it will defrost and liquefy and dissolve. It will collect and rush into gutters before joining a charging river on its way to the ocean. I promise it's only a matter of time until the waxy leaves puff out their colorful chests and whistle a sidewalk breeze for your pleasure. And you'll just flop along, happy to forget certain frozen moments. But you can't just box that stuff away. We should not be satisfied by the presentation of our ever-posturing person: this disease of disguise is spreading.

The Probably Magical Wheelchair
(True Story)

The story begins when I sit down to write it—as the factually worst song ever recorded plays, on repeat, in my head. "Barbie Girl," by the band: Aqua. Except I edit the only lyric any of us has ever known, the chorus, by adding "You Bitch," in parenthesis after the "Come on Barbie, let's go party." When I hear Barbie respond, "ah-ah-ah-*yeah*," to me calling her a bitch, over and over, I add ALL-caps to the parenthetical section to see if she'll notice. She doesn't.

Then I think how I'd better erase this because while that is actually happening, it probably doesn't have anything to do with the real, true story—that started last week, and is, in fact, *ending* as I write it.

The first time I drove past the garage sale I almost didn't notice. I pass that house every day and it's a shabby house, one you'd look at just to find something to criticize, but I'm not one of those people. It is an incredibly short, one-story house. I feel like I could clean their chimney on my tippy toes. The yard is equal parts grass and mud and I'm pretty sure a few graying tires are scattered here and there. I idly scanned the garage sale, feeling a little bad— nobody wants to put all their crap out on the lawn for judgment; they do it because they need a few extra bucks. If they needed only space, they'd throw the shit away and save themselves the hassle of haggling with neighbors who are really just strangers anyway.

Just before returning my eyes to the road, I noticed one particularly interesting item at the garage sale: a wheelchair. "Oh . . . fuck, they're selling a wheelchair," I thought. It's hard not to notice an empty wheelchair. Especially one that is stuck in mud instead of on a ramp where it belongs—empty, a wheelchair is simultaneously symbolic of past and future tragedies.

Over the following week, I thought up some important questions regarding the wheelchair that just wasn't selling.

Why don't you need it anymore?

And who, needing one, would ever get it there? Or even think to.

Can't you just donate that to a hospital?

Is it there to elicit pity from garage sale customers?

After how many days does a garage sale become an open-air market?

I wanted to believe that the former wheelchair resident had at least graduated to crutches. My favorite image was of the rider finishing his or her first marathon, as a runner. I wanted the wheelchair to be there as a symbol of something *good* that happened.

After four days I made a note in my house with prearranged duct tape and wrote in thick black sharpie the word: **WHY?**

And leaving room for a reply, I stuck it to the wheelchair seat. I sealed it on there good and ran to my car and drove away *fast*.

The next day when I drove past, the paper was gone. I cursed those bastards for not playing my game how I wanted.

The day after that was Saturday. I knew that if I could summon the courage to have an extremely disappointing conversation, that'd be the time.

I went over at ten am sharp—the prime hour for garage sale shopping. I pulled up and saw a rotund gentleman, probably sixty-three, sitting on a quivering plastic folding chair. I worried that if the chair dumped him, he might roll all the way into the busy street in front of his house. I parked in his driveway.

He didn't get up from the seat when I approached him. He lit a cigarette. I lit one as well, to show him I'm a real man too. So obsessed with the purpose of my visit I totally forgot to walk around, act normal and look at the stuff. I instead stood there smoking and watching him smoke, about four drags when I realized how strange I must have seemed showing up in the yard like that.

"Well . . . what is it?" he asked me.

"Why are you selling that wheelchair?"

"You're the one that put that fuckin' piece uh paper on it."

"No," I said. "Okay, yeah," I said.

"We don't need it anymore," he announced.

It wasn't so much that his answer could apply to *any* item, at *any* garage sale on earth that bothered me. It was the word we, and that he didn't seem to care.

"Why don't you need it?" I asked again.

"You thinking about buying it?"

That actually had not occurred to me. Finally, I just decided to ask him, "Were you healed? Is the person who needed this better now?"

"You wanna buy it?" he asked again.

"Can you just *answer* me?" I said.

He stood up. "YEAH," he shouted, "I'm *cured.* . . . It's a magical fucking wheelchair, now you wanna buy it or what?"

"Well, how much is it?" I asked.

"Thirty bucks," he said.

"Thaaaat's pretty steep," I said.

"I'll go to twenty-five."

"Deal." We shook on it there in the yard. He helped me load the wheelchair into my car and I drove straight to the hospital. The nurses thanked me profusely, "Oh, Bobby," and I felt really magical.

When the Wells Run Dry

I confess: I had sex with the married woman who first brought me to the stream. Please forgive me, for it was good. It started out innocently—this married woman had just finished grooming my dog, Chubs. Chubs needed a bath, but he needed the haircut even more. When we first pulled into Yamar, NY, he was panting convulsively, sleeping in fits and hanging his head out the window, gasping for air. I remember the AM radio flickering in and out as well. The host spoke of drought and despair, an all-time low harvest of grapes and almonds. He mentioned moderated, alternating, appointed times for watering the luscious green lawns of Yamar. A translucent heat wave lingered like a ghost over the car's hood.

"You know, my husband's been messing around on me," the groomer said, looking at me.

"I know," I answered, though I didn't.

"If you don't mind Chubs getting a little dirty, I could show you where the stream is. It's cool there, Gogifu and I are heading over now," she pointed to her dog, Gogifu, the black standard poodle. I knew what she was getting at, so I went.

"You've gotta climb up and around this hill, then down the backside to get to the stream," she said as we walked from our cars. The trails were covered with woodchips, easy on the paws. Trees wobbled back and forth on either side, creaking wearily like old bones, hundreds of these looming pines shading the entire way. Herds of adolescent track boys jogged passed, also breathing heavily, pounding their feet, wafting of Mom's Sunday laundry, checking their watches. Beyond the forest, a neighborhood of houses defined the circular park perimeter. The houses had crisp, bright siding, in-ground sprinkler systems, and hammocks that would dry by the early afternoon.

"That one's ours," she pointed at a house, with hammock. She'd removed her wedding ring since leaving the grooming salon. She told me about how it hadn't rained in almost two months so the stream might be a little low for tall Chubs' enjoyment, but the shade is good, she said, and the mud very cool. She did not ask what I was doing in Yamar.

We did it down by the stream, peaceful and shallow, rocks seen easily beneath the water. There was a small, red bench for people to rest on while their dogs lapped up the water and played. The groomer gripped the corner of the bench with all ten ringless fingers. Her hair fell all around her face when she presented herself to me. The dogs chased each other up and down the hills that surrounded the water and when they crossed through the stream, the slapping made by their paws sounded just like the adjacent sex.

"Oh *my God*," said Gogifu's owner, "*ah* . . . yeah, ah . . . Jesus." "Fuck me, oh my God," she added, bouncing athletically. Mosquitoes were landing all over her and likely enjoyed a memorable feast. Miniscule black gnats hovered around my ears and in front of my eyes, sometimes landing in the eye, sticking to the moisture, joyously wriggling along irises and inspiring a quickened conclusion.

Still, she did not ask why else I'd come to Yamar, just buttoned up and thanked me.

"At your service," I said.

We climbed the inconsistent terrain leading away from the stream. Logs had been placed across the steep path to guard against summer mudslides that never came. Two girls stood at the top of the hill, nearly out of sight. They started skipping down the hill, something lusty in the freedom of their movement. I was drawn to them, one blonde and one brunette, both tan, gleaming, shapely thighs gliding impossibly over the chunky ground.

"How long will you be in Yamar?" Gogifu's owner was talking.

They laughed as though they were born to. The laughter quivered and rattled in their bellies as they negotiated the path, "Tee heehee, tee heehee, mmmhahaha." No way to tell the source of that laughter, they hadn't said a word that I could hear, innocence and purity, glossy, tight ponytails pulled back and adorned with bedazzled purple ribbons, teeth shining from the shade, "Hi," they said in unison. The brunette held a butterfly net. I turned to watch. Their shirts had numbers on the back—twenty-one and twenty-two. The brunette swooshed the butterfly net through the air overhead, ha-*whooosh*, the blonde laughed. When they reached the flat bottom, she swooshed it again, this time in continuous orbit with her spinning body. "You'll never get any like that," the blonde told her, "you have to wait until you *see* one." "If I'm meant to get one I will," the brunette replied, still spinning. They went to the edge of the shallow stream without removing their sneakers. Running shoes, a little mucky, skin-tight tube socks reaching for their knees.

"It's hard to say yet," I told Gogifu's owner after a noticeable delay, still concentrating on the noises coming from the stream. They splashed through the water, "There's one," I heard the blonde yell, more laughter before chasing after the flapping insect, presumably. It sounded like they were running up the hill behind the stream, leaves and sticks crunching underfoot, the net still swishing the air, "You had it," "You got it," "Hurry up," and more cackles rolling down the leafy hill and gaining momentum over the stream before rising to our ears up the other side. I drifted back to the car alongside the groomer and our dogs, stricken—were beautiful people running around the world like this? Clueless about what might become of them? What if they'd arrived a moment earlier, would they still have bothered with the butterflies? Would they have giggled so?

The girls' presence hung over me into the night, suffocating and constant like Yamar's humidity. The hotel clerk told me running water would be available for the next three hours only, so if I wanted to shower, best do it in the next three hours. I thanked him for the information and he replied by saying that he had been praying for rain and that he could feel it coming. The concierge, seemingly annoyed by the familiar phrase and perhaps the hitherto ineffectiveness of prayer called out, "Cut it wit' dat bullshit." The hotel atmosphere had indeed become tense during the drought; you could see people shaking their heads no-no-no without cause. Old ladies carried handheld fans, both the traditional Japanese and the modern motorized American—some even equipped with affluent misting action.

I must confess: in the shower I masturbated—not to the Groomer's fine body, but to the two girls. I thought about how sweaty they were probably getting, chasing the butterflies like that, also the shape and color of their legs. I wished they'd seen my performance by the red bench. I imagined it would've given them ideas and desires. I exited the shower in the state of sweat with which I entered, having accomplished nothing.

My dreams did disturb me. Me with the girls, both girls at once, each girl at a time, the girls together and me watching. . . . I couldn't believe that this madness was mine. I felt somehow invaded and invading. They were young and I wanted to corrupt them—pools of perspiration collected in the valleys of flesh between my neck and shoulders, almost drowning my earlobes. I woke up in the middle of the night to strip the bed, put towels down everywhere and sap up all the moisture I could. Those dimpled smiles played in my mind and prevented rest. I got up and looked in the mirror, turned faucet C to no avail, ran the sweat from my forehead back into my hair. I'd set aside three glasses of water for drinking but chose to dump one over my head, drink another, and leave the third full for whatever came next.

***

A screeching threesome of waterfowl ripped me from sleep. Their callings were unusual. They sounded trapped, desiccated, and cooked. They didn't cue the blessing of another sunny day but instead cried of thirst—a distress signal wrenched from their thin, rickety throats. I left the last glass of water on the windowsill for them and went to the lobby for continental breakfast: All Things Bran. I drank coffee and scanned the Yamar papers. The too familiar sun burned into the lobby and every single person shook their head no-no-no and commented on it—the word scorcher was used by half, sizzler, a third, burning toasty steaming roasty boiling scalding muggy humid, even sultry. People not designed for linen shirts faced forced acquaintance with the formerly foreign fabric. You could recognize the uninitiated, or recently initiated, swinging their arms wildly through the air, invading others' space, surprised by the newfound freedom characteristic of the material. Though the slightly see-through quality of linen did escape them, terribly: sweat stains appeared in inappropriate places, bellies and hair and nipples could all be seen sliding along the breakfast line, clawing at the bran medley while swallowing more caffeine. Telling by the papers and their chatter, they'd be heading to the races today. Wagering hard-earned dollars on galloping animals while guzzling alcohol in the heat— one should never bet on anything that sleeps standing.

I returned, instead, to the stream. Every single day for the next week I did return to it, looking for the girls. I didn't know what I planned to do, or that I'd do anything at all, but something about them brought me back. On Monday I learned from Terry that a family of Snow Owls had taken residence at a nearby airport. The first time she went to see them she brought her dog Pippin, but was denied—"Who knew you can't just walk around the airport fields with yer dog," she'd said, "seems like uh big enough place," she added. I agreed. On Tuesday, I met a state worker who was out early because she was sick, said nice to meet me and shook my hand. Told me that her dog, the cleverly named Buddy, "had rolled around in a bunch of shit and corpses yesterday," and on cue Buddy rolled in another something a few feet away from the woodchip trails—a skunky smell did rise. "Buddy!" she yelled. "Buddy, get *the fuck* outta there, Buuuuddddd," and she ran in after him, "Ah, *shit*," she yelled, stepping in something, probably shit. Buddy then took off toward a friendly and clean looking older couple walking two polite Golden Retrievers. "Get back here Buuud," screamed the state worker. But the beast, immune to the constant calling, was already rubbing the recently acquired grime on the woman's khakis and launching from his hind legs to lick the husband's pleasant lips—what a mess, they all quarreled over it. Wednesday, it reached triple digit degrees and Chubs more or less got free run. He rolled in the stream, as it'd become too shallow to soak and so cool much above his ankles. A constant and gory haze played between the thin rays of sunlight that pierced the thick canopy of leaves and branches above the stream. Plants sagged, wilted and lifeless. The few faces we saw were unseasonably pale and drawn down, yawning away from the nose, bubbles of sweat dotted their foreheads like their brains were condensing. I lingered by the stream for twenty minutes Wednesday, wanting to make this trip worthwhile and feeling guilty for subjecting the large K-9 to the nasty afternoon. But the laughter did not arrive. No bobbing ponytails bouncing down the hill, no rolling cackles. Just the trees and the stream and the heat—the wide-open terrain also seemed lone, also seemed to be awaiting their return. The trees peered over one another toward the parking lot where the girls might arrive. The stream, nearly nodding off to sleep, held its eyes open just a few moments longer and a few more after that, as long as it could, to the edges of daylight before calling it quits.

On Thursday I followed Chubs down the hill to the stream and I heard splashing. I heard the cackling, the whisk of the butterfly net thin through the air awoke nervous flappers in my stomach. Chubs, undeterred by the Sirens, plunked down and lapped up some water. The stream had run so close to dry that if he drank for an hour, he might finish what was left. They stopped laughing when I got there. They didn't speak to each other, or to me at first, but watched the dog.

"He likes the water," the brunette announced.

"Dogs do," I said, "especially when it's hot out."

"Barely any water left," the blonde said, sulking, "we can hardly keep the garden alive anymore."

"Garden?" I stuttered.

"The Parish garden," the brunette jumped in. "Father just refuses to run a hose, he only uses well water."

"Of course . . . *now* . . . there isn't that much water in the well at all," said the blonde.

I figured they were working towards a donation—the way they kept adjusting their hair and bending at the hips to stretch. They had the same shirts again, softball shirts, the front said: Saint Edward's Softball. I assumed he sponsored the team.

"Do you sell the garden vegetables to raise money for your team?" I asked.

"No, our dinners are free; parishioners may choose to donate," replied the brunette.

"I see," I said, "well I'd like to help out if I could." They looked at each other. "In, any way . . . that you might need help," I added, running a few fingers through my haircut.

"Well," the blonde mumbled, looking down her tube socks, "we could use a strong man to help carry buckets of water, maybe help with a small harvest we're having for Saturday's dinner."

I liked being called a strong man. I liked that *they* considered me strong, and a man, "At your service," I told them.

"Come an hour or two before sundown," they said and waved goodbye to Chubs, thanked me and ascended the hill behind the stream. I watched them climb, their ponytails bobbing in rhythm with their strides and when they reached the top they jogged out of sight and did giggle without ever looking back.

***

Three hours before sundown I asked the hotel clerk to direct me to Saint Edward's Parish. "The Confessor or The Martyr?" he returned.

"Cut it wit' dat bullshit," croaked the concierge.

"I don't know," I replied. "The one that has a garden?"

"Ah, The *Confessor*," he said, "but dinner isn't until tomorrow."

"I'm going to help them water and harvest."

"I see, Father just refuses to run a hose," the clerk told me. He gave me an intricate hand-drawn map before adding, "It's just up the road."

I went up the road, the road flanked by hanging oaks, driveways rolling to garages at strict intervals—one, aaaand a-*nother* aaaand a-*nother*, and then the vast clearing. Twenty yards of clipped yellowing grass on either side of the paved church entryway that ran at least the length of a football field back to the church positioned in the absolute center of the whole space. Parking lots to the side and the rear, cars parked on the side now and an assembly line of men passing water buckets from the well to the garden and back. Bent women weeding and harvesting the garden popped up like moles to look at my car. The collected stare made my approach feel more like lurking—this unfamiliar car driving slowly to join us for what?

It had never occurred to me that my sudden presence might strike these parishioners as odd. Could they identify a sinner as easily as I could identify One Who Has Never Sinned? Here, a sober virgin and *here*, a guy hunting two virgins, same bastard who sullied a married dog groomer earlier this week. Her husband had it coming. Eye for an eye, that's in one of the bibles isn't it?

By the time I got out of my car, they'd all gone back to work. The women wore hats on their heads and put lettuce, carrots, eggplants, cucumbers, tomatoes, and peppers into cardboard collecting boxes. These mothers were really going at it in their jeans, faces serious and aglow in the setting sun; you could see a lot of the forearm-to-forehead sweat-wiping action going down. Twenty other strong men humped the buckets of water back and forth from the well. Like I said, they passed each bucket (there were a total of two—one always going out, one always coming back) along their line instead of carrying one at a time and in this way fostered communal feelings. By the way, the well had a Holy Cross attached to its roof, just like the looming church.

I got out of my car and walked slowly toward the

garden. I noticed the father standing at the other side. I could see but flashes of him as the women worked back and forth through my line of sight—his bald head separated two waterfalls of thin black hair hanging like curtains over his ears. He wore khakis and a white golf shirt. He tucked a book under his arm. He walked into the garden. As he walked, I searched for the two girls. I examined each of the women's hats, anxious to find the familiar ponytails bobbing out below. Every woman turned to say something to the father as he sauntered majestically through the garden. They tilted their cardboard boxes to display the contents for him and he nodded, pleased by this. I couldn't tell him what I'd come for, who had invited me—I'll just say I was driving by, a curious out-of-towner, hoping to help, no, inquiring about Sunday's Mass, no, hotel man told me there'd be a dinner tonight. Oh, it's tomorrow? And then I could leave and not come back tomorrow or ever. Or I could ask about the girls' softball team. . . .

As he reached the edge of the garden, I panicked. You couldn't tell where he was looking, if he saw me, disapproved or approved—he had this nondescript face, a featureless peach impossible to read, just staring into boxes and nodding.

"Hello father," I said.

"*Father*," he laughed, "call no man on earth your father, you have one father, who is in heaven—I am a priest, but call me Tim."

"Tim . . ."

"You are here to help harvest?"

"I wanted to inquire about the girls' softball team."

His blank face paused. He looked down at the book,

"Softball team?"

"The Saint Edward's softball team, I met two girls—"

"We haven't sponsored a softball team in fifteen years."

"Oh," I replied, a bit shaken, and offered, "but they called you father . . . do you have daughters?"

His shiny, flesh mohawk stared, disturbed, thin lips zipped shut, blank and fixed and stopped by the queer questions. I tried to avoid his gaze. Could feel him calculating possible reasons for my arrival. I looked beyond the bucket assembly line to the tall oaks waving and taunting my moronic inquiry, too distant to hear the leaves whispering to each other. No cars came up the drive or passed in the road out front. No softball team for fifteen years. Perhaps Saint Edward the Martyr had a church that sponsored softball.

"Why don't you go give ole Peter there a break," he pointed to the man rolling the handle that dunked and pulled up the bucket.

I rolled the wooden handle until my shirt was soaked through, until my hands calloused and the sun had nearly set. All I wanted was a drink of the outgoing bucket, yet no one else took even a sip. I wondered how the garden could possibly need so much water. The depth of the well made me bitter. The priest would stroll alongside the factory line to let us know that we were almost there, "Yes, we're alllllmost there," he'd say.

"Okay," the priest announced. And at once the men dispersed to grab up the watering cans we'd been filling. Without a word the women started trucking all the cardboard boxes into the church and so clearing the garden for the men to come through and water. I observed each man standing over a particular plant for ten methodical seconds before moving to the next. I grabbed two leftover cans and entered the garden. The soil was moist and conceded inches to my sneakers. The priest stood in front of the garden with his back to everyone and watched the sun issue its violet goodbye behind the oaks. The garden smelled dank in the fresh dusk. The water appeared more vibrant in the flat, faded light. The priest turned back to the garden like he'd just personally tucked the sun in for the evening.

"That's perfect, *perfect*," he said. And at once the men now exited the garden, stacking their watering cans on the lawn. The women watched them do it. It became clear to me that these were mostly husband and wife tandems, especially when they all joined hands at the last strip of lawn before the asphalt. The priest then made the sign of the cross before them and said a few things. I stood awkwardly apart from the scene, looked to the parking lot in search of purpose, but none came.

"Go in peace," the priest said. And they did, all waving 'goodbye Tim' and 'see you tomorrow' and all that; my return waves went unnoticed.

"Give me a hand with these," he said to me.

"Sure," I grabbed up as many of the cans as I could and followed him not inside the church but to the other side of the garden, to a large wooden box with six stones on top to hold the lid down.

"If you knew where you were going, maybe you wouldn't have struggled to carry so many watering cans," he told me.

"Maybe," I agreed and placed the cans inside.

"Will you join us for supper tomorrow?"

"Okay," I said. He nodded, "Good," at me and went inside the church.

The hotel lobby reeked of armpits and cigars in the dry night. The number of hungry guests swarming inside the lobby bar caused the decibel level required for intelligible conversation to rise considerably.

"I hit the pick four *straight* away and slammed the fuckin' exacta in the ninth, baby," a man told his wife, "*straight* away," he reinforced the boast. She did look pleased. He showed her a clever wad of money and fired a few bills at the bartender, instructing her, "Whatever they're all havin'" pointing to everyone sitting at the bar. And everyone sitting at the bar appreciated the free cocktail. A few held up a current beverage for salute, others yelled, "HEY NOW JACKIE BOY," and Jackie Boy took a showy slug of ale, pounded the empty pint onto the bar, "You fuckin' got it," he returned.

I walked up to the clerk, "Just two hours of water tonight, this and the next," he said before I could ask him anything.

"No, no," I replied, "I wanted to ask you . . ." here I paused, felt a discomforting stare from the concierge over my left shoulder, "is there, a-uhhh-nother Saint Edward's church in Yamar, the Martyr maybe, like you said?"

"I told ya," croaked the concierge.

"Shut up, Joey," the clerk retorted.

The clerk now looked at me, "I'm sorry," he said, "people go crazy during track season, they're all wasted and asking for refunds and discounts because of the water situation. . . . Couldn't've come at a worse time, really."

"I can see that," I sympathized.

"Anyway," he said, "yeah, there is only one Saint

Edward's church in Yamar, The Confessor, only one anywhere remotely close to Yamar as far as I can tell."

"Then why'd you ask me if I meant The Confessor or The Martyr?"

"Just to entertain Joey there, sorry about that."

"What?"

"Lately a lot of people have been asking me that, if there is a different Saint Edward's church in town, other than The Confessor. So finally, we decided to double-check just to make sure and found out that there are two Saints named Edward but still only the one church. It's kind of an inside joke now, I've said it to, like, the last four people who asked."

"I see. Are any of those people still at the hotel?"

"They all checked out."

"I see." I thanked him and went to my room. Roars from the hotel bar rose up through the floor all night. Bastards down there mother-effing and sonofabitching and coughing, chugging, back-slapping, and smoking. These are the people that give birth to beautiful virgins, same people who eventually ruin them. Though I'd never seen anything quite like those two from the stream, I started to forget about them and wonder more about Tim. And how the parishioners reacted to his blank face—the married tandems moved with a purity of purpose, elegant and quiet and calm, not asking questions, not stricken by the drought, but taking it in stride. Is it that they're just *good*? I didn't want to believe that. They were weird and quiet, passing those damn buckets around in oppressive heat without thirst. That's strange. Ladies separated from men, aged asexual vibes—how's that any good? That's the kind of thing that turns men into sex-crazed beasts, capable of God knows what. What *is* good in the world but slamming exacta boxes and cocktails and public adultery? When Tim watched the sun go down, what could it possibly be that he wished for if not money, booze, and sex? How the hell to satisfy or reward his faith while still on earth? Why even bother?

***

Twelve elegant serving platters set along the middle of a twenty-foot folding table. White tablecloth. No meat, but fish. "Bless us O' Lord for these thy gifts," the priest began with the usual. I glanced up and around the room at all the down-turned heads. No ponytails and no dimpled cheeks. Sets of clasped hands rested uniformly on the edge of the table just below mumbling mouths, "herbaderbderbderb," verses in collective monotone, eyes closed, pinched at the corners, maybe even sadly. I wondered if these same words, spoken so many times, at every single one of every single person's meals, could retain any weight rolling out like that as though the entire prayer were just one word— blessusolordforthesethygiftswhichweareabouttoreceive . . . rolling out like an unfortunate reading tick. The autopilot mouthing masking actual brain activity. The group murmur has all the force of an active vacuum cleaner two rooms away.

It is entirely possible that some of the parishioners thought evil things during grace—'I don't see why we can't just have some damn steak. What'd'ya know, the room smells like wax again. Billy got caught smoking weed in school, I bet that bastard Mikey made him do it, that little sonofabitch is such a bad influence on my boy and look at

Marge just sitting there praying like she doesn't know what happened. Dolores smells like mothballs, I'm losing my appetite because the selfish bitch refuses to use running water.' But they were probably just being really mentally thankful for the food and for not starving like some other people in the world.

When Tim finally reached The Amen, everyone, including me, moved their right hand generally around their head, chest and shoulders. They filled their plates in the orderly manner with which they tended the garden. Each man grabbed the serving platter in front of him, took a modest portion of whatever vegetable or fish, then moved it to the right until every person had his or her share. No one spoke during the rationing and not a lick of skin could be seen anywhere at the table, save for their faces. They'd worn sweaters and long sleeves and pants, despite the oppressive heat. I had a lot of forearm on display, the mark of a stranger, I felt anxious that when the time came to dig in, I'd have to justify my place at the table. The girls were nowhere to be seen. I thought maybe I'd lie and say I was starving.

"Ruth, I understand you have a grace moment you'd like to share with us," Tim said.

"Yes," everyone turned to look at Ruth, 75, of Yamar, NY. She sat not directly across from me but diagonally, one to the right. I could see most of her face from the slight angle—her lips were all dry, crusty and cracked, she'd pulled her gray hair into a bun so tight it took her eyelids back with it. She had dark blotches of skin about her pale cheeks and a dangling Turkey's chin that wobbled back and forth along the upper rim of her black turtleneck. This tight turtleneck filled open holes in her white sweater to form floral patterns in the negative space.

Ruth kept hold of her utensils as she began. Her hands were crooked and veiny and shaking. The knife and fork scratched her plate like two hungry mice throughout her story. Her scabby lips did not separate much as she spoke, "A few weeks ago, when I went to Pennsylvania for my sister Irene's funeral, an old grave marker leapt out at me. It said: '**Sister, Ruth Marie**,' which is *my* name. I felt that maybe *my* big sister, Irene, was trying to tell me something. Now this was almost three hundred miles away from here. Me and Irene used to talk on the phone a lot, our beloved brother Joe had passed away just a few months before Irene had her stroke, we've always wondered which of us would be called home next. Now I've been blessed with good health my whole life. I joked with my family about the grave when I got back to Yamar, told them I really thought Irene might be trying to send me a message. One of Irene's favorite hobbies was scratch off lottery tickets. Lord, I never had any luck with 'em, but Irene? Irene would purchase them when she needed money to pay her bills—she'd just walk into the store, buy one of those tickets and so many times she'd win the amount she needed. I don't like to leap to conclusions, but last Thursday I stopped to get gas on my way home from lunch with my grandson. I told him I was going in to buy a scratch off lottery ticket and that if I won more than five dollars, I'd make an appointment with my doctor."

"Tell 'em what happened," Ruth's husband said.

"I won a hundred dollars," Ruth's husband nodded his head proudly at this.

"Oh, Dear Lord," another woman exclaimed, crossing herself.

"Tell 'em what else," Ruth's husband said.

"I'm *gonna*," Ruth said, continuing, "So I went to the doc. He asked why I had made the appointment, given my good health. I told him the whole story and he smiled at me. He'd known about my spirituality and though I was symptom free he said he'd order an ultrasound of my carotid artery."

"Tell 'em what he saw," Ruth's husband said.

"I had a ninety percent blockage of my carotid artery. My doctor couldn't believe it. He scheduled an appointment with a vascular surgeon, who did more tests to confirm the blockage because I was symptom free. But it was true, I needed surgery—it saved me. I never would have gone."

"Bless you," a woman said.

"Doctor Richards told her he's gonna make a few changes to his practice too, didn't he?" Ruth's husband asked.

"Yes, he did."

Most of the parishioners put down their utensils to perform the sign of the Holy Cross, more precisely than before. Priest Tim did not remark on the celestial message. Though he did shovel an impressive portion of haddock into his mouth. It was difficult not to laugh at his thin hair swishing back and forth over his ears as he ate.

"Tell me what you think of this," announced the hungry priest, between bites. He took a sip of (white) wine. "After her mother's passing, Josephine, you all know Josephine?" They nodded. "She kept thinking about this one phrase: 'Are you thirsty.' *Now*, throughout their lives, Josephine had heard her mother repeat this phrase to so many homeless people she grew to hate it. Her mother would offer the homeless some of her drink, or the whole drink, and then when she got old and sick she would buy the homeless their own drink. She'd sometimes work at local shelters. Other times she would bring whole cases of water for the homeless, always asking, 'Are you thirsty?' I ran into Josephine a month or two ago, around the start of the drought. I asked her how she had been doing since her mother entered God's Kingdom. She said she'd been traveling with her husband. She visited her mother's birthplace in Alabama. She and her husband drove past a convenience store with a homeless man sitting on the curb out front and she became suddenly *very* thirsty. She thought it might be a message and told her husband to pull into the convenience store, which he did. On her way in Josephine asked the man, 'Are you thirsty?' She told me how he sat there and just stared at her, a black man, 'Are you thirsty' she asked him again. She stood over him for another silent moment as he shook his head. She said, 'It's okay, I'm thirsty too, I'm going to get a drink, would you like one?' And do you know what that man said to Josephine?" Priest Tim asked.

"What did he say?"

"He said, '*Fuck you*, I work at the garage right next door, if I want a drink I'll go in and get it myself.'"

"Oh, Dear *Lord*," a woman cried, Holy-Crossed herself. Tim took another sip of wine and waited. Not a word, and I saw Ruth shaking her head, her eyes even wider than before.

"Well?" Tim asked.

"Some people don't appreciate their blessings when they receive them," Ruth said.

"Ah, perhaps, but who would you say was blessed in

this situation?"

"The man," Ruth said.

"Yes, the man," a few others agreed.

"The *woman*," I spoke, "Josephine." I could feel their faces turn to me, perhaps noticing me for the first time.

"And how is that?" Tim asked.

"She learned her lesson."

"What lesson?" Ruth's husband inserted.

"That you shouldn't just assume someone is homeless."

"Right," said Tim, "a humble perspective is . . ."

Before Tim could finish, Ruth's husband jumped back in, "Josephine was only just offering the man a drink. She was doing a good deed, she had a message from her mother—she got *really* thirsty, remember, she told her husband she became suddenly thirsty."

"Can't thirst just be thirst, George?"

"What do you mean?" George asked.

"I mean that if you go around constantly searching for the message, desperate to find some-*thing*, some . . . *connection*, isn't it possible you've invented meaning to fulfill your needs? Your desperation sees only what it wants to see and clouds your vision, desire dilutes the purity of experience—a simple local mechanic on break becomes a thirsty homeless man and divine message."

"Are you saying that Irene didn't send that message to Ruth?"

"I *know* she sent me a message," Ruth added.

"I'm saying that Ruth was saved and blessed. And that we are all thankful, that's all I can know and all I need to know."

"Ah-men," said George, just like that.

After dinner, three youth volunteers boxed up the leftovers for donation. Each of them shook Tim's hand upon arrival and again before leaving, "Father," Ruth said. "Eck heh hem," Tim replied.

"I mean, *Tim*," she continued, "what will your sermon be about tomorrow?"

"I think . . . water," he announced.

"Or lack thereof," said George, snorting a guttural post-meal laugh.

"When we need rain, it will rain," Tim replied. At this, Tim looked off in that way that signifies the finality of an unanswerable inquiry, the empty gaze of empty resolution. The parishioners fumbled around with their napkins and coughed and rearranged their silverware until George eventually stood up from the table and said, "Well, I sure hope so," and reached over to shake Tim's hand, thanking him for the delightful and informative evening. Ruth mentioned her excitement for Sunday's mass and others agreed saying 'yesyesyes' as they shuffled to the exit.

Tim turned to me and asked, "Are you coming tomorrow?"

"Yes."

"Why?'

"I don't know."

He waved at the last few folks leaving. The Church's heavy front doors closed behind them. One last gust of wind snuck inside and whooshed through the bare hallways. Papers posted to a corkboard by the front door ruffled then relaxed and the only sound left was the exit sign's neon buzzing.

"Why are you here?" Tim asked.

"I'm not sure."

"No, you can't be sure. That's true. But why did you come here, in the first place?"

"It doesn't matter why I came."

"It matters only that you are here?"

"I think so."

"I know why you're here," Tim said.

"How can you be sure?"

"I can't," he said, but nodded his head yes. The fine black hair draped over his ears shifted back and forth like two wide tassels and the corners of his mouth turned up a tad, "no one is ever sure," he said, and repeated, "no one's ever sure." He put his palm on my knee to test my nerve against silence. The exit sign kept time as the flat face hovered two feet away, seemingly examining my classically contoured face like an enthralled alien. He did not move but stared, his hold on my knee soft like he wanted to pass something on or receive something. "I can finish my sermon now," he said, with that got up and left. His heavy black shoes clop-clop-clopped down the still empty hall and I heard him call out, "We'll see you tomorrow," as I walked outside where the concrete parking lot now felt like an intrusion. It suffocated the earth in its absoluteness and threatened to overtake the garden. The garden looked so small from the parking lot. It looked like the past, something people grinned at the thought of before getting into their jacked-up rides and pushing a pedal to go away. It's so cute the way they walk around in there, growing their vegetables—any number of things are possible in a garden. From a garden, things sprout and they feed and they live and then die and the people walking there are part of it—there are things they must do, the garden makes demands. In a parking lot only one thing happens. They flatten it and pave it. People come, they park and they leave. They turn their headlights on and the drone burps up from the metallic underbelly and disturbs the snoozing oaks. That crass echo evokes final evening chirps from the birds before they decide to go do whatever it is birds do so silently all night long. I drive along more pavement back to a hotel. Thank God.

There is commotion in there. A big, fat, sweaty, disheveled guy is waving his glass around in the air above shoulder height. Joey the concierge is after him with both hands. It's Jackieboy, he's yelling, "That pipsqueak motherfucking motherfucker. Fucking Jockey? The fuck is *that*? Jockey? That pipsqueak motherfucker," he's yelling and spinning, "He wouldn't give him the whip, he had it, *had* it on the inside, he just hadda give 'em the fucking whip." The doors slid open automatically and I walked inside. Jackieboy's wife was crying in the corner, not loudly, just the welling eyes like she'd seen this too many times and expected it at some point—here-we-go-again tears. Joey locked him up with an arm grapple and handed the drink away to the clerk, "Get OFF me," Jackieboy yelled, flailing, "You shoulda seen this bullshit. It's fixed is what it is. It's fixed!" A police cruiser arrived outside and two uniformed policemen entered through the automatic doors. Jackieboy went to retrieve his drink from the clerk but the clerk hopped over his big desk just out of reach. Jackieboy's belly bounced into the desk's edge again and again as he lunged to steal back the drink, grasping like a kitty at a yarn ball, he yelled, "Give it here, you fucking pipsqueak." Then one of the cops swept Jackie's legs out so his head cracked against the desk edge, knocking him out as he fell flat against the thin lobby carpet. Jackieboy bounced once before his overstuffed stomach decompressed, which released an air bubble through his nose and mouth in the form of a great awakening burp that delighted the gathered spectators.

"You have the right to remain silent," one cop said, perhaps referencing that burp.

Jackieboy mumbled, "It's all fixed," into the carpet and the officer responded cleverly with, "We'll fix ya all right." Jackieboy's wife followed them out barefoot with her high heels hanging from her two fingers.

I wouldn't see that darling couple again until the next morning when they walked into Pastor Tim's church. Jackieboy shuffled painfully with a Band-Aid on his head and a pissed off wife on his arm. They moved in a trance to their seat like everyone else, all there for something, wanting something—the same thing? Old folks with gray hair they never wanted, limps they didn't deserve. The invisible organist played them along boringly. The music floated down from the ceiling with the weight of a feather. The parishioners would Holy Cross themselves before sliding into one of the rows. Row after row of long, wooden, unpadded pews. The dog groomer walked up the aisle holding her husband's hand. They slid into the unpadded pew in front of me without acknowledgment. They rejoined hands after Holy Crossing themselves, they held each other tightly, like they *needed* this, like they were trying to meld their skin together to show just how close they really were. That was the first time I'd thought about her since we'd done it.

The song changed as Pastor Tim began his approach up the center aisle. The aisle separated the two sections of pews and led to the pulpit. Ahead of Pastor Tim was his Deacon who held The Book way up in the air. Both the Deacon and Pastor Tim donned green robes with white satin stoles—Pastor Tim's stole was clearly more ornate than that of the Deacon. A semi-circular clan of children called, 'The Youth Ministry,' walked ahead of the Deacon. Pastor Tim was followed by a couple of nuns in black and when they all got up there the place grew silent with anticipation that had seemed more casual up to that point.

"Peace be with you," Pastor Tim said.

"Andalsowithyourholyspirit," the parishioners gurgled.

"Lift up your hearts."

"Weliftthemuptothelord."

Then Tim outstretched his arms and turned his palms upward, or towards heaven you might say, "*Through Himmmm in Himmmm with Himmmm in the unity of the holy spiriiiiiit, all glory and honor is yours almighty Father, forever and everrrr,*" he said. Then the organ fired up again. A plain woman in long white sleeves and long black skirt with black stockings and black shoes took over the pulpit and sang some tune about abundant fruit and peace and salvation. When it came time for the chorus of the song, she lifted her palm at one side of pews and bounced upward from her knees, to lift them and inspire a bit of mumbled singing. She'd alternate sides each time the chorus came around and she'd recount this performance to her family at brunch and again later at dinner.

Then everyone sat down in the pews. No sound but surrounding exit signs, coughing, and a few babies. Pastor Tim walked up to the pulpit, he paused, he looked at the parishioners in the pews to his right, the parishioners in the pews to his left, he smiled and began, "In 1964, I was sitting down for lunch with my father when my sister came home from school crying, 'It's just a story,' she cried to my Dad. 'What,' he replied, 'what story?' 'The Garden of Eden, they told us it's just a story.' Now . . . being that he sent my sister to *Catholic* school, I could see my father getting red in the face over this, mumbling this or *that* under his breath," Tim paused to allow laughter, "But it's true. The Garden of Eden, it's just a story. That's part of the message I want to share with you today. A message about the literal meaning of a text and the metaphorical— science asks *how*, but philosophy and theology, they're all about *why*," Tim clenches his fist, not raising it much from the alter, "Theology asks of us to find meaning in the words outside of the text to understand truth. You see, fiction equals truth here, each one of you must discover what a text, what a story, means for you—but you must also remember that a text or a message may have a different meaning for someone else. I've often told many of you that my favorite prayer spot, the place where I think most clearly, is by the ocean at night. I feel closest to Him there. And in this way, I've found hope in the stories of Jonah and Noah, stories that involve water. And that's fine, for me. But I was reading the paper yesterday and I read a story about an Indonesian girl swept up in a Tsunami ten years ago. She was just four years old when it took her away from her family. She survived. A fisherman caught in the storm had found her and pulled her into his boat and brought her to his village. A few weeks ago, she was just walking through that village when her uncle spotted her. Not wanting to create any immediate fuss, doubting it could really be his niece, whom they'd presumed dead, the man began to ask around the village about this girl. Eventually he realized that it must be her—and she was reunited with her family; her mother and father had also survived. But her seven-year-old brother did not. Almost two hundred thousand other people did not. How do you think *she* feels standing on the edge of the ocean? For her, water brings sensations of unfathomable terror, the pain of great loss. In the stories of Jonah and Noah, she doesn't find hope for the future—she is reminded of a singular tragedy in her past. And that's what I want you to be aware of, always. That message: All Great Things, is a dangerous one. It is too simple. It is preached far too often. It says that all these stories are hopeful. It wants you to believe that if you follow God, all will be good. It never considers that water, for some, is wretched and torturous. You're all conscious of our lack of rain but never consider that other places might be flooding. You're frustrated that you can't shower, but you forget that much of the world is still without clean water. You never consider that *this*, this *test*, could instead be a blessing. God tells us that those who drink of the water that I give them will never be thirsty. For each of you this water, this drink, is a blessing that quenches a thirst inside you—it is unique to every one of you. I can't tell you what it is and I can't promise you that it is good. But the journey, the righteous path you take trying to answer *why*, is what defines you."

The dog groomer looked up longingly at her husband's shaved face. She unclenched their grip, ran her fingers up the back of his neck into his blonde crew cut. He rolled his head back and maybe looked at the red beams running across the ceiling. His neck spiked with goose bumps at the sudden sound of thunder.

"Ah," Tim said from the pulpit, raising his arms to conclude the sermon. Bidding the parishioners to rise.

A second crash of thunder rolled through the room, almost rising from the ground and sticking in their throats. Parishioners recoiled their necks down into their shoulders, hair follicles prickled on edge as the musky smell of rain seeped beneath the church doors. "Our father, who art in heaven, hallowed be thy name," they said in unison as *rain* pelted the red, metallic church roof. These folks' combined smiles kept the church lit and battled gathering clouds that extinguished the seemingly eternal sun. Entire empires of rain blasted onto the roof. Squalling scores of barrel-chested kamikaze water warriors exploding upon earth, a united thud, "Thy kingdom come, thy will be done, on earth as it is in heaven," they said. The people from the last pew filed out and did not make their way to the pulpit but turned their backs to it and went outside. When they opened the door, the foreign sound of water hitting sidewalks and pavement and car windshields swept through the parish in one great wave. The whole community fled to the exit and Tim followed them. They did not remain under the awning's shelter but went all the way to the parking lot and in a long line they walked to the garden—the leaves hanging from the ears of corn waved welcome. Toothy yellow grins sprouted above the peeled back husks. The wide, gray sky revealed reassuring bits of blue. Rain sparkled like glitter in the streets and rolled into thirsty drains all over the property.

The parishioners stood with their soaked shoes in the grass and continued their prayer, "Give us this day our daily bread; and forgive us our trespasses as we forgive those who trespass against us; and lead us not into temptation but deliver us from evil." Then they all said The Amen and Holy-Crossed themselves as the rain came and came all over them, soaking their heads and clothes and their faces and fingers. They seemed suddenly so happy and did go in peace to their cars. The dog groomer hugged her husband. She rubbed the crew cut again with her ringed finger. She pressed their wetness together, making it one wetness. A rainbow of butterflies flew out from several lettuce heads and danced around the wet couple. One onlooker gasped, "Oh Dear Lord." A purple one landed on the husband's head for a time. He could sense it and so gazed up goofily—the butterfly wings tickled his eyelashes. The dog groomer whispered in his ear, "Oh my God," and he held her some more.

Pastor Tim approached, "How do you feel?" he asked.

"Comforted," I said, "but . . ."

"But?"

"Can't water just be water, Father?"

The Juxtaposer; or, The Final Paper

Philip Picot's head looked like a glistening mound of oven-ready pizza dough. His pointy, red, rough, and long beard had grown in a way so distinguished that it actually concealed, by way of distraction, the odd and ugly head from view. Truth be told, he looked like an inverted treasure troll from the nineties, without the everlasting smile. Philip was someone who never went by the name "Phil," who knew neither the cost of diapers nor condoms.

On the wall of Philip's room, a corny cat clock "coo-coo-cooed" attention to the new day. Philip and his crunchy beard rose from bed, leaving behind the lingering appearance of a wild paprika accident upon the sheets. On a calendar behind Philip's desk the words, "write final paper," noted this day. The subway rolled below his apartment, clickclick-clickclick-clickclick, and combined with auto horns in the street to further the reality of impending scholarship. Feral cats meowed behind an unlocked door in Philip's room that lead out to what his landlord referred to as a "backyard."

The burning hot shower water pelted his pale body in a pleasurable way, the color of his skin tone now beginning to match his burnt orange beard. He thought about the final paper, he considered a post-modernist psychoanalysis of the forces driving gender relations in

Drown, he wondered if a subconscious male inferiority complex forced those moronic spics to treat their women like dogs as they simultaneously lamented about a world that treats *them* unfairly. He thought his professor might read this as elitist, or even racist. He thought about a French Feminist reading of, "The Darling," with Luce Irigaray's, "Women on the Market," as the informing voice. He thought this might score him some points with some of the babes in class if he could find a way to casually bring his paper topic up in conversation. He thought, yeah I could say something like, 'I really think the darling character should be read as a hero and inspiration for all women. Yeah, I actually juxtaposed Chekhov against Luce Irigaray's feminist treatise "Women on the Market," to defend . . . and really, *elevate* her character.' He thought this idea might be better suited when juxtaposed against the themes in *Drown*. 'I was raised by a single mom so I can relate to trying to rise up in a male dominated world in which those in power will fight forever before they relinquish it—I think the study of women is important to becoming a truly informed member of society. "The Darling," in my opinion,' he would say, 'is a tale of perseverance and caring and the ability to adapt and flourish against all odds.' He thought about how this one girl in class might eat up some real scholarly shit like this. Thought about the way her clothes seemed to find her body by accident, hanging about with an aloof nature that told Philip the clothes could stay on, or easily come off, either way would be fine.

"Christ," she'd say, "I didn't know you cared so much, that sounds really *fascinating*." Philip's mind wouldn't allow her to use the word 'interesting'.

And then she'd look at him. He could see her eyes widen, longing for more scholarly diction, searching for the miniscule eyes hiding behind his enormous spectacles. He imagined the feeling of her lips snuggling into his "beard gap," a phrase used by Philip's acquaintances to describe his mouth. He thought about how smart their children would be. He gripped his beard, wringing out the water with both hands. He enjoyed the feeling of the wet beard hanging down against his bare chest, resting between his small nipples like a forward-facing ponytail. He looked down at his penis and began to juxtapose furthering his morning pleasure against saving his energy and time for writing the final paper.

An hour later Philip stepstepstepstepped down the iron stairway into the subway with a shoulder bag on his shoulder, black cap on his head, brown cords, nice boots, umbrella just in case and a boring blue blazer. He looked up at the fancy timer counting down the arrival time of the next train, "3 Minutes," and blew a plume of reactionary air that manifested itself to the others looking on as an air of great importance, his air stressed that three minutes is unacceptable. So, for three minutes Philip thought about the tiles lining the subway walls as Satan's shower—grimy, underground, a dirty home for people with dirty minds, no doubt perpetuators of myriad crimes. When the cars clickclick-clickclick-clickclicked their way into the station, the passengers looked like members of a quarantine. Their wretched faces pressed against the doors and windows, the disaster of modernity, not the smallish nature of the cars but the mounting pregnancies—all those fuckers fucking for a higher cause. Mom and Dad meet up for dinner, they look at each other over candles for three hours, their skin looked much different at dinner than it does now on the train, especially when they're squeezed this closely together, especially when the wine has turned their teeth purple and the meat rumbling in their belly whispers hints of instability that elevates their heart rate and forces each forehead to concede sweat. They spill out of the cars in a way that predicts the forthcoming bowel movement and after a shower or two they decide it's time to make a baby. Everyone else shuffles in gently, yet aggressively. Philip doesn't make it far before colliding with a giant beast man. Those following him into the car are desperate to make way for the closing doors. They pile atop one another to form the posterior wall of Picot's imprisonment. The man attached to Philip weighs four hundred pounds and smells of discarded summer vegetables. Sweat cascades from his face and drips in a perpetual ooze that weaves its way through his prickly black neck hairs and eventually down through the collar of his black shirt, finally coming to rest at his chest in a sweet saturation that forms an impressive archipelago of salty sweat stains seen easily against the black shirt. He huffs yesterday's breath into Philip's face and glasses, fogging and defogging the spectacles with each audible effort.

"I'm so sorry," he says.

Philip makes a funny face, responding in kind to the breath, "It's okay, man."

"God bless you, son," the man says, now trying to collect some sweat himself by rubbing the collar along his great neck, wiping it against his forehead in a precise janitorial display. His absurd forearm brushes against a headphoned alien who shakes her head in disgust and inches further away. Philip's fine eyelashes wilt under the pressure of the beastly hot breath while words like "ewww," and "gross," run amuck through his mind's eye.

"So sorry, I'm exiting at the next stop," said the beast into the fog of Picot's lenses. Philip wondered why in hell this man insisted upon using so many words with an 'S' sound—these seeming to elicit the most putrid odor from somewhere behind his teeth. The head-shaking alien who'd not heard this announcement tried to make eye contact with Philip in order to establish a bit of negative group sentiment in regard to the big man's odor. But Picot could not see through the fog, perhaps would not have partaken anyway. The head shaker was pretty and vane. The narcissistic production of a mechanized age of ideal types. She wakes up in the morning, her face lit by a Light Emitting Diode and through the little screen she immediately starts judging all of her half relations and acquaintances from the privacy of her home. Philip considers the implications of socializing in private. She's been doing just that all her life. Every single free moment is another opportunity to pull out an electronic device used to reinforce the societal standard, all her friends are pretty, take sexy pictures on the weekend to make people like the beast jealous of a world he will never know. Bunch of lumps, lumping around, her lumps of course are very nice indeed, she's not fooling herself there. Picot himself would like to get into the bed and lump around with her lumps for a while. But first he'd want her to consider the life of the beast man. He'd want her to juxtapose it against the privileges of her own world to make her further appreciate the opportunities afforded her. The opportunity to fall in love and take glorious sweat-free photographs in sunny, sandy locales. He's worrying that that statement is the antithesis of Irigaray's treatise. He's worrying that *their* children would only have a fifty-fifty shot at being intelligent, also a fifty-fifty shot at being attractive.

As the man barrels out of the subway car, Philip contemplates the career of such a beast. Fancies him a balloon man perhaps, wouldn't that be fun? That his gift is master craftsman of the first balloon order? He could be a damn revolutionary for all anyone else knows. He could be an educational balloon man even, using encyclopedic interplay to describe the lives of the animals as he fashions them. He's got the rare gift of being immune to the balloon sound, balloons and Styrofoam, Philip thinks—God's fingernails along his spine's chalkboard. A lot of former balloon artists got down with the dog and cat, so what? The beast came through with a giraffe and a lion. 'You see kids, the giraffe is native to Africa, his long craning neck that you see here,' and here he blows the neck with deft artistic brilliance and timing, given his unique ability to store lots of air, the children rear back in delight and laughter as he attaches the newly inflated neck to body, 'gives him the ability to reach way up into very tall trees to find his food. The giraffe survives off leaves and plants kids, this is called *herbivorous*.' The parents are just eating it up, 'Pay him anything,' they say, next thing you know he's doing shows all over the USA. He's opened a school, teaches groups of hopeful balloon disciples and then one day he invents the balloon *Elephant*. It's so revolutionary he transcends the traditional balloon audience and starts playing adult parties, the whole damn nation, balloon euphoric. You've got to understand, the giant ears, the tusks, the dangling mollusk nose that he miraculously forms into a water balloon so that it can arch and blow water over the balloon elephant's back with striking realism is quite the complicated process. Maybe he's wealthy and his former disciples are now instructors able to run the balloon school without him: the disciples go on tour, maybe he writes a few balloon books and being so damn rich and comfortable in NYC what else is there to do but go out to eat a lot and gain weight. Perhaps he was just now in the middle of a healthy walk but got really tired. Being so far away from his home on the Upper East Side, the beast thought it best to take the subway back to his apartment and avoid any risk of heart attack. This explains the sweat and shortness of breath.

Normally Picot takes a seat on the subway as soon as one becomes available. But in honor of his newly formed Feminist thesis he continued to stand, stewing in the wake of the great beast. He plugged some headphones into his earlobes. Fantastic guttural grunts overtook his entire psyche.

Rah! Yeah, come on, yeah. Ack . . . heyyyy yeah, come on, babyyyy.

People continued to push in and out of the car, treating Picot's boring blazer like a turnstile. He of that nominal class of folks who spend a lifetime without getting much notice—inside the car Philip didn't think much about the hooded hustlers taking naps next to him. Never wondered about their familiarity with crack, coke, heroin alleyways. He wrote off the two couples sitting opposite each other, each girl had her head on her man's shoulder, some queer mirror competition for America's next cute couple. A load of Amish piled in, hats that connected to the ceiling of the car like electric powered bumper cars from the days of amusement parks, when families took pictures with their kid's skinned knees and grass stained shirts all Sunday. He didn't even consider that he was riding in the middle of two other cars all filled to the brim with other people, or that this grouping of cars flashed by stations as though they were just a bunch of characters stuck inside a two-dimensional flip book. Above the stations were people walking, people in automobiles, hemming and hawing and carrying things and smoking things and probably all making important plans.

Ahhhhh yeah baby, yeah, I'm a backdoor man. . . .

One Amish gentleman carried a suitcase with a neon green sticker: "Skydive." He was staring at his cellular telephone. Luckily, he was also reading his prayer book, probably even say a few before he goes to sleep tonight.

Hey all of y'all people trying to sleep. . . I'm out to make it with my midnight dreaaaamm.

The doors at Wall Street remain open for an incredible amount of time before the stiff suits enter. After a long day of deciding the nation's fiscal fate, they feel those in the car should excitedly anticipate their entrance? They walk in, finally, with a distinguished air that promotes the opinion, 'these doors will never shut on *me*,' and take any seat available. Look around at the rest of the tired citizens in the car as though they're the only ones just finishing a long and frustrating day at work. One of the hooded hustlers cracks an eyelid to inspect an adjacent Wallstreeter's watch, chuckles, goes back to sleep. The man then checks the time in that particular way that requires him to stretch his arm *all* the way out before bringing the watch back to his face. Realizing the time, his mouth opens to yawn like a Precambrian drawbridge and he falls asleep. The inferior rural world would certainly imagine someone with a little more energy, perhaps someone who spends his money on a proper timepiece instead of prostitutes and cocaine.

The men don't know . . . but the little girls understaaaaaaand.

Picot considered this last line, felt it decidedly un-feminist and so stopped the song in protest. 'Can I be a feminist and still listen to songs about having sex with married women,' he asked himself.

"People! People! *People!* Just a minute of your time *PUH*-lease," began a gentleman from the back of the car, "marijuana . . . is *not* a drug. It's an *herb*. You wanna be fifty-four and look like me? Motherfucker start smoking weed today!" Philip laughs, he doesn't know how to buy weed, always been too nervous.

"No one on this earth dies from smoking weed," he continued, "I gotta watch out for the police . . ." he looks out of the car doors as they open to let more people on, "Oh, hello, pretty white girl," he says to a pretty white girl. "Now I got two girlfriends, one is twenty-five and the other one is twenty-two—wait a minute, wait a minute now, I gotta check for the police . . ." he checks, "You wanna be fifty-four and look like me then *start* smoking weed today." The crowd mostly enjoys his rant, he does have that Christmas cheer about him, wrapped in a green scarf and all. Chris Kringle for the new millennium, Chris Chronic maybe, sounds like a rap name. The doors open again, the car is getting crowded, "Hey, white girl," he yells on his way out the door, "I'm your Uncle!" The whole car laughs. It is doubtful either of the adjacent cars had this level of entertainment. Philip doesn't quite get it, labels the man anti-feminist/chauvinist.

A flock of holiday shoppers enter the car next: bags, scarves, sweat, anger, fatigue, frustration, the doors try to close once, twice, three times, the atmosphere is getting thick, finally someone is left out.

"That dude was no New Yorker," someone said, Philip couldn't be sure who said it.

"Oh, who *cares*," mentioned an Eastern European woman next to Philip, "what's the *point*," she seemed grumpy, ready to take it up with this man.

"Guy just lost five minutes of his life," Philip said.

"What?"

"Well, he's stuck standing there in the station now for five more minutes," Philip said, in his most feminist voice.

"Is it worth it?"

"In New York it is," retorted the disembodied voice.

"Okay," started the Eastern European, "what if *this* car crashes, now he's not lost five minutes but saved an entire lifetime."

This line ruffled the feathers of the holiday flock, who all gesticulated their disbelief.

"I think that's a little hyperbolic," Philip said.

"What the fuck does that mean?" asked the woman.

"Yeah, the fuck does that mean," asked the disembodied voice.

"This car isn't going to *crash*, all right?"

Now people were looking at Picot as well. He could hear someone whispering something about a 'fucking beard.'

"Well, it *probably* won't, but I mean, still, is it worth it?" The woman continued on, surprisingly, Philip thought about her perseverance and strength—he was one-hundred percent certain they'd make intelligent babies.

"I guess that depends if you're a *real* New Yorker or not," Philip said, alluding to and insulting the disembodied voice.

"You look like uh upside down treasure troll, motherfucka," replied the disembodied voice. Having heard this one, Philip replied simply, "Perhaps, but I do not have the everlasting grin," with that he smiled cleverly and left the train, thanking the Eastern European woman for giving him a wonderful idea.

"I'm a feminist," he said to her, "if you ever want to have dinner and make some intelligent babies just give me a call, okay?"

He ran off the train. 'I've got it,' he thought. He'd finally realized his idea for the perfect final paper. He'd forgotten his notebook computer in the bathroom of his apartment, so returned home to write. He dictated some notes into his special telephone, "Okay . . . okay . . . okay . . . " the trains can be heard clicking in the background as he fumbles over the start of his notes, "It's like, scholarship okay, does it matter? Yes, it matters, but to whom . . . only to the enclosed environment of academia, no one else even cares, so what does *that* matter? What if I take my reading skills and apply them to the world . . . read people like characters. . . . I can imagine any story . . . the most wonderful stories are possible . . . isn't that what writing is . . . isn't that what authors *do*? What is the role of the scholar . . . in the actual world . . . answer this without answering it . . . because it's not there, there is no exact answer—the answer is anything new . . . anything fun and creative . . . can this allude, metaphorically, to the outer world's influence upon scholarship and reading? Feminist readings were part of the feminist movement . . . politically, and that was important . . . that came from the real world . . . not from a way of looking at fiction . . . a gun control reading of Joyce's *The Dead* . . . No. . . . What . . . No, but that's it . . . that kind of thing . . . something new from the outside world that inspires a reading . . . Am I going to write an *essay* about this . . . a postmodern psychoanalysis of *scholarship itself* in the twenty-first century . . . how's that possible? What does it say? What the scholar fails to realize about his isolated world. Something like that. . . ."

Philip took his computer from the bathroom and returned to his desk to write his final paper.

The Juxtaposer, he typed.

I entered his room through the unlocked backdoor and pushed a polished pistol against his doughy head. I'd been picturing it exploding all day, interested in the way that it might ultimately look like a cooked pizza, spilled all over the floor.

"What the heck are you doing in my room, *Bob*," he asked, his head beginning to perspire.

"This is going to be your final paper, Philip," I told him.

"Please don't kill me," he begged.

"Well, write your paper and we'll see."

"Are you really here for my paper? Why don't you just write your own?"

"Because I can't think of anything."

In Your Dreams

It was just too nasty out to continue working. My job was outside in the nasty weather, it wasn't like I was just sad or something. I guess the weather was probably making me sad. Gray and damp and smelling like cardboard. You'd have to be some kind of excellent to be having a good time in the weather I'm talking about. Some people are so excellent they're immune to the effects of weather. I'm not one of those people. For the most part, my job never matters. Imagine that. Yours probably doesn't either. If you're being totally honest. The kind of immune-to-weather excellence I'm talking about is reserved for people who are even intimidating while being kind.

Who am I then? It doesn't matter. I'm you. Okay? I'm a projection coming from your mind, so, it doesn't matter what I tell you my name is. Call me Hue, if it makes you feel more comfortable. Huh-*you*. Like a sneeze that turned into a yawn. That's me, you.

I left work and went to see a movie. It's a great place to get inside and the theaters have coffee now. I told myself I'd go back to work after the movie and work really hard but that's not what happened at all. They also have pretzel bites with nacho cheese dipping sauce at the theaters—all the entrées are accompanied by a calorie count on menus comprised of light emitting diodes.

I'd been excited about the movie for a while. It'd come out a week ago. It had a young, visionary director who I admired. I don't say that to be clever. She was only thirty-one and already doing stuff like transcending genres—this is the kind of excellence I was talking about before. The visionary director did not disappoint. The film had within it several levels of truth and the action-packed happenings did heighten the actual story being told, which was a perfectly nuanced exploration of race relations in America. That's too simply put. The truth is I will never fully comprehend everything that went into making a piece of art so close to perfect. Even the freaking comic relief. The comic relief was some of the funniest I'd ever heard. Wonderful jokes with flawless timing. At one point I was so blown away by the level of entertainment that I got sad. I just thought about all the people around me in the theater on a gray, cardboard Thursday, who were going to talk about this film later and say things like, "I didn't really like it," or, "it was *okay*," or, "it *sucked*." My sadness turned to anger then because I know people say that stuff. They will find other people who will even agree with them. And they'll go around saying it sucked without ever thinking about it. Without ever considering, not for one second, that maybe they did not comprehend what they saw. What else do they go and do without realizing it? Sitting there chomping on nine hundred and seventy calories worth of pretzel bites with nacho cheese dipping sauce as the genius stuff in front of them goes unnoticed. I think about my life like that all the time—am I fully and properly comprehending what's happening around me? Am I understanding what is and is not happening to me and why? Am I reacting properly to what is and is not happening to me? Are these people reacting this way for the reason I think, or is this all a complete misunderstanding? How many vitally important communications throughout our lives are perfectly perceived by both parties? In real life it's okay to be this way, it's called paranoia, but there's simultaneously so much and so little going on it's probably stranger to be unafraid. Like, you can be on the verge of blowing your brains out over something that turns out to be meaningless, or, a tiny occurrence that slips by unnoticed ends up mostly deciding what happens to you in life.

I left the theater and went back outside and the day hadn't changed at all. I stumbled while pulling my headphones out of my pocket and fumbled them into a sewer. I wanted to listen to music about the summer months. The last earbud hung on the rusted grate long enough to tempt me and so I dove for it, but, alas, my earbuds went for a terrible swim.

I scraped my hand trying to rescue the earbuds. My jeans were really wet down the front. I stood up and thought about how headphones were a mainstay of my existence and how the store that has the best ones is back inside the mall I just walked out of. I went back inside, appearance be damned.

The store that had the best headphones is lit like you're trapped in an alien space beam. And the beam is filled almost to the brim with people, circling, wondering about things, searching for insane explanations and making wild purchases. They ask your name at the door.

"Hue."

Then they write a description of you. You are a

combination of male or female, old or young, heavy or skinny, tall or short—if you are five feet ten and a half inches tall and weigh one hundred and sixty-seven pounds with flat, brown hair and clear skin and no glasses and carrying no bag and displaying absolutely no body language then you have wet pants and a bloody hand.

"Hue?"

"Yes."

A female employee smiled at me and held out her hand. Her round, happy cheeks had dimples in them that made you smile reflexively, like a contagious yawn but way better. Her face made me feel weird. Something was happening. But I knew I should be perceiving an interaction that happens to her, here, almost two thousand times in a given year. The tag on her shirt said, "Sue, 3yrs. experience," so I calculated that meant around six thousand interactions just like this. When I went to shake her hand she said, "Ew," and recoiled. I forgot about the sewer incident. I wiped my hand on my wet pants, nervously, which did nothing more than smear the blood equally between my pants and hand. The interaction had started off odd. I wondered, maybe, just *maybe* . . . unlike any of the other six thousand.

"I fell outside."

"Oh, *no*. What happened?"

Did she really care? Did she really want to know? That sweet voice. It sounded caring. Do I tell the truth or just move on? Shouldn't I realize that I'm only here for new earbuds and that any ancillary items are not only probably unnecessary but maybe even annoying? You have to realize that people say unnecessary and annoying things to pretty girls all day long every day. You see a pretty girl and you start dreaming. But what if she thinks I did it being nefarious? The bloody hand is also an entry point into the reason for my visit. It should be fine.

"You see, I scraped it diving for my earbuds."

"Diving?"

"They fell into the sewer."

And then she cackled at me and I almost fell on the floor and she said, "What are you even talking about?" and kept laughing. I noticed a few people looking our way so I laughed too and said, "I was just taking them out of my pocket and I stumbled a bit on some uneven pavement and they slipped from my fingers and fell down on a sewer and hung there long enough so I dove, trying to save them, scraping my hand with the effort, but ultimately I lost them forever."

"And that's why your jeans are all wet?"

"Yes."

"I figured you were doing something nefarious."

"I wasn't."

She showed me to the headphones. When she walked past, I smelled a field of flowers. I didn't understand what was happening.

"If you get these ones that can't fit in your pocket you won't be as likely to drop them into the sewer. Also, they are too large to fit through ninety percent of the sewer grates along the eastern seaboard. Says it right on the box."

I knew the large, wireless headphones that she pointed to cost three times as much money as the ones I always get. But I didn't want to seem like I didn't have a lot of money. I was dreaming. I started thinking about somehow asking her on a date or for her phone number. I wondered how many times that'd already happened in her previous six thousand interactions within this store. How could I do it better with great authenticity and caring? What special thing could I say about myself to entice her? Not entice, this isn't a trick.

"What do I do with them when I'm not wearing them if I can't put them back into my pocket?"

"You just hang them around your neck."

"Wouldn't that look weird?"

"Is looking weird something that you worry about?"

"My heart is telling me to ask you on a date or for your phone number."

"Well . . . you must be *lucky*. I get lunch in fifteen minutes. You can meet me. Is that a date?"

"Yes. Meet you where?"

"In the food court."

I knew I didn't like to eat in the food court. I'd never done it, but I've watched it being done. The people in the food court always made me feel sad not because I knew anything about them but because the food was of such a low quality and yet they looked happy. I guess people can be happy eating bad food. That shouldn't matter. I'm happy smoking cigarettes. But I'm not oblivious to the fact that they're unhealthy, low-class, and gross and killing me and ultimately, they don't contribute to my happiness or sadness. I thought perhaps this is the same for eating in the food court—your life shouldn't be defined by a meal in the food court. But still I felt a little sad knowing that really excellent people don't ever eat in a food court.

"You're not happy?"

"No. Yes, I am. I don't, I've never . . ."

"I don't really want to go to the food court either but

they're not going to let you in any of the restaurants bleeding and looking like you peed your pants."

I felt a lot of warm fluid rushing around my brain thinking about Sue's thoughtfulness.

I paused on the runway that led to the food court and surveyed the landscape. I'd need a plan of what to do so I wouldn't get flustered in the thick of things. Eight restaurants on either side. Two pathways flanked a central corral of black, hard-plastic, wiry tables like sewer grates. Each table had four chairs of the same design. Rows and rows and rows of ravenous mouths in motion, bobbing up and down to eat and looking up to chat. A hungry human jambalaya. How can any one person smell or taste or hear a specific thing with all the food and people mixed together so tightly?

I removed my wireless earphones from the box and put them over my ears and everything went silent. It was as though I'd entered a soundproof glass box. I put the place on mute. I watched them moving and it felt weird, like I wasn't even existing. I could just sit there watching them come and go forever, every day, young and old, tall and short, heavy and light—coming and eating and going and coming and eating and going. The two fellas on the outside pushing toothpicks topped with miniscule morsels in your face for infinity. I switched on that summer song I'd been dying for. Now they moved like a symphony and made me smile. Sweet satiation. All these drooling beauties in congress.

I entered the court.

I grabbed a toothpick sample. "Oh, *YES*," I said.

I put my hands in the sky, triumphant, "Give me two orders!" I moved to the next restaurant before they could serve me and poked my head forward, requesting, "Two of your very best." Before they could ask what exactly I meant I moved to the next, "Two, please." And so on down the line. Then I crossed to the other side and did the same. And as I circled to return to the first side and pick up my items, I saw Sue approaching, laughing. I knew I wanted to do something sincere, so I held out my arm like you have to when you're in a wedding. She looped her elbow through. The smell of flowers was upon me once again. I could tell she'd been in a wedding before, "What have you been up to?" she asked. I put my earphones around my neck and called, "The LADY has arrived in court," and escorted her to the place where I put in my first two orders. We moved to the next restaurant and I announced, "LADY SUE HAS ARRIVED," and, not caring or expressing himself in any way, a man with a hat he did not choose to wear handed us two items. Soon we had to unlock elbows to allow for all the trays. Sue kept on laughing and smelling like flowers. I never thought her floral essence could transcend the plethora of beef preparations filling the arena. Gentle citizens lining the perimeter of the seating corral cheered as we progressed through all the restaurants. As we crossed to the east-facing establishments I blessed a foursome of patrons with two random items from one of our trays and they said, "Oh, *THANK* you," and I said, "The Lady Sue blesses thee."

As we completed our tour of the east-facing establishments, people beckoned us to sit in their section and we obliged them. I had the feeling they caught a waft of flowers as we sat down—they were smiling and holding their noses in a welcoming way.

"Why did you order all this?" Sue asked.

"I thought it'd make you laugh."

"I never thought of ordering food as an opportunity to make someone laugh."

"I was feeling excitement," I said, sincerely.

My jaw had joined the great herd. There was an ecstasy in sitting across from her that made my mouth chomp wildly with chatter. What was I saying? What was she thinking about the things I was saying? Was she thinking about other, better, more important things? I envisioned the inside of my skull like a hyperspeed lava lamp, globules of thought colliding and knocking off the walls and rising and falling but never going anywhere definitive. As we talked about our lives, saying our hopes and dreams, I started to wonder if anything was happening. Anything more than just two people talking in the food court. Something really significant, you know? I had probably less than ten minutes to decide if this was a meaningless lunch or the most important moment of my life so far. I made sure my eyes looked normal even though they were relaying intense messages to my brain like: this is the sweetest girl you've ever met. That is the prettiest smile you've ever seen. Her eyes are looking at your eyes. The most likely reason for this interaction is general kindness. You are in love with this person. You are thinking this person is the most wonderful person you've met so far on the planet. You must at least pronounce these feelings to avoid future feelings of sorrow.

I looked at Sue with a tender expression on my face. One of our table neighbors was showing her the secret of putting chopped up chicken nuggets into a folded piece of sausage pizza. I could tell she didn't really need to do that, but she wanted to partake in the food court camaraderie.

She took a bite and said it was amazing and thanked the person who showed her. She passed it to me and I took a bite and agreed that it was amazing.

"I'm in love with you," I said.

She covered her mouth in an attempt to stifle a great cackle then noticed my look of tender sincerity and asked, "What are you talking about?"

"My brain keeps thinking about love when I look at you."

"That's really something great, son. That's *special*," said one of our table neighbors.

"Okay," Sue said, "what am I supposed to say to that?"

"Let's go on an airplane to somewhere tropical and maybe get married."

"I only agreed to this because I wanted you to buy the more expensive headphones."

Just kidding, that's not what she said. That wouldn't happen to you. I mean, Hue.

She really said, "Seriously?"

And I said, "Yeah."

And our neighbor's wife now said, "That sounds like a *dream* vacation."

And Sue said, "Okay let's go then."

It was the best time to be in a mall. We needed all sorts of stuff for our trip and we could get it all right there. I bought new clothes from a popular store and threw away my bloody and wet clothes in a popular garbage barrel. Then we procured casualwear and swimwear and formalwear and luggage and sunglasses. We wheeled our items into a travel agency and booked a trip and called a cab.

All the people inside the airport were complaining

about something—they had the exact opposite attitude of the people in the food court. These people were staring at screens and shaking their heads. A great many of them sported U-shaped pillows around their necks with their heads tilted back, against the pillow, making them look freshly anesthetized. They did not walk to their destinations but were transported, like hovering ghouls, by motorized flooring. Perhaps, many of them were headed to evil destinations—impossible to be sure, the mood had become debilitating.

But then Sue grabbed my hand and pushed her shoulder into my shoulder and everything smelled like flowers again.

"Have you ever been to an airport?" she asked.

"No," I said, "not for flying."

On the airplane we drank champagne with wet, hot towels draped over our faces. I made a sound like a tired cow. One of the employees fastened and unfastened a seatbelt for everyone's approval while a different employee demonstrated the proper technique for hitting mescaline. Someone made a joke about death over the intercom and soon we were on our way to a tropical destination.

Sadly, on our way to the tropical destination an otherwise wonderful bird flew into one of the jet engines. After it happened the plane shook so horribly the towel fell off my face. An unnerving beeping sounded throughout the tube and confirmed something bad was happening. The way the airplane suddenly turned toward the earth did not seem appropriate. People were screaming, "OH NO," and asking for God to save them. Employees were running up and down the aisle helping to affix the masks to all the panicked faces. All the people were screaming and crying please as the jet plummeted for the ground at a rate of hundreds of miles an hour. The wind resistance coupled with the exploding engine multiplied by the alarms and oxygen masks and desperation of the remaining engine should have been enough to drown out the sound of human crying and screaming but it wasn't. All the zipped-up luggage toppled from the overhead bins and rumbled down the aisle and collided with the unattended beverage cart. Sue squeezed my hand. I wanted to say that we were going to make it, but everyone knew we were going to die. I stared at Sue's face and accepted that it would be the last thing I see. I felt really bad that if she did not decide to look elsewhere, my face would be the last thing she sees. I tried to smile and make my face look as good as it could for her. But I think the look we shared was disbelief, and, correctly so, because that's not what happened at all. That shit never happens, especially to huh-*you*.

What really happened was we landed safely in our tropical destination and lots of people clapped their hands with excitement and filed politely down the aisle, careful not to harm anyone with the jagged edges of certain carry-on items. The beautifully tanned pilot told us to enjoy our trip, flashing his cloud-white teeth anew for every exiting passenger.

The hot, tropical air enfolded Sue and I like an electric blanket made of baby-soft wool. The air urged us to relax. We made our way to a row of hammocks. Together, we laid within a hammock, looking at the sky, which was blue—how else can you say it? With her breathing in my ear so sweetly, under the sky, rich and blue, like angel wings dipped in melted marshmallows, I figured I must have died. I had indeed heard the word "paradise" used over forty times in the first twenty minutes of our visit. The place did have many qualities one might associate with the more desirable side of afterlife. For instance, I could see everyone's feet. Citizens seemed to hover slowly over the pure, white sands in a way not dissimilar from walking on clouds. Palm tree trunks shot for the sky at interesting angles. The burly, green leaves waved gently, fanning us, mirroring the never-ending ocean edge sauntering up the beach, framing the forever feeling, blessing all our eardrums. Heavenly sailboats grazing on wind in the distance. Thoroughbred horses trotting at the request of excellent riders. Rainbow-colored kites. Hang gliders shooting cupid's arrows. I think one hit me. I melted into this life, into my partner—more like melded. I'd seen it written somewhere at every wedding I'd ever been to: Two become One. Sue and Hue become Shue. Shue has a baby and names it Lue. Shue and Lue live a life of innocent bliss and experience reality without terror or the threat of deep thoughts. They contract the entire universe into this existence, green grass, simple. Earn. Spend. Sleep. Wake up, always feeling normal, discussing fashionable worries inside a homogenous social circle. Complete disregard for the unfathomably massive aspect of everything that is not Shue and Lue. Time marked by major events between long periods of unremarkable routine. Safe, unthinking movements along one tiny stretch of land. Waking life like a dream. An existence that makes so much sense there's nothing left to question. Nothing left to dream. Horses on the beach and skiing. An appetite always answered and washed down with a smile.

They call this well-rounded. I say it has no edge. *You*, Shue and Lue, roll into infinity without leaving a single meaningful thing behind, like a dream, your memory clung to by few for a moment after you're gone but then entirely forgotten by the afternoon. What is that? What is this? Here. This is a love story, between me and you, from me . . . to you, or, Hue and Sue, if it makes you feel more comfortable. This is my dream. I dreamed it on a bus, asleep against a warm window, with the sun shining on my face. Sitting next to an old man with only one sock and Velcro sneakers who poured barbecue sauce into iced coffee with great care. I dreamed of the girl I wished had sat in his seat. I wondered if the only thing that separated me from you is that I keep getting the old man and so many of you saddle up next to a perfect partner. I stared at the old man some more and eventually decided that I could love him. That him and I could easily be Hue and Sue if I'm writing to entertain you. It's no sillier than any other love story. Imagine me as I sensually unvelcro his black sneaker. He enthusiastically sips his iced, barbecue coffee. His eyes widen as I remove the sneaker and admire his foot. I say, "What's your name, sugar," and he says, "Hue." He tilts his head back and moans as I slide his foot into my mouth. He puts the leg with the sock on my other shoulder and kicks and shakes like an infant. I slide both hands up into his shorts and bring my head up for a kiss. But I decide to tease him. I kiss and lick and breathe heavily into his ear and whisper, "Hi . . . I'm Sue." His ear is thick with hair and wax, so he can't hear. He moans, "Whaaaa?" I answer, moaning, "I'm *SUE*," and caress his cheek. And as I move to mount him, I think of the possibility of you. Laughing at me, this absurdity, these chance happenings that lead only, truly, to the chance happening of that bit of laughter you let slip at the idea of an age-inappropriate, homosexual, public encounter. That's my dream— tiptoeing across the thin dimensional line of fabric between dreaming and reality. Dreams do happen, in a way, so are they real? These projections of Hue, us meeting here, inside fiction—is a reality. Now. I made this come true. I shared my dream with you. I tickled you from an infinite distance. We were together, in your head. That was my dream . . . becoming you, fantasizing about all the love and life I see, for a moment, before fading, pointlessly away forever again.

Beautiful Delusions

If you sat down and really thought about it, how many days of your life can you actually remember? If you're honest, if it even *matters* to you, you'd have to admit the answer is very few. And even those supposedly memorable days have been worn down to dim recollections, foggy flashes of cliché events like weddings, graduations, birthdays, funerals, and miscellaneous holidays—basically, if you gave or received a card, you have a memory. It's also quite likely that you've molded those memories more to your liking as life leaves you. And so when you do finally die, and your life flashes before your eyes, those flashes might be as fanciful as someone who would tell you "my life flashed before my eyes." What's even worse . . . something you really should consider . . . is the extreme likelihood that when you're about to die, you won't know it . . . and that your last thoughts might be as trivial as all those days you can't remember.

I'll never forget his silhouette. Even now, it feels stamped to my skull, ink tattooing bone behind forehead. Of course, I can't remember *for the life of me* what I was doing driving down the road that night, Halloween, during a torrential downpour, but I do remember the moon—a massive, tawny globe, casting a creepy glow over the soaked sprawl of dead leaves blanketing either side of the street, with him in the middle—black, unmoving, and umbrella-less, a lunar pupil.

His lack of foresight should have been a warning . . . well-adjusted people don't walk around in the rain with no umbrella. They really don't walk around in the rain at all. They take taxis to predetermined locations and breathlessly ask, "Can you *believe* this weather?" whenever they get there. Usually, someone will reply, "No . . . it's crazy," or, "No . . . it's insane." You could probably collect an endless highlight reel of this exact exchange across the globe as people come and go in hard rain. Many of these same people would be horrified at the thought of picking up a stranger walking along the side of the road at night. And yet, bringing attractive strangers *home*, from bars, for freaky-hot-naked sex is, while not necessarily encouraged, much more reasonable. Anyway, this guy had his hood pulled up over his head, which showed a certain level of awareness, and regret. I couldn't leave him there. The moon projected a steady spotlight, signaling, lighting the stage for this fated interaction. No one on the road but us. All signs pointed in the same direction.

I eased my car to the side of the road, about ten or twenty yards ahead of him. I pushed the button for hazard lights and waited. I examined him through the rearview as he approached, getting closer with every pulse of red. Given the circumstances, it was difficult to be certain of anything, but he looked BIG and seemed in no rush at all to get out of the rain. When he did finally arrive at the passenger door, he opened it without hesitation or any type of feeling out process. In one coordinated movement he landed in the passenger seat like a felled oak, the tires bounced to support him. I immediately discovered he'd been carrying a black leather duffel bag below the line of sight provided by the rearview mirror. He dropped that onto the floor between his feet. It landed with more force than anticipated.

I turned to look at him, but the hood from his jacket concealed his face. He just *sat* there, like he'd been expecting me. His oversized frame dominated the car interior. His left shoulder almost touched my right shoulder and wasn't nearly contained by the backrest. I tried not to choke on the thick and musty aroma seeping from his soaked clothing. Clicking windshield wipers dutifully tracked the length of this strange and terrible silence.

"Anywhere, um, you'd like to go . . . in particular?" I asked.

Incredibly . . . after *five* more seconds . . . and eight wiper swipes . . . he took his left hand and casually waved forward in a way that suggested he'd been seriously debating if he should have me drive, or just sit with him in the car, unmoving, for eternity. The absolute lack of enthusiasm in his motion told me two things: first, that having me drive him somewhere, instead of remaining motionless, had *barely* won the debate. And second, that the decision was entirely up to him.

So I drove.

I drove up a hill, into the deluge, toward the pale, yellow orb overhead. If I could have wished for anything, I would have wished that I never turned the radio off as I waited for him to enter the car. I figured he'd come in and say thanks so much and we'd comment on the terrible weather and exchange names and say what we all did for a living and he'd tell me where he was going and why he was walking there and why he *had* to go there *now* and without an umbrella and what was in his bag.

But he didn't say anything. Not one word. He hadn't even looked at me yet. I could have been toting an entire arsenal of weapons pointed at the side of his black hood and he'd have no clue.

As we reached the top of the hill a traffic light came into view. The red light alone flashed from each of the four faces, blinking like a lighthouse at the edge of hell. Behind the light, three houses stood on a hill, powered-out black, terrible and inanimate like the light itself, alternately alive in red intervals before vanishing black with a sickly consistent rhythm. The same cadence filled the car. A countdown. When the car stopped he would have to tell me how to proceed—left . . . right . . . straight? Somehow, I wasn't exactly in a *rush* to get to the light, but I did. And when I did, he reached to pull back his hood. As the hood came down, he turned toward me and that's when I noticed for the first time the eye patch covering his left eye. His other eye was blue and so bright that it seemed to glow in the dark. As with everything, he took his time in directing me, maybe to give me a chance to look him over, maybe because he didn't have anywhere to go. And so I looked him over. He looked weathered, as though he'd walked clear across Texas. His mostly bald head absorbing years of sun, wind and blowing sands that carved many pockmarks from his temples down to his neck and outlined the tiny ears. Ears that did not make sense. Ears insufficient for walling in that dome.

"LEFT," he yelled into my face.

I recoiled, frightened by the sudden volume.

"Sorry," he said, "I'm almost deaf . . . I've trouble with

. . . um . . ."

"Volume?" I asked.

"The appropriate, you know . . . "

He didn't hear me. And couldn't see me unless he turned his head a full ninety degrees.

"VOLUME?!"

"RIGHT . . . *VOLUME*," he replied.

"Where do you want to go?" I asked.

"DO YOU MIND IF I SMOKE IN HERE?" he asked.

"NO!"

"NO . . . I CAN'T? OR NO YOU DON'T MIND?"

My throat was already getting tired. He was soaked all the way through, dripping wet, and when he turned his whole head sideways to yell, I was pelted, in the face, by mixed particles of spit and rain. So, I lit one of my own cigarettes and he got the point.

I took a left and drove some more.

Strangers smoking in silence, on the road to nowhere, bits of rain steadily sneaking through cracked windows, a flood upon armrests. I could feel the forceful nature with which he smoked. His chest huffed . . . and heaved. It took a while for the exhaust steaming from his mouth to exit the car. Each of his drags resulted in three to five seconds of blind driving, so when he flicked his cigarette out the window and yelled, "HERE," I had no clue what he was talking about.

"AT THE SIGN."

Once his final mushroom cloud cleared, I could see the sign, "Candy 4 Cans," which had on it an arrow—pointing at a supermarket. Why he didn't just say, 'Take me to the market up the road,' in the first place, I'll never know. He didn't have any trouble instructing exactly where I should park. He did not seem to even consider the possibility that *this* might be the end of the road for him. It would have been at least cordial to confirm with me that I'd wait, or ask, maybe, if I would like him to bring me something from inside the market. Instead, he grabbed his bag and exited the car. That's when I first noticed the spectacular Tiger's tail attached to his buttocks. I watched that tail swing gracefully back and forth as he walked toward the market.

All around the parking lot, crazed citizens were doing everything they could to protect themselves from getting wet. The rain had really come as a shocker this time. I saw a sexy leather kitten with a plastic bag over her head, she pulled the handle holes tight below her chin; a portly Captain America jogging toward the store, wearing mismatched boots of red and blue, splashing in the water, holding his child overhead for cover; a glamorous Jessica Rabbit saw me staring and made a pretty pouty face; four strawberry cupcakes scampered along, distraught, clutching twelve packs in the air like championship trophies. I found Waldo, Wonder Woman, Batman, Beetlejuice, Scorpion, Spider-Man, seven stupid zombies and Superman, a skeleton, Luke Skywalker, a hotdog, four more zombies, a few Spice Girls, a bag of skittles, Hunter Thompson, David Bowie, Richard Nixon and OJ Simpson—hell-bent for shelter, reacting to water—the giver of life, as though it were Sodium cyanide.

A massive 747 airplane launched into the sky from a nearby airport. An aircraft, filled to the brim with people, eclipsing the moon as it ascends virtually unnoticed. There is an angry Chewbacca pushing its shopping cart at warp speed who is mystified by the onslaught of precipitation but accepts modes of transport that fly out of sight. Here on the ground, my car was threatened on all sides by lunatic behavior. But the people sitting a bit uncomfortably, flying through space to a destination possibly thousands of miles away, over entire oceans of water, are calm and cool. *That*, is the casual setting. I've seen pictures of them. Palms flat on pants, possibly bored. Cocktails and neck pillows and blankets and socks. I've heard of reclining chairs and personal television screens that play films still in theaters. What? They should be going *buckwild*. When that spaceship launches successfully into the sky, everyone should unbuckle their safety belts and scream and dance to loud music and make love, baby, because that is not normal. I remember this feeling viscerally. Twisted thoughts started to pour over me like the storm. I'd never felt so abnormal in my whole life as I did waiting for the tiger-tailed pirate. I realized, as another zombie squad hotfooted through the lot, that it wasn't even "normal" that I was alive. *Alive* . . . and overwhelmed by zombies and superheroes and flying modes of transportation, silent in the face of a future no one cares for but to complain. Before this Halloween voyage, I never thought much about waking up every morning. The fact that I was here, alive, was good enough. It seemed so obvious that as long as I stayed alive, life would turn out good, swell—isn't that what happens? I assumed every morning that I would wake up, go to my job, eat and drink over the course of yet another pleasant day, and eventually enjoy a comfortable sleep. I assumed one day I would wake up and find love. I hoped to have enough money, sometime, to fly in the sky over an ocean and land in a hot place to chill. I never worried for one moment that I wouldn't end up normal. It always seemed that as long as you are born and keep working that good things will happen. Like everyone else, I moved through the world fully confident that A plus B equaled C. I never conceived of the possibility that that B might actually be an 8, or that C might stand for cemetery, or that the entire equation is arbitrary, or even worse, wrong. The craziest thing of all might be moving through the world in this way—under the guise of normality. If flying comfortably across the sky is considered normal, what could ever be extraordinary? You'd have to make it up. The only thing we can't believe is hard rain.

I turned on the radio.

"This is a warning from the national weather service."

I turned off the radio.

I got out of the car—I had to get out of the car. I must have been in there for a long time. I didn't know about the wind. The wind was so strong it had a voice. Not like a sweet breeze, not whispers playing through eyelashes, this was a gale-force growl, "Go *HOOOOOME*." It roared across the blacktop like the collected chorus of ghouls throughout history. Objects not normally designated for blowing in the wind were being tossed about effortlessly— a Poodle in a scarf inside a shopping cart jetted overhead and landed on the market roof, futilely howling for help. A box of vinyl records had been unleashed on the scene, from a neighboring establishment perhaps, the discs were slashing dangerously about the lot and joined by an increasing amount of discarded costume accessories—you can imagine all the hats and masks orbiting two stories above ground. For a moment I locked eyes with a plastic, disembodied Elvis, or, through the open holes where his eyes should have been, I witnessed a stampede of shoppers headed my way. They looked terrible and pained, eyelids wrenched beyond open disappeared into the skull's hidden chambers, soaked faces twisted by the wind in a manner that recalled candy too sour for safety. I could see the eye patch hovering above them all. A slow-moving, self-assured Cyclops plodding upon massive, booted feet, stomping with an unnamable yet undeniable confidence in the midst of panicked freaks in disguises.

"GET IN THE CAR!" He shouted, loudly, too loudly. Was this his intended volume? I couldn't be sure. If he *meant* to sound like that, the timbre of his voice thundered above the crowd and storm and conveyed a sense of urgency I didn't think possible.

I got back in the car and waited. If the tiger-tailed pirate's voice suggested urgency, his movements refuted it. That tail was a-swingin' in the wind like an abandoned hammock in August. He *moseyed* his way to the car. He *plopped* into the passenger seat . . . and handed me a handwritten note: *Take a right to exit the parking lot. Make a right at the first light and then your third left onto Locust Rd. Drive about six miles and wait for the signal.*

I sat there staring at the note. The handwriting, cursive, was kind of beautiful—written in pencil with a steady hand. Though the words conveyed no tone, strictly instructional, the dark, unwavering lead path carried a sense of force. This note was not to be questioned. It left no room for interpretation. Although I had to wonder . . . he couldn't have begun his walk from this destination. The *signal*? He'd written it—

"DRIVE!"

Right. Engines were firing up all around us as records

and masks constantly pelted my windshield. As I made my way out of the lot, I couldn't avoid the sickening cold gaze of Michael Myers stuck behind one of my windshield wipers. His thin, unwashed, black hair, very wet, swished back and forth with the wipers and the wind. I felt like commenting on the unlikely arrival of our new companion, or at least asking the pirate if he could believe these weather conditions, but he just smoked cigarettes out the window, riding more like a prince than a fortunate hitchhiker.

By the time we turned onto Locust road, all other vehicles had disappeared and the storm had subsided. I rolled the window down, lit up, and listened to the tires purr along saturated pavement. Driveways had become an infrequent occurrence. Streetlights were a thing of the past. There was nothing but the car's headlights, Myers, the pirate and I, cruising incognito, blending with the sable nature of Locust road.

"Turn at the hammer," he said, flat and quiet, like making a note-to-self.

Unsure how to respond, I nodded. Before I could complete my evaluation on what instructional road signs "The Hammer" might be slang for, I saw it—a mailbox, in the shape of a giant hammer, where the head opens up to receive mail.

So, I turned and drove up what I assumed to be his driveway. Tires crackled along the gravel path. But this wasn't that shabby gravel, the car did not bounce and bottom out but instead rolled smoothly, delighting upon the soft, consistent terrain, the product of millions of gentle pebbles laid together. The manicured drive demanded the respect of patient navigation. The car's beams did not penetrate much in any direction, but from what I could tell this pebbled path had been curated to allow guests ample time to admire the surrounding landscape. The car was flanked on either side by never-ending rows of kaleidoscopic shrubbery, pruned to perfection, perfuming through our open windows. And though they couldn't quite be seen, one got the sense that ageless oaks snoozed somewhere beyond the shrubs with their branches reaching out to create a leafy canopy. All these thousand leaves issued gentle droplets that landed and ran down the windshield, each weaving a unique path like all the infinite rivers squirming erratic blue across paper maps. The branches and shrubs eventually subsided to reveal two still ponds. The crisp, post-storm atmosphere clashed with the warm water to create a dense fog that surrounded the car. A bright yellow light radiated from an unidentifiable source somewhere behind the fog.

"Stop here."

The car stopped and for some reason I felt like I should shut the engine off. It was like we were sitting in a cloud—the front and side views were uniform, pale gray. You'd go snow-blind trying to focus on any one thing. Nothing to be heard but the leftover rain dripping and dripping into the ponds, the little individual pellets rendered unidentifiable in the pond's comparative vastness, a terrible harmony. All the tranquil, peaceful nothingness infected my mind's ability to think anything. It raced in a million directions searching for some bit of interest. No weather to wonder about, no masked, agitated people to critique, just this silent stranger sitting like a depressed mannequin, leaving me to myself—fog blocking light and dark and nothing. An empty brain floating in prenatal liquid, a consciousness in search of signifier. I wanted him to reach for the bag and he did. I wanted him to pull a weapon. "What's in there?" I asked. I closed my eyes, the ultimate anticipation. I hoped that some kind of interesting life would flash before me, quickly, a bountiful, meaningful existence summed up in these final milliseconds . . . but no, it went wild with everything, a psychedelic panorama that blended into nothing soup, the most impressive organ on earth, a singular gift rivaling the universe itself, unable to arrive at anything spectacular in the most important instant, another cloud, this bulbous hoax, the physical manifestation of emptiness. What a fucking day.

"What a day," I said, opening my eyes.

He pulled back from the bag, lowered his hood and turned to look at me, holding something in his hand. With his free hand he removed his eye patch to reveal a second, beautiful, glowing, blue eye.

He smiled a kind smile. Warm.

"Trick-or-treat."

He handed me a candy bar and left as casually as he arrived.

The candy bar was a Whatchamacallit.

For The Birds
(Time Flies)

"We're existentially alone on the planet. I can't know what you're thinking and feeling and you can't know what I'm thinking and feeling. And the very best works construct a bridge across that abyss of human loneliness."
    -David Foster Wallace
    (True?)

"People say that your dreams are the only things that save ya."
    -Arcade Fire
    (Untrue.)

Winter

If it weren't for the headphones, he'd have more fear of cars sloshing from all sides. Huge red headphones over a forest green wool cap. He trimmed the tips off matching wool gloves so his hands wouldn't slip from the handlebars.

If it weren't for the headphones, he'd hear people voicing profound opinions. Get out of the road. It's god damn freezing out fer chrissakes. What are you? *Stupid*? He kept his head down to shield his eyes against all the miscellaneous wet flung up by meaty rubber tires. And still the slush slapped his cheeks and froze there, stuck in his hat and to his gloves, but he concentrated on the rock 'n' roll music and the way the headphones' cord turned white and stiff under his chin as he pedaled. The cord maintained its shape as he looked up to check for the turn. He spotted the turn and also the people frowning at him from behind their windshields, pointing at the road rebel— who is this fool using an alternative method of transportation in utterly unadvisable conditions? Leonard Smock, thank you very much.

Smock lowered his kickstand in front of the store. He pocketed his gloves and used his bare hands to ring out his ponytail. He pulled a pretty blue beach towel and plastic shopping bag from a seemingly empty knapsack. With the towel he dried his hands, his hair, the bicycle seat. With the bag, he wrapped the seat and secured it with a red rubber band from his hair.

Leonard held the door for a couple shuffling in from their car. They blew into their hands like that'd do anything—these strange, ineffective rituals. They rubbed their hands feverishly up and down their arms, looked at Leonard and said, "Burrrr." Entering the store after the ungrateful couple, Smock was struck by the glimmering birdbaths—sturdy and strong but with a polished sheen and rounded, inviting edges. Come on, slip in here, take a dip. A few were solid in color—evergreen and midnight blue. Others kaleidoscopic, transitioning between rich greens and blues and purples, probably giving an impression of the soothing Mediterranean Sea as far as the little birds were concerned. Still other baths had sweet painted pictures on them of leaves and big nuts and one with a Cardinal in a tree and one of a tree with no birds in it.

Behind the baths, a central desk/checkout counter lined with knickknacks—postcards and pens and compact discs, field guides and mugs and jars of hummingbird nectar. Disembodied birds chirped and chortled from speakers arranged strategically around the store and frightened some of the children.

Leonard recognized the owner, from her TV ads, helping a few customers. He moved toward them, lingering idly on the periphery of their conversation, a classic indicator of One Who Needs Assistance.

"Oh sure, right, if you don't want to get a red feeder you can just put a few red flowers there . . . or hang a red ribbon. Once the hummingbird has found the feeder you can remove the red items."

"And what about nectar?"

"I sell nectar in the store, over there on the counter."

Leonard whistled, non-aggressively, seeing how his rendition of The Stones' "It's Only Rock 'n' Roll" might play with some of the bird rhythms. He covertly observed the owner interacting with the couple. All three faces strained with tension abnormal for the subject matter. The owner, Dianne, did look orange and fuzzy like a chickadee necking over the egg's fresh edge. A splash of tangerine hair twisted above and around her face not unlike a bird's nest. If it weren't for her frustrated demeanor one might expect her to break into song or develop wings and fly away.

"Isn't it just sugar water?"

"Basically."

"How long before it ferments? And what's the proper ratio of sugar to water?"

"I'm sorry, I have another customer waiting," the owner said, moving Smock's way.

Still whistling, pretending he hadn't been listening, Leonard did not turn at first when she asked, "Hello?"

"*Sir*, can I help you with something?"

"Oh, hello," said Leonard, holding out his hand.

"Christ, man, you're *soaked*."

Leonard apologized and tucked his hand back inside his jacket pocket.

"I wanna buy a house."

"Great," said Dianne (unenthusiastically), "for what species?"

"Oh," replied Leonard.

"You don't know?"

"No."

"Where do you live?"

"Just a few blocks that way."

"What the hell'd you do, walk here?"

"Rode my bike."

"Well . . . you'll probably have some wrens, Eastern blue birds, tree swallows, and maybe some purple martins."

"What's the difference?"

"What do you *mean*, what's the difference?"

"Which one's the coolest?"

"I think they're all cool. . . . The martins live in communities. See that white house with the four holes in it?"

"*Yeah*."

"Different families will move into and nest in each apartment, if yer lucky."

"I'll take it."

"Yeah?"

"*Oh* yeah."

"Martins can be pretty loud ya know, their songs are oh, well . . . okay, I see you like music anyway," nodding at Smock's fire hydrant headphones.

"And I like it *loud*."

Dianne scooped up the house with a finger and brought it to the counter.

"Wait," Smock called.

"Yeah?"

"Don't I need some feed to put in it? What do purple martins eat?"

"No. You don't ever put *feed* in a bird-*house*. You put

feed," pointing at the bags of feed, "in a *feeder*," and pointing at the feeders.

"I see," Leonard sighed, a little upset that Dianne's personality in no way reflected the on-screen persona from her smiling singsong TV ads. But that's nothing new. Smock transformed his arms into wings and flapped his way to the front counter behind Dianne. A passing child pointed and cackled. Her mother pulled her away from the strange, wet man. And just as Leonard went to chortle for the child, Dianne turned, "*Hey*, what are you doing?"

"Huhwhat?" replied Leonard.

"Were you going to chortle at that child?"

"No, absolutely not. Of course not."

Dianne punched her fingers into the old cash register. "Seventy dollars."

Smock handed over his bills.

"It's gonna get all wet ya know. Why don't you just come back and grab it tomorrow or something?"

"I have a bag with me."

"Oh. Ya know, you're not as dumb as you look."

"Thanks. You look pretty dumb yourself."

Dianne went ahead and threw in a CD of smokin' bird tracks and a small informational booklet about purple martins.

Leonard raced home with the house. The trip more workout than simple transport—fierce leg pumping, cold sweat, heavy breathing. A familiar, vigorous journey. He could feel his blood running through his body and warming it as he leaned into his neighborhood—a spout of water streamed from his back tire into the air behind him, as if the guy were shredding a skidoo.

Music roared from the headphones, had his guts

jumping, the lanky worm-body becoming a loaded bundle of kinetic energy. His mind slipped the scene, daydreaming of past performances—nasty clubs and screaming, horny people. He remembered their foreheads bouncing, arms reaching for his face, fingers squeezing the empty air. Eyes that were open, focused on his playing. Sweat poured down his arms, glistening the guitar, dripping onto the worn wooden stage. His Converse left an imprint there as he stood in the sweat, bowing polite response to massive applause. And though he was one block from home he could hear them so clearly begging for one more song, begging him to keep riding, keep this dream alive. . . .

But in the next instant he saw his landlord, Jean, smoking on her porch. Her lips already flapping despite Smock's giant and clearly affixed headphones.

Jean didn't move or make kind gestures or smile or wave. She looked and smoked and the cords in her neck stretched out and recoiled with the mouth motioning. She got up from the step and continued toward Smock as he dismounted.

Finally, Leonard lowered his headphones.

And Jean, in her terribly loose-fitting wrangler blue, *men's* blue jeans: ". . . better not be, I swear it better not. What *is* in that bag, Lenny? Hope it's not another dog. Hope yer not tryin' to sneak another dog by me. Filthy fucking creatures," she blew out some smoke. Jean owned this two-story house—left to her by dead parents. She'd lived there with them her entire life, into her thirties, until one evening they were crushed by a falling tree while walking their dog through the woods. So, they left the place to Jean, noting in their will that Leonard Smock need not pay rent. Leonard had considered them friends. They considered themselves fans and supporters—of Lenny's singing and especially his songwriting. Jean was never a fan. Jean was never anything, was never going to be anything. Smock called her "Mean Jean," but never to her face.

"It's not a dog, Jean. I wouldn't put a dog inside a wet knapsack."

"What the hell is it then?"

"It's none of your business."

"Sure as shit it's my business. Everything you do up there is my business."

"It's a birdhouse."

"A *what*?" She laughed, and with the laugh a cough, and with the cough some smoke.

"It's a birdhouse."

"What are ya gonna do with a birdhouse, Lenny?"

"I plan to provide housing for several purple martin families."

"In the winter?"

"In the spring. They were having a sale, ya know, for the holidays."

"Listen Lenny, I'm having some people over tonight."

"Okay."

"So don't be playing your guitar."

"Okay."

"And no smoking grass neither. One of em's married to a cop I think."

Smock (and Jean) lived in a neighborhood called Hamilton Hill, though there wasn't any hill to speak of. They split this mold-white, shutterless, rectangular abode—imagine stacked trailers with Leonard Smock on top. The same shabby setup went up and down either side of the street forever. Each residence separated by slender alleys lined with garbage barrels. Too narrow for cars, each alley offered a glimpse into the backyards of Hamilton Hill that sprouted thin, piss-yellow grass from dusty dirt. Dead trees and strange metal fences bowed to each other. Here and there a run-down Big Wheel quivered into view, the rotting plastic wheels paralyzed by weeds. Squirrel apartments under the hood. Boxy adult cars parked all over the street had hubcaps and mostly faded paint, graying tires. Telephone wires tangled everywhere overhead. Like so many shitholes, it is true that this place used to *be something.* Hill residents talked about the town mill like a family keeping alive the memory of a relative who died too soon. Only this relative was made of bricks and shadows. The lights went out for good forty years ago but they don't let go, there's nothing else. The giant façade sheds bits of flesh every day, collecting on the pavement below, a merciless public decomposition— reminder that they were the ones left behind. Most weekends, angry adolescents drink skunk beer and smoke pot with seeds and fire rocks through the windows for fun.

Leonard Smock's bachelor pad might also be referred to as a shithole. Not like it was dirty or gross . . . just, empty. Plain. Possibly undeveloped. Possibly like Leonard. The tri-fold dining room table had one metal folding chair that faced into the living room at an old television. "Why don't you get a *flat* screen, high-def, man," guests often suggested. The tri-fold table surface had rubbery padding like those unsettling exam room chair/beds, or like how toilet seats used to be. Maybe the padding was put there to protect penniless eaters when they inevitably passed out, forehead first, from the shame of ramen noodles again.

But the table was also great for rolling joints, usually the first thing Smock did when the sun went down. Freed his hair from the red rubber band, combed it out, sweatpants, the lit J and his acoustic—Martin d45, purchased for him by Mean Jean's parents around five Christmases ago, "Nothing says you've arrived like a d45." Every time Leonard started strummin' he thought about Jean's angry face, "How much *was* that?" And her mother Pat shushing her, "We got it second-hand, Jean, calm down." Jealous Jean.

Smock stubbed out his joint at the sound of boots thudding up the stairs. At the sound of dog paws and the clinking collar, he relit it and went to the door.

"My brother," Smock announced as he opened the door for his giant black friend (and former drummer) LaTroy and his smaller black friend Bobby Dog the Labrador.

"How's my boy doing?" Leonard asked, handing LaTroy the joint.

"He's great man, been bringing him to work all week too."

"Awwww, whooosagudboyyy," Leonard said, rubbing Bobby Dog's ears (after the unfortunate incident in the woods, Jean turned even meaner and came to resent Leonard and Bobby Dog and all dogs. She obsessed over how much her parents had enjoyed Leonard's music. She called him "Lenny the Loser," but never to his face. She hated that she couldn't make him pay rent. She felt lonely and purposeless and took her frustrations out on the innocent Smock by imposing new house rules: no music, no smoking, no pets—"I'm gonna get this shithole cleaned up, sell it, and move south," she said.)

"Ha, dude, you bought a birdhouse?" LaTroy asked, returning the joint.

"That's a purple martin pad, man. They live in communities. They are *very* loud singers."

"That'll show her."

Another set of feet moved up the stairs, smaller, gentler feet.

Pat-pat-pat on the door.

"Put that out."

"WHO IS IT?"

"It's Patty."

LaTroy smiled, "Get in here, girl."

Jean's daughter walked through the door in tight pink sweatpants and a thick black hoodie that failed to conceal her post-adolescent bloom. Her presence wasn't uncommon; she liked Leonard and LaTroy and especially Bobby Dog, who hopped over to greet her with his tail going.

"Do you guys mind if I hangout here a while? This cop's wife is getting drunk and weird because her husband won't stop staring at me."

"*Shit*," said LaTroy, passing the joint to Patty.

"Thanks." She blew out some smoke, immediately calmed, "Nice birdhouse, Leonard."

"Why thank you," said Lenny, nodding, strumming his guitar with rhythm and purpose—a place beyond tuning.

Patty and LaTroy smoked and listened and waited, knowing that once Leonard stopped tuning he'd reached his splendid disposition and would soon play sweet music.

"So . . . like, did I just happen upon The Rollin' L's first reunion show?" Patty asked.

"Nahhh," answered LaTroy, not looking at Leonard.

"We've been thinking about getting back into it," countered Smock.

LaTroy seemed surprised by this, but happy.

"Well then play me something already . . . *Lenny*," Patty said, teasing Smock, mocking her mom. "Play me a *bird* song," she exhaled, standing and flapping around the apartment.

And so, Smock took up a soft rhythm, "Little sparrowwwwww, little sparrow."

The room went silent around him.

Bobby Dog curled up at Leonard's feet.

Patty spun and swayed toward the living room, circling Smock's furry blue couch, the pads of her bare feet made no noise, her sweatshirt off, arms above her head.

"Precious fragile little thing, flies so high and feels no pain."

During the solemn introductory section, the burpy inflections of drunken debate bounced off the ceiling below. ARGLE FARGLE GOBARGLE-BARGLE.

The monotone cries couldn't spoil the quickening melody or the ticklish image of slow-falling snow that freckled Smock's black bay window.

Leonard's d45 lit the room, his lean stomach flexed and drew air for his lungs as he belted . . .

If I were a little sparrow,
O'er these mountains I would fly.
I would find him, I would find him,
Look into his lying eyes.
I would flutter all around him,
On my little sparrow wings.
I would ask him, I would ask him,

Why he let me love in vain.

"HEY BABY," LaTroy shouted, stomping out the beat and clapping his hands as Smock picked purely the strings. The joint rested in an ashtray on the table, one strand of smoke pirouetted like Patty there with her eyes closed.

I am not a little sparrow,
I am just the broken dream,
Of a cold false-hearted lover,
And his evil cunning scheme. . . .

The snow came quiet yet abundantly through the night. Lighting up the world for no one's notice. Burying all the cold cars in gorgeous fat masses like two opposing barricades in the street. Nimble piles balanced impossibly along the power lines overhead. Evergreen trees wrapped in fabulous white fur, porches and rooftops and windowsills all freshly framed and ready to sparkle in the morning sun.

When the Hamilton Hill residents woke up Monday morning they were fucking pissed. Smock slid his curtain to the side and watched them working in the street. He slurped at his mug, yum, wiggled his frozen toes. They were out there thrashing. Bodies bending up and down, painfully at the waist, multicolored shovels stabbed into the air with delicious consistency. Those who had to be to work early were already inside their cars, rocking from drive to reverse as their tires spun a moonwalk along the icy street and kicked crusty snow into neighbors' cold, red faces. Smock could see Jean inside her car, slamming the steering wheel with her palm as she lurched forward and back, begging for inches. Leonard laughed at his vantage of Jean's silver, midsize car—she was too short to shovel the roof and her car had on a very classy, all white top hat.

Once all the superior neighborhoods were cleared, the big machines came and plowed the hill; and Leonard rode his bicycle to work.

On Monday all the employees were dressed in heavy, dark, sexless clothing. And their hair was a bit messy, messier after lunch, a mess by the end of the day.

On Tuesday they looked at the Internet: two celebrities got together. A kitty did a new trick. Someone people kind of remembered died last night—they sent thoughts and prayers all across the Internet. Everyone spent at least twenty minutes worrying about local shootings and fires before debating the best methods for resolving various global conflicts.

On Wednesday they sent emails throughout the office. There will be a meeting after lunch. The meeting will have food. So, should we go to lunch? Well, yes, still go to lunch but don't eat too much. Will there be enough food in the meeting if one should choose to eat lunch exclusively during the meeting? Probably. Will there be vegetables? There will be a vegetable platter. Maybe I'll go for a walk during lunch and then eat during the meeting. It's probably too cold for a walk today.

On Thursday there was a lot of work to do. Phone calls were made. Site visits were coordinated. Data . . . was entered . . . into spreadsheets. Site visit follow-ups were coordinated for the previously coordinated site visits. A meeting about the meaning of the data. Emails about the meaning of the data. Digital filing. After lunch, everyone was exhausted.

On Friday there was a big surprise. All the departments filed into the basement cafeteria at noon for catered lunch and a magic show. The boss took the microphone first and thanked everyone for all their hard work during such a stressful and busy time. He knew it wasn't easy, getting up, going to work—when it's so cold and nasty outside.

A balding man in a black suit seated next to the boss nodded his head. Like most bald men this guy had grown a beard and he kept it manicured. Next to the manicured man was a giant sign with his face on it. The sign said "Snacktastic!" and showed him pinching an Ace of Spades with his fingers in the foreground. It's likely that the smile on the poster was meant to convey something magical, but for most in attendance it read as a warning that one should not inquire about the magician's personal life. His eyes were a dreary gray blue and he shouldn't have matched his tie to them. He looked more like a funeral director. A funeral director who hobbied in magic. A funeral director who bankrupted his business after several ill-timed, poorly performed magic tricks. Leonard sat in the back staring at him while everyone else dipped pizza crust into Blue Cheese dressing. Smock knew this couldn't have been the magician's dream, playing a basement cafeteria at noon to a chorus of smacking lips.

"My friend . . . the magical . . . Jim Snack." Four people clapped, twice each. Smock offered a sturdy but appropriate round of applause. The magical Snack opened with a card trick. He fanned the deck for a woman sitting at a table up front. She did not look up from her submarine but stuck her hand out, like searching for a light switch in the dark, until her hand met a card and she pulled. "Okay," she mumbled. Then Snack fooled around with the cards a little bit while the woman went back to eating. After about ten seconds of fooling she reacted, screamed "What the *fuck,*" while pulling dramatically away from her submarine sandwich. Coworkers all turned to discover the playing card, with mayo, peeking between her lips, which she spat violently onto the table, "That's fuckin' dis-*gusting,*" she shouted. "Your hands were on that."

"Is that your card?" asked the magical Snack.

"Who gives a shit, you ruined my sandwich," she got up to get another.

"Looks like somebody just had a Snack-attack," Jim announced, while casually grabbing a toothpick from the table, "Check this out," he said, moving smoothly around the basement cafeteria. He took the toothpick from his mouth, and pinching it between his fingers, showed it to the employees, "Just a regular toothpick—you saw me grab it off the table. . . ."

"*Ah, shit,* there's no roast beef left," the woman called.

"Just a regular . . . used . . . toothpick," Snack tried to regain as much attention as possible as the sandwich-less employee rambled about her abhorrence of ham.

"VOILA!" Snack shouted. He clapped and the toothpick disappeared. Wow. A few people jumped at the sudden noise, but all did wonder—where did that toothpick disappear to? "VOILA again," Jim yelled, clapping again, boom—the toothpick materialized from thin air and he stuck it in the corner of his mouth while bowing to minimal applause.

Leonard noticed Snack look over at the boss, who replied with that impatient, finger winding 'finish it up' motion.

"For my . . . *final* trick . . . I'll need a volunteer."

No one moved. The boss looked at his unwilling, unmotivated, unimpressed, unimpressive, unenthusiastic group of hires, eating submarines and pizza and bullshit salad. He knew everyone would view catered lunch as the real gift for all the hard work, but he truly did believe they'd enjoy a little side of magic.

"I'll volunteer," said a blind woman.

"Oh," replied Jim Snack.

There was a lot of time to cringe as the blind lady poked her way towards the front of the cafeteria—perhaps she likened any magician's abilities to the work of Jesus, or at least figured it worth a shot. Her long stick clinked and clinked and clinked off the legs of each and every chair, a holiday ghost working its way so slowly up the staircase for inevitable soul sucking.

"*No*, ummm," Snack looked at the boss, "this won't uhhhh, this won't. . ."

And still she poked, "I'll do it. Just hold on a minute."

"No that's really all right, Dorothy, I'll do it," said the boss. He took Dorothy by her shoulders and put her in his vacated seat. No miracles today.

"Hey all right, let's hear it for Mr. Chickles everyone," and mostly everyone clapped for the awkward boss.

"Now please, Darren, inspect this top hat of mine. . . ." Mr. Chickles turned the hat round and round in his hands, mmhmm-ing and nodding his head. "Looks normal to me," he confirmed. Leonard, who was about the only one paying attention, noticed the magical Snack shaking from his ankles. He instructed the boss to try the hat on and to show it to the audience. Turn it around. Show 'em the inside. Smock thought the magician might be experiencing some sort of personal earthquake the way his body trembled.

"Now . . . you're *sure* there's nothing in there, Darren?"

"Yeah, uh, haha, I'm pretty damn sure."

"Let me take a look." The magical Jim Snack put his hands, forearms, and elbows inside the top hat. He started convulsing from the torso as though puking into the top hat might be the finale. But, after far too long, once any suspense had been sapped from the room and it was obvious that this magician was working to get something out of his clothes and into the top hat, the magical Snack reared backward and held aloft a beautiful white dove, which, in truth, is really just a breed of pigeon. And so, like his cousins, once the "dove" flapped from Snack's grasp it began to defecate nervously all over the lunch buffet, spoiling anyone's chances at finding that last roast beef. "Oh, Christ," Snack said. The dove flew up and smashed into the tile ceiling, then darted across the room and just missed crashing into the wall before it turned again and brushed one employee's pretty, brunette hair. She shrieked as the bird landed on the adjacent table. That table of employees screamed and stood and fled as the bird flew away again. The blind woman sitting in Darren Chickles' chair asked, "I hear flapping. There a bat loose in here again?" and started swinging her walking pole through the air with surprising aggression. Leonard Smock wanted so badly to shout "VOILA," but felt awful for the magical Snack, who now chased the bird, holding the top hat forth like an inviting nest or birdbath. Chairs went everywhere as employees sprinted for the exit, dropping food and drink all over the floor—blessing the bird and fucking the janitorial crew.

Leonard pedaled home in the black night. On deserted streets, he'd pull his headphones down around his neck and listen to the natural sounds of the winter world—wind, the familiar drone of his lubricated chain, nothing. He'd take an empty whiff—the smell of cold? An occasional evergreen? They call it fresh air but it has all the invented qualities of fresh water—what is refreshing about absence? He studied the nothing and the dark—the dead world awash in white and waiting.

Going to work and coming home and waiting.

Eating and sleeping and watching a screen and waiting.

The first puzzle is labeled: Song Title. Obscenely dramatic music plays as the letters reveal themselves to the contestants and the at-home audience. Nancy, an eighth-grade teacher from Ludlow, Illinois shouts, "Great . . . Balls . . . of *Fire*!" and as this is the correct answer the crowd cheers. Nancy claps and jumps up and down while smiling a smile that is the epitome of pure joy. The immortal, wrinkle-free host approaches Nancy and asks, though he already knows, "What do ya do there in Ludlow?" "Well, Pat," she swoons, "I'm an eighth-grade social studies teacher!" Her voice is monotone but loud, she is shouting, although the immortal host stands only inches from her face, "You married," he asks. "YES I AM, PAT. I WANNA SAY HI TO MY WONDERFUL HUSBAND MATT!!!" "Thanks Nancy," the host begins to move away but is mistaken, Nancy isn't finished, "AND OUR THREE WONDERFUL KIDS BLUE, GREEN AND CHERRYYYY!!!" The host flinches and turns to Todd, "Hi, Todd." "Hi." "Todd Shide from Milton, Massachusetts—a customer support director for a lubricants company." "Yessir." "Married?" "Yes I am . . . uh, my beautiful wife Amy, we've been married for about five years and I'd also like to say hello to my two beautiful daughters, Nora and Laura." "Great." The host slides a bit closer to the final contestant who is younger and more camera-ready than her opponents. "Julie Abernathy," he almost sighs. "Hi, Pat," she hugs him. Though the host does not age, the audience is aware of his tenure and that he has in fact been alive for a very long time, easily twice as long as Julie—so this interaction is awkward because Julie is naïve, she doesn't think for a moment that he's sniffing her hair and studying the curves of her body as it presses against his, but he is. There is an obvious pause that should have been edited before he asks her where she's from and what she does: consumer events manager from Flagstaff, Arizona, "And I wanna say hi to my two beautiful children—Great Garrison and *Marvelous . . . Madison*!!" The host did not ask if she was married.

After a good deal of give and take, *Nancy* has reached The Bonus Round. She's already won $18,367 and a dream vacation to The Bahamas. The host tells us that if one were to look up the definition of "firecracker" in the dictionary there'd be a picture of Nancy there. She laughs so hard that she bends over at the waist and then returns to an upright position with her hands on her cheeks. The Bonus Round is very intense. The puzzles are much more difficult and an even more dramatic (yet hushed) instrumental track is enlisted. The wrinkle-free host holds an envelope that could potentially give Nancy up to a hundred thousand dollars in cash or even a brand new car. The at-home audience derides her choice of three consonants and a vowel, no matter which she chooses—D, F, W . . . O.

This works out quite well for Nancy, as the unremarkable _ R _ _ T _ _ _ _ magically becomes D R _ F T W O O D. The wrinkle-free host asks the audience for complete silence before they start the timer. Nancy's eyes are enormous. She is bursting at the seams to solve this puzzle.

"*DRIFT . . . WOOD!*" She screams with perfect annunciation and leaps into the air in a way the at-home audience didn't imagine possible. She hugs the host but does not stop jumping, is she trying to mount the host? He struggles to push her away so he can reveal what's inside the envelope, what she's won . . . and wouldn't you know it . . . another hundred grand. This added information sends the firecracker into the sky, she's gone to eleven, the already burning fire stoked with another colossal log, she runs in circles around the stage, her arms spread like wings. Blue, Green, and Cherry rush down from their seats and chase after their mother. Nancy's wonderful husband Matt nearly falls over as she embraces him at full speed and proceeds with the traditional mount—this time with a kiss. The camera is too close and the at-home audience can hear Nancy whispering, "Oh thank you, Jesus," over and over again. Her grand total of cash winnings flashes in golden numbers at the bottom of the screen: $118,367. Not to mention the dream vacation.

Leonard isn't really watching all this with his guitar and notebook on the couch. He's got a joint going. He's putting pen to paper. He's also not watching ninety percent of the neighborhood out setting up their holiday lights in observance of a god, who, even if he or she does exist, clearly doesn't favor the citizens of Hamilton Hill. And yet they proceed, into the basements and out with the boxes and on with the unravelling. Pinning and pinning these uninspired, uninspiring, multicolored bulbs to dead bushes and rusty handrails as the silent snow blesses them again. The decorations convert the uniform white into inconsistent rainbows up and down the street. The commotion and temporary camaraderie drown the sound of a sparkling original rhythm drifting from Leonard Smock's window.

Spring

On the first official Sunday of spring, Leonard Smock woke naturally, sniffed an invigorating breeze. He'd slept with all his windows open. The previous evening, preparing to smoke, he'd ritualistically opened just one section of his front bay window (allowing the joint smoke to bless the neighborhood). But upon smelling the *fresh* . . . *air*, upon realizing that that fresh air was *warm* fresh air, Smock went ahead and cranked-to-unfurl the other two sections. And then, just minutes later, he momentarily postponed his practice session to go open every single window in the apartment—a total of two and a half other windows. He looked out one of them—all the people's cheeks signaled a jubilant spring mood, half the neighborhood on a porch or in the street, relishing the sun's violet goodbye. And so, Smock played the old Sol away, sitting on the ledge of his bay window and blessing the neighborhood. More than a few neighbors did comment on the superb sound of that guitar coming from . . . somewhere.

Spring air wandered all through Leonard's apartment. It smelled dank, heavy with the weight of reincarnated earth. Leonard's little black arm-hairs stood up to acknowledge the changing tide. And outside his eyes took in, what? Color. Insects buzzing from bush to bush. Neighbors, whole troops, walking so fast their bodies could be seen bouncing under Sunday sweat suits—oh how they laughed and spoke with a passionate cadence and without mumbling and their joints felt loose and rejuvenated by the rising temperature. It was pretty obvious kites were flying everywhere.

Lenny mounted his classic roadster bicycle, just for fun—chrome pedals sparkling against muted rosewood frame. His seat gave way to his ass for the first time in months. When he went to put the red rubber band around his ponytail he thought: nahhh. When he went to put on his safety helmet he thought: nahhh. Be free.

The first three pumps of Leonard's pedals *swoosh . . . swoosh . . . swooshed* like igniting a great wind turbine. He blazed from the alley and out into the street, streaking under the unfamiliar azure sky, his flashy mane flapping in the heated breeze. The jet-black hair, to be sure, had adopted a touch of gray, but none of the locks so jaded that they couldn't relish a moment in the Sunday sun. Smock picked his head upright and with his back vertical took a moment to acknowledge the simple pleasure and purity of swift movement, the way the wind whistled in his ears and lifted his hair and not only his hair—but the rush of all things. He sensed the great migration, could almost hear all those birds calling to each other and playing in the sky, drawn north magnetically by something that preexisted being. And as he pushed his bicycle faster, he imagined himself as one of the flock, performing for earthbound crowds along an infinite, crystal clear stage, their million wings spiked the air with a sweetness that brought everyone outside to see—and not simply outside, but together.

How could it be that something so routine as a few added degrees affected a new attitude in all humans?

It can't be that a thing this simple is responsible for such complexities as kindness and activity.

Smock parked his bike, inspired. He hurried to his notebook. He took up his guitar, put his hand gently to its neck and with his clammy hands he played. He played to the great migration. He played them back home. He played some old things and was reminded how even the aged wood of his Martin breathed a sigh of relief as it defrosted—something richer in the sound. He tried out the beginning sequence of his new tune and realized that it was good. Outside on the lawn some creeping and crawling things shuffled to the soggy surface. Those passing below Leonard's window listened to the Martin d45's melody and thought that it was good. And he could feel a small crowd beginning to assemble outside. He began to play louder, and more beautifully—the clammy hands and moisturized air, there was a sultry pulse in his fingertips and as he started to sing his body took off.

You were only waiting for this moment to arise. . . .

Young Patty swayed in the apartment below. She moved her math homework out of the way. "Listen to him," she said to her Mom, Mean Jean, sitting on a brown sofa, blowing out a cigarette hit, coughing, coughing the word, "What," coughing the question "Who?" She looked at the TV.

"It's Leonard," Patty said.

"*Leonard??*"

"*Shhhhhhhh,*" answered Patty.

You were only waiting for this moment to arise. . . .

Mean Jean stuffed her cigarette into a crowded ashtray and went to the kitchen and returned with a broom. She walked toward her own bay window and stood there with the broom a moment. She watched her daughter sway. She smashed the butt end of the broom into her ceiling four times—*butt butt butt butt.*

"LENNY," she yelled, "LENNYYYYYYYY."

The playing persisted.

"LEN . . ." she coughed, "*ACK*—UCK, ACK, UCK . . . SHUT THE *FUCK* UP, UP THERE."

"MOM," Patty yelled.

The music stopped.

And in the night just after bedtime it started raining, gently at first so that you could sense it in your body and then audibly onto the roof and against the windows; so loud it couldn't be ignored, so loud that people even woke up from all the splashing. They grunted and rolled over. But the plants absolutely loved it—being alive, getting fed, awesome.

When the Hamilton Hill residents woke up Monday morning, they were so fucking pissed you wouldn't believe it. It was *still* raining. They were irate under umbrellas and apoplectic at the traffic. Their windshield wipers went wild. Feet squish-squish-squished into the office and a few daring employees did slip off their socks, airing out their puppies in a public place—top five on the office no-no list. There were arguments and emails about bare feet and wet socks all day long. Leonard Smock contributed to the office email, a rarity: "On particularly rainy days, I bring an extra pair of shoes and socks in my bag. . . . Not a bad idea. – LS." Well, nobody enjoyed this pompous ass email. Everyone said that that's Leonard's responsibility and 'what he gets' for riding a bicycle to work—wet feet are not something 'we' ever have to *deal with*, Leonard.

That same Monday, Nancy Dowling drove her family to the airport. The gray and modestly priced CUV was filled with an entire family of not-pissed people— wonderful Matt and Blue and Green and Cherry (also all wonderful) smiled huge smiles. They passed their passports around the car and looked at them and laughed at the funny faces. They couldn't wait to get away. They talked and talked the whole ride about how they couldn't wait to get away.

The airport was filled with people wanting to get away, many of them pissed. There were terrible things inside the Chicago Midway International Airport: delays, cancellations, security checks, low-class dining, groups of intoxicated spring breakers, urinals sprinkled with pubic hair, general crowding.

In the airport several people recognized Nancy and yelled either, "Driftwood," or, "Oh thank you, Jesus," at her family. Though some non-pissed people did tell the Dowlings to enjoy their trip and/or congratulations. Nancy enjoyed the attention.

To the shock and dismay of all Dowlings, the game show provided only economy class seats—not first class. Wonderful Matt made a wonderful joke about what would happen if the host and hostess were forced to fly coach, everyone laughed.

Everyone stopped laughing when one of the Bahama-bound spring breakers recognized Nancy.

"HEY, there's uhhhh, HEY—fucking *driftwood*," he exclaimed. Everyone laughed.

Not Nancy's family.

"Mommy, what's that word?" asked sweet, sweet Cherry.

"Nothing honey, it's just wood that the waves wash ashore."

"Not *that* word, Mommy."

"OH, *thank* you Jesus, OH, OH, OH, JESUS, OH *FUCK*, OH *THANK* YOU, JEEZUSSSS," someone shouted. Everyone laughed. Girls giggled, "*Stop* that."

After four hours of this, the Dowlings got off the plane in a pretty pissed-off mood.

On Tuesday, the hot Bahama air and bright Bahama sunshine had the Dowlings in a really wonderful mood and they all went to lie by the pool, to decompress. Once Nancy, Blue, Green, and Cherry fell asleep, wonderful Matt crept away to the beach. He lit a cigarette and exhaled the words, "Oh . . . thank you, *Jesus*," with that first hit. And laughing almost hysterically he started down the beach. Everyone kept saying this place was *paradise*. Wonderful Matt figured: they probably have awesome weed in paradise. He asked and asked and no one had any to sell. He hit a few joints on his way through the sand. The waves sounded louder, clearer, they crashed crisply in his ears. He wanted to laugh at some driftwood, but they didn't have that shit in paradise—just the soft sand, the sun, the perfect sky, gleeful seagulls flapping and calling quietly, his feet never felt this way. The hard-bodied spring breakers poured everything down their throats and danced and swam and fell and probably later fucked, tan on tan, wet shorts on the floor, maid ladies outside getting aroused, paradise.

Finally, Matt scored. He rolled a joint and smoked it to the bone. The guy said meet me here tomorrow if you want more, this is all I have on me. Then he said, meet me here tomorrow if you want some coke too.

Arriving back at the pool everyone was burnt—Nancy, Blue, Green, Cherry, and Matt.

"Ohhhh, no," Nancy said, when Matt woke her. "Why the fuck didn't you wake us up an hour ago?"

"Mommy, what's that word mean?" Cherry asked again.

"I went for a walk."

"A *walk*?" Nancy pointed her eyes at Matt in a way that suggested she'd accurately read 'walk' as a codeword for 'smoking cigarettes and pot.'

At dinner, being so burnt and stiff and uncomfortable, nobody talked much and mostly everyone was pretty pissed. Except for Matt, who was not pissed, or stiff. Matt enjoyed his meal, and most of Cherry's and all of Green's.

On Wednesday everyone was still badly burnt. Most of the Dowlings stayed inside and got room service and rubbed aloe vera all over their bodies—taking turns getting each other's back.

Matt went out to get some weed and coke, which he called "aloe vera."

Matt had had another idea last night, once again when Nancy was asleep. He went ahead and helped himself to a heaping portion of Nancy's winnings, maybe twenty grand, which he planned to spend on "aloe vera."

"Oh, *shit*, I didn't think it was like that," said Matt's guy, looking at the twenty grand.

The guy brought Matt back to his house. And the guy let Matt sample his aloe vera, which turned out to be really top quality. The guy asked Matt if he wanted some girls, or something. Matt said he better not, but then decided to anyway.

Then, while Matt was balls deep in this tan Bahama babe's ass and this other Bahama babe had her tongue in Matt's ass, the cops busted down the guy's door and started yelling and pointing their guns around and smashing and breaking more stuff and asking "What is this," "What is this," "What is this," eventually they opened the door to the room Matt was in and asked, "What is this?"

They made Matt put his clothes back on so that they could arrest him, for solicitation and possession. They looked through his pants first, pulled out all his aloe vera and asked, "What is this?" When Matt answered "Aloe vera," they didn't believe him. Then they slapped the cuffs on him, read him his rights.

On Thursday Nancy received a phone call. It was the wrinkle-free host!

"How's life in paradise?"

"We're burnt, peeling, and my husband has disappeared."

"Oh, Jesus," replied the host. Then he said he had to go and that he was sorry and that he hoped it all worked out for them, though he did not care at all.

On Thursday Nancy received a second phone call, this one from Matt, a.k.a. "an inmate at Her Majesty's Prison."

"It really isn't as nice as the name makes it sound.

They're feeding us bologna, with like, tomato paste. . . . You gotta come get me."

"What'd you do, Matt?"

"Pot, blow . . . and two," he coughed the word: hookers.

"That's wonderful, Matt."

On Friday, Nancy's family flew back to Chicago—the hot Bahama air and bright Bahama sunshine weren't so much fun anymore, kind of like God shining a spotlight upon their suffering. The Dowlings sat in silence as the airplane fired up its engines—sickening unearthly gas turbines that nearly pierced Matt's overly sensitive eardrums. And so, Matt, facing extreme mental and physical fatigue, applied some massive, noise-canceling headphones to his ears and shut the strange, stiff plastic curtain over the window to spare his tender eyes. Nancy immediately leaned over Matt and pushed the curtain back to its upright position, clicking emphatically into place. Matt countered by lowering a cheetah print sleep mask over his eyes, thinking, divorce might not be the worst thing ever. And as the plane burned down the runway and lifted from the earth, Nancy remembered herself, arms spread out so wide, running all around the game show stage with her family smiling behind her. Her shining moment, it seemed like forever ago. She shook her head. Cherry slept on her shoulder. Matt burped, mumbled, "You know, humans were never meant to fly."

Birds chirped and chortled all about Hamilton Hill. They pushed their spectacular bird breasts out proudly, announcing the season. Leonard noticed them always landing or flying, always having lots of fun. They hung out on handrails and lined up along telephone wires for morning roll call. Though none of them had taken residence in Leonard Smock's purple martin pad. Leonard and LaTroy sat smoking by the window, looking at the house, waiting for some action. So many birds blew right by the house without a second look. Some even landed in the same tree, lo, the very *branch* from which Leonard's house hung.

"Look at that shit," LaTroy said.

"What?"

"That's a boring ass house, man, it's all white. There's nothin' to it. I wouldn't want to live in that house."

"What should I do?" asked Leonard.

"Make it a rock 'n' roll house, man. You said purple martins are rockin' singers, right? And they live in communities? They want to live in a party house."

And so, Leonard Smock took the house down from its tree and brought it inside. It sat there for a week while he smoked, practiced, wrote and just generally thought about what to do. How to transform the drab pad into a real rockin' domicile? How will the birds know?

It's the white they don't like. . . .

It's boring. . . .

Paint it. Yes.

Put *food* in it. No, you don't put *feed* in a bird-*house*, you put feed in a *feeder*.

Instead of just painting it, Smock had another inspired idea. He would paint the logos of three of his favorite rock bands of all time, rock icons. He would incorporate the four holes (or, doorways, if you're a bird) into his design.

The top hole became the black, empty brain of The Grateful Dead's steal-your-face skull design.

Using the middle two holes for the letter "O," Smock wrote the word "Z-O-S-O."

The bottom hole served as the gaping mouth for the Rolling Stones' unmistakable tongue and lip logo.

Smock looked over the house and decided the fresh exterior did rock. He lit up a joint and let the house dry—blowing some smoke (drying agent) over it as a blessing. The more he smoked, the better the pad appeared. And before putting it back in the tree he decided, yeah, put a little food in it.

But Leonard didn't have any feed. He had a two pack of chili beef and cheddar Hot Pockets and some fresh broccoli. He put just one Hot Pocket in the microwave for 2:47 and watched it spin around and around on the plate. Imagine being a bird; inside a house painted with rock 'n' roll icons, filled with Hot Pockets and broccoli. That'd make anyone want to take up residence, sing loudly about it. Also, Leonard noted, these new Hot Pockets are filled with 100% Angus beef and *real* cheddar cheese and thus, he concluded, most likely safe for birds.

The Hot Pockets came out steaming, oozing real cheddar cheese from all four corners and looking delicious. Leonard decided to boil the broccoli as the Hot Pockets cooled. And removing the broccoli with a slotted spoon he put all this food onto one plate and cut everything into bird bites—tiny specks of sustenance. *Then*, Smock went into the bathroom, his ponytail bouncing off his back as he walked, grabbed his tweezers, and used them to place the food into the little doorways, providing between five and ten tweezersfull per residence.

Smock went out and restored the rockin' house to its original branch, using a ladder and everything. Climbing down the ladder he heard the terrible noise of Jean's bedroom window screeching open. It faced their shared backyard, she coughed the question, "Well, the fuck ya got there now, Lenny?"

"It's still a birdhouse, Jean."

"What's all that shit all over it?"

"Those are rock icons."

"What's that?"

"Logos, you know?"

"Yeah, I see the Stones on there I guess."

"Right," Leonard folded up his ladder, hoping to signal an end to these pleasantries.

"You don't think that's gonna make the birds wanna come live there do you?"

"I don't know."

"I got more tenants than you, *Lenny*," she laughed, blew out some smoke, ashed onto the backyard, "And I only got one . . . *YOU*," Jean laughed even more at this, coughed, wind gusted through her window and caused her dry, black hair to flutter as one bunch.

Moving away with his ladder, Smock replied, "A very astute observation, Jean."

Jean tossed her cigarette out into the yard, mumbled something and shut the window.

Leonard went up to his apartment and played guitar and waited.

He waited for the purple martins to arrive.

He waited for the martins to sing.

He waited for them to serenade Mean Jean to hell.

He ate Top Ramen and Hot Pockets and waited.

He looked out the window and waited.

It rained and the flowers blossomed while he waited.

The bees buzzed and pollinated while he waited.
He wrote a sweet new tune and waited.
He smelled all the fresh smells and waited.
He rode the rosewood roadster and waited.
He went to work and came home and waited.
Looking out the window and waiting.
Waking and sleeping and waiting.
With the whole world in bloom, he's waiting.

Summer

By midsummer Leonard Smock had waited long enough. Birds chanted morning torment and he woke up dripping. His waterlogged locks had formed an everlasting bond of moisture with his pillow and sheet overnight. His bright red sleeveless shirt had become a dark red sleeveless shirt. It clung to his back when he pulled it over his head. Smock let the shirt plop onto the floor and left it there. He pulled down his shorts so the goddamn shirt would have some company.

Outside an army of sprinklers tick-tick-tick-ticked before machine-gunning back into place. All the lawnmowers got fired up, rumbling like tanks, decimating nasty looking, overgrown lawns.

Leonard saw no point in showering. Toweled the sweat from his body, for now, and pulled the red rubber band tight around his soggy ponytail—grabbed his bicycle helmet and knapsack and headphones on his way out the door.

"I just *love* what you've done with the place, Leonard," Patty said, out sunbathing, watching Leonard unhook the purple martin pad from its branch.

"Well . . . thank you, Patty, but I'm returning it now."

Leonard tried to avoid staring at Patty in her white bikini. She would be able to tell he fantasized about her. Maybe the not looking would be a far worse indicator.

"Because no birds came?"

"Yup."

"My Mom is absolutely *loving* that, by the way."

"Your Mom is a mean person."

"I know," Patty sighed and lay back on her towel. Her flat stomach looked fine in the sun. Leonard noticed her spectacular tan and how the angle of the sun's rays highlighted the normally invisible fuzz around her pierced navel. Her little legs looked more muscular than he'd imagined. He reaffirmed his opinion of Patty's petite feet, made even cuter by the pink polish, the fourth toe of each foot actually painted purple. She had sparkles around her cheeks and eyes and . . .

"*So* . . . you were going back to the bird store then?" Patty asked.

"Oh, yeah, shit . . . I'm sorry. I didn't mean to, uhh," Smock stood there holding the rockin' birdhouse in one hand, his knapsack in the other.

"It's okay . . . *Lenny*," she laughed, "away with you now, shoo-shoo-shoo, fly away, fly on ya big *BIRD*."

Leonard stuffed the birdhouse into his bag and flew back to the store.

There were about no people at all inside Backyard Birds.

Smock peered through the front door and swore he saw that Chickadee Dianne drinking from a jar of nectar.

A little bell on the door alerted both parties. Ding-ding-ding.

"Well, the soaked man returns. Soaked again."

"Good afternoon," Smock said.

"Soaked Two: The Sequel . . . Soaked in Sweat."

Smock pulled the martin pad out of his knapsack. The sight of the rockin' domicile was nearly enough to cause Dianne's collapse. The back section of the counter saved her.

"What the heck did you *do*, man?"

"What?" answered Leonard.

"You can't *paint* the house, especially with black paint . . . *especially*."

"Why?"

"Didn't you read the book I gave you?"

"Obviously not."

"Obviously. Listen . . . uh . . ."

"Leonard."

"Listen, *Leonard*, the house was white for a reason. Purple martins are attracted to white or pastel-colored housing."

"Well even when the house was still all white they weren't comin'. They were even perched on the same branch, sometimes, and nothing."

"Where'd you hang the house?"

"In my backyard."

"How far from your house . . . and your neighbors houses?"

"I dunno, not that far, I guess."

"A hundred feet or so?"

"Ten."

"Were there other trees around too?"

"Yes."

Disembodied birds chirped and chortled from the speakers. The jar of nectar lay open between Leonard and

Dianne.

"Where exactly do you live, Leonard?"

"Hamilton Hill."

"Oh furchrissakes, Lenny, you can't have a purple martin house on Hamilton Hill."

"Why?"

"You're all packed in like a bunch of sardines up there. It would never work. Martins need clear thruways, a large open space, at least forty to sixty feet away from the next closest tree."

"Shit."

"Shit is right . . . housing a community of martins is a very fickle situation, Leonard."

"A fickle situation?"

"*Very* fickle."

"I guess I'll paint it back to white then."

"Oh don't bother with it now, Lenny, it's way too late. They stop nesting in mid-May."

"Shit," Leonard looked at the floor.

"Why'd you want to get the house in the first place, Leonard? If you wanna see some birds, if you wanna go bird watching, I'll take you. We have a little club in town."

"That's all right. I really just wanted to piss off my landlord. She lives downstairs."

"Why?"

"She made me give my dog away. I mean, he stays with my buddy, so I still see him and everything, but it's not the same . . . you know?"

"And you wanted the birds, the martins, to be screaming outside her window all the time?"

"Bingo."

"That's a damn good plan, Lenny. I'll give it to ya. Just

too bad you live up there."

"Guess I'll paint it back to white."

"It's too late, Lenny."

"Give me a bag of the feed. I'm gonna put feed in it."

"If you do, the sparrows'll come and bust the thing all up. Might even get an infestation of squirrels in your yard."

"I already had Hot Pockets in there."

"You're kidding me."

"Angus beef and real cheddar."

"Birds don't like Hot Pockets, Leonard. Purple martins feed primarily on flying insects."

"How's that even possible?"

"Read the book."

"It's too late."

Lenny left with his vacant and now mobile bird home, his knapsack made heavier by the pointless feed that Dianne, to her credit, donated to his cause.

Sweat oozed from the foam-padded helmet down Smock's forehead as he pedaled home. Perspiration collected in his eyebrows until they soaked through, the dam broke, and the flood rushed into his eyeballs—"*AHH* . . . *SHIT*," he said, attempting to blink away the terrible stinging. The twin hallows dripped from his face like inverted puddles and sizzled down his red, peeling nose, already burnt raw from the summer sun. The sweat slid between his lips and tasted salty on the tongue. He tilted his head back and sucked in a stream from his water bottle, the liquid too warm to be really refreshing, he took a squirt to the face anyways. He added another squirt through a hole at the top of his helmet. The warm water drenched his ponytail and squeezed behind the massive red headphones and gave the impression of listening to music underwater. Monstrous, air-conditioned SUVs towing boats swerved around Smock as he pedaled, "These bikers take up the whole damn road," a driver said. "Mmmm-I know," responded a passenger, without really removing his or her lips from the straw of some tasty and fantastic iced coffee drink. Leonard's waistband collected all the sweat cascading down his back and eventually, deposited it into his asshole. The foam-padded bicycle seat became waterlogged, squishing audibly along inconsistent pavement.

So much liquid pooled inside his headphones that all Leonard could hear was the sound of his own breathing—heavy, heavy breathing and a heightened sense of his pulse. The straps from his knapsack rubbed and chafed his tender shoulders. A corner of the birdhouse foundation bounced sharply against his lower back, tick-tick-ticking into the base of his spine. This was no joyride, man. He hadn't taken a nice trip. It occurred to Leonard, drowning in his own perspiration, that he'd just completed a circular . . . useless . . . errand. It wasn't only that he'd gone out and returned home in the same condition, the same predicament—a bird-less man, but that, perhaps, the entire bird experience went beyond failed experiment. The sharp pain in his back a cruel reminder that this futile scheme had backfired—add it to the long list of failures and embarrassments, his hopes and dreams squashed by something completely out of his hands.

Leonard leaned his red roadster on the side of the house and studied his backyard, determined. There was a tree set back from the others. While it did not have what Chickadee Dianne called "clear thruways," it was a suitable distance away from the house. And it did seem, supposing that these martins could really wail, that the tree was still close enough that the birds' morning cries would drive Jean nuts.

Smock filled all four holes with feed and hung the domicile (still rockin') on the new tree, upon a very high branch to get everyone's attention and, of course, also to prevent potential squirrel infestations.

LaTroy pulled up in his air-conditioned car with Bobby Dog sticking his head and hanging tongue out the passenger window. The dog barked and wagged at the sight of his owner, Leonard Smock, who yelled, "BOBBY DOG," as the dog clumsily leapt out the window and the drummer went to the trunk to unpack his portable drum kit. On Sundays, in the summer, Mean Jean liked to go to the races and gamble her meager inheritance on the animals. This gave The Rollin' L's opportunity to practice at full volume.

"Now *that's* a rockin' ass house, man," LaTroy said, looking at the domicile on its new branch.

"You like it?" Leonard asked.

"Love it, dude. You're a brilliant birdman."

"At least somebody does."

"Huh?"

"Ahhh, I just got back from Backyard Birds. This chick who owns the store said they don't like black paint, or tight space, or the kinda food I put in it."

"She doesn't know shit, man."

"Yeah . . . but no birds came."

"Dude, chill, it's gonna be all right. If you build it . . . they will come."

"Do you even know what that's from?"

"Nahh. But I heard some people sayin' it before."

"It's from Field of . . ."

"Who gives a SHIT what it's from, it's time to play."

As The Rollin' L's set up another rehearsal in preparation for their Fall Tour: ReRollin' It, the scent of fresh feed spread through the backyards of Hamilton Hill. And from Leonard's front bay window, the scent of fresh marijuana.

Neighborhood birds chirped and chortled with excitement, drawn to the feed, they inspected the scene from nearby branches. Downstairs, Patty took a break from painting rainbows, drawn to the marijuana and music.

LaTroy kicked off rehearsal with a hot beat. Leonard's foot kept time, beads of sweat slid down his bobbing forehead. When Smock stroked his d45 everything sounded right. The Rollin' L's played with purpose. They weren't just fucking around now. They were jamming, but this wasn't just some old Sunday jam. This was the new shit—fresh, unique, rhythm and blues with soul and spunk. Smock belted acapella from his living room out into the street. His neck flexed. His fingers slid up and down the guitar as though guided, by something, an unnamable element granted to those who have the passion to practice as much as Leonard.

Patty tiptoed into the room. Her eyes, still framed by all those sparkles, lit up at Leonard. She grabbed a joint from the ashtray, sparked it and moved coolly around the padded plastic table. She went to the back window and exhaled. The Rollin' L's had reached a crescendo and started to let the tune fade away. Something outside had Patty's knees bouncing. She smiled and pointed but didn't want to distract the practicing L's. She hit the joint again and mumbled, "Oh my *goddddd*," below the music.

When the L's finished the new song Patty did applaud, but almost just out of courtesy, kind of like yeah yeah yeah that's great but, "Hurry up and get over here," she waved at them. With an L over each shoulder and all three looking out the window, Patty passed back the joint and LaTroy exclaimed, "YO . . . I *TOLD* you, dude."

Indeed, there were birds everywhere—a world of wings. The rockin' domicile hosted its first bird bash. Wrens and blue jays and cardinals and martins and sparrows, even an oriole, all chirping and chortling and pecking feverishly at this feast of feed. No squirrels to be seen.

"You see? If you fuckin' build it . . . they will come."

"*Field of Dreams*, LaTroy?" Patty chuckled, exhaled.

"What?"

"That's from *Field of Dreams*. Have you seen it?"

"Nahh. Should I see it?"

"It's stupid," answered Patty, "and kind of sad."

"Fuck that," answered LaTroy.

"Yahhhh," replied Patty, the word fading as she danced away from them. "Lenny, my big bird, play me another bird song—let's celebrate. Play my *favorite*."

"Will you sing it, Patty?" Smock inquired.

LaTroy went *pot-budda-dot-dot* on his drums, imploring Patty.

"Come onnnn now," Smock insisted.

Bobby Dog jumped up and barked for her.

"*Fine*," Patty said, taking two long, dramatic pulls off the joint. She let the L's jam the beginning of the tune slightly longer than normal. Waiting to find her way into the music, Patty walked and stood face to face with Leonard Smock (lead guitar, vocals). He tried again to avoid drooling but did become slightly aroused when Patty put the joint into his mouth and held it there while he took a drag. Leonard smiled awkwardly and let it go, still playing, Patty put it to his lips a second time, whispered, "Don't worry . . . about a thing," and sang her favorite:

Rise up this morning,
Smile with the rising sun,
Three little birds
Pitch by my doorstep
Singin' sweet songs. . . .

"THEY'LL HAVE TO CATCH MOJO RISING AS THEY TURN FOR HOME. IT'S ALYSHEBA, MOJO RISING AND SUNDAY SILENCE ON THE INSIDE . . ."

"Come ONNNNNNNNNNN, MO-JO. COME ON SIX, YOU BASTARRRD," Jean screamed. Strings of saliva flew from her lips into the air. She slapped her thigh with the day's racing form. She flipped her black gas station sunglasses from her eyes to her oily black hair. She let her plastic cup drop to the ground with three good sips of warm ale inside. The sips splashed onto an adjacent ankle, but the owner of the ankle didn't notice. The owner of the ankle jumped and screamed, "SHEE-BAAAAA," instead.

The horses' heads bobbed frantically from the neck, their nostrils flaring, sucking dirt kicked up by the leading horses. Forty-eight horse hooves pounded the track with animal force as they raged forward—a thunderous herd, with every horse and jockey desperate for individual glory.

"ALYSHEBA IS DRIVING *HARD* UP THE OUTSIDE, STEVENS GOING TO A VIGOROUS LEFT-HANDED WHIP

FOR THE FINAL FURLONG. . . ."

"NO . . . NO . . . NOOOO," Jean pleaded as she strained to see the race on her tippy toes. The area surrounding her head had become a battlefield of elbows. Spectators knocked hips all around, dizzy from winning, losing, booze, and the sun. Everyone's eyes fixated on this last race. For many, including Jean, the day's outcome depended almost entirely on this final result.

"AND NOW IT'S THE SUPERSTAR . . . SUNDAY SILENCE IN AN ALL . . . OUT . . . DRIVE! GIANT STRIDES ON THE INSIDE, SHE *SURGES* TO THE FRONT, BAILEY'S ASKING HER FOR EVERYTHING SHE'S GOT. IT'S A SPELLBINDING STRETCH RUN WITH MOJO RISING NOW FADING FROM THE FRONT. . . ."

"NOOOOOO," Jean jumped and jumped and jumped two inches into the air, "COME ON, SIX, YOU MUTHUHFUCKUHHHH. GET UP THERE BABY, PLEASE, BABY PLEASE. . . ."

"AS THE HORSES HEAD FOR THE WIRE IT'S SUNDAY SILENCE AND ALYSHEBA WITH LESS THAN A LENGTH ON MOJO RISING, PAT DAY GIVING MOJO THE WHIP BUT IT'S TOO LATE, IT'S GONNA BEEEEE . . . SUNDAY SILENCE BY A NOSE."

"Shitballs," Jean said, throwing her racing form and betting slips right on the ground, littering in despair.

Jean got another ale and sulked the whole way home. Then, she smelled a forest fire of fresh marijuana three blocks from her house and had a good bet on its source. Verified by the rising sound of that stupid hippie music she hated so much. But, a female voice? A familiar female voice. . . .

Of melodies pure and true,

Sayin' this is my message to you-ou-ou.

Jean littered another plastic cup and quickened her pace. With a strut now bordering powerwalk territory she lit a cigarette and turned the last block to gaze on her own rockin' residence. She saw the bird bash happening in her back yard—wings everywhere, the chirping and the chortling.

Every little thing is gonna be all right. . . .

Jean couldn't miss the smoke basically billowing out the second story window, which caused her right eye to wince with fury. The melodic reggae rock mixed pleasantly with the smoke and kind of poked Jean in the ribs when she just wasn't in a joking mood.

She stabbed her cigarette into the porch and marched through the door that lead to *Leonard's* apartment. . . .

Neighborhood squirrels took notice of the noisy bird bash. They deliberated with their tails pointing at the sky, gnawing their greedy teeth; their bodies gyrated with fast forward animation. Their non-existent legs rushed toward the lone tree.

Jean's drunken lumber up the stairs *did not* mix well with the melodic reggae music. Actually, it stopped The Rollin' L's (feat. Patty) dead in their tracks.

When Jean saw Patty, she stopped dead in *her* tracks.

"Patty . . . ?" she asked.

"Hi, Mom."

"Patty . . . what are you doing up *here*?"

"Just playing music. You know . . ."

The entire apartment reeked of marijuana smoke, mostly because there was a lit joint smoking away on the padded table.

"What else are you doing. . . ."

Everyone in the room could feel the frustrated tension seething from Jean's body. She stared at the joint like it was a fresh corpse and the trio held knives instead of musical instruments. Her clothes looked bad on her—jean skirt, button shirt with uninspired flowers, those flip-flops with the *thick* rubber soles. She totally ruined the mood. She seemed so utterly unhappy. It felt like she might be gearing up to use the word "drugs" on her daughter.

LaTroy put his hand over his mouth to stymie a burst of laughter, but some did slip out and everyone heard it. They all turned to look at LaTroy—chaos building in this silence. Seconds passed. Birds cried for help—the sounds they made unlike any chortle heard before, followed by the horrific scratching. An armada of miniscule squirrel claws tearing along the tree bark, coming for all the feed.

"Were you doing these drugs, Patty?"

"No," Patty answered.

And LaTroy did burst out laughing.

And so did Leonard.

And so did Patty.

But Jean did not, "You think this is funny?" she asked.

"It's not a big deal, Mom."

"Oh, you think so?"

No one answered.

The birds' cries receded quickly into the distance, only echoes reached through the window. The once beautiful bird music now replaced entirely by that incessant squirrel scratching.

"Well, *you're* drunk," Patty stated.

"So?"

"It's the same thing."

"No, it isn't."

"Yes, it is."

"I'm uhh-*llowed* to be drunk. It's . . ." Jean withheld a belch, "legal."

"So, you're allowed to get drunk and gamble away your money, but I can't smoke pot?"

"You can . . . if you wanna end up like these *losers*," Jean pointed.

"They're not losers."

"Yes they are. This guy's pushin' forty and still thinks he's gonna be some kinda rockstar (meaning Leonard). It's too late. He's a fucking dreamer, Patty, look at 'em. He's not even any good at it."

"At least he's nice."

"He's a fucking asshole!" Jean shouted.

"Grandma and Grandpa thought he was really talented."

"They're dead. They knew about as much about music as Lenny here knows about birds. Look at all those damn squirrels out there you dumb bastard."

"Ohhhhh fuck *YOU*, Jean. Seriously, fuck *YOU*! It's not my fault your parents died, okay? I'm sorry. I loved them too. I'm sorry I let Patty come up here, she enjoys it, the kid loves music and art, you should encourage . . ."

"Don't tell me how to raise my daughter!"

Jean lunged at Leonard. Leonard moved to the side and Jean fell. She fell into LaTroy's drum kit. Cymbals clashed. LaTroy laughed again, almost in shock. Bobby Dog went to lick Jean's face and make her feel better, but she smacked the poor pup hard in the face, "GET AWAY," she growled. Bobby Dog whimpered and ran into Leonard's bedroom.

"Jean, calm down," Leonard pleaded.

Drunken Jean scrambled to her feet. Not even noticing her sunglasses still on the floor, she announced, "That stupid dog isn't even supposed to *be* here. You're not supposed to be *smoking* in here. You're not supposed to be playing *music* in here. You're out, Lenny. I warned ya. I'm fucktin' evictin' ya."

"Oh . . . *fucktin'*?" LaTroy chimed in, "You can stay at my place, Leonard."

"Mom, you can't!" Patty yelled, grabbing her mother's arm.

Jean slashed sideways to remove herself from her daughter's grip and caught Patty's face with a sharp elbow. Surprised that she freed herself so easily, the unexpected momentum sent her to the floor once again, this time she brought the padded tri-fold table down with her. Spending a moment or two dizzy on the ground, Jean roused herself to discover the half-smoked roach by her side. She picked it up and threw it out the window, "Here, I'll help you get started movin' out." Next, she folded the tri-fold table together and went for the window, the front bay window. It looked like a tight squeeze, but Jean went in full bore, fearlessly, and jammed the table through the window. But it didn't slide right out. It got stuck. Jean grunted and shoved, the glass broke and people enjoying a Sunday stroll looked over and pointed and laughed. Jean grunted the words, "Here, I'll help you," she pushed, "Here," she pushed harder, "Help you get started movin' out," and there it went down onto Jean's front lawn with a bunch of glass from Jean's bay window.

Jean turned around. Her face had sweat on it and her

hair tentacled about the room. Three frightened faces stared back at her, stunned.

"You got until tomorrow night to be outta here," she grabbed Patty and went for the stairs, turned to add, "Fucking loser."

On Monday, Jean woke up and went into her bathroom. She was not entirely surprised to discover reddish pepperoni pizza vomit splatter on the rim of the blue toilet bowl and some on the white tile floor. She felt relieved that she'd put the seat up. She put the seat down and peed and after that took a shower. She got out of the shower and dried herself without ever looking in the mirror. She left the bathroom without ever cleaning the vomit.

Sitting on her bed, wrapped in a brown towel, Jean opened the window and lit a cigarette. She thought, "This tastes like shit," and noticed that it was particularly hot outside. This realization of the hot day neither pleased nor disappointed Jean—it served as the determining factor for her choice of work attire. She dragged a terribly thin, brown sock over her left foot and up her left leg. The backside of her thumbs brushed along her calf. She noticed a sandpaper quality to her skin and knew that she hadn't shaved her legs in a week or so. After a similar situation involving a right sock, Jean went to her wooden dresser drawers and opened the top. She grabbed a pair of white, cotton underwear, looked them over, put them on, again starting with the left foot. The aerobic movement coupled with the oppressive humidity made Jean break into a slight sweat. She leaned back and squeezed some moisture from her hair. She did this twice. Then she picked up the brown towel and dried her hair until it was dry enough to put on her outfit—white, cotton bra, blue t-shirt, breathable khaki slacks.

Walking to her car, Jean did not look at the glass all over her lawn. Nor did she look at the padded, tri-fold table. She was aware of these out of place objects, though they neither pleased nor disappointed her. She was aware of several squirrels curiously inspecting the tri-fold table.

Jean got into her car and started it. She pushed the buttons to make all the windows open all the way. She didn't turn the radio on. She lit a cigarette and exhaled. At a stoplight she sipped from her coffee mug and took another hit from her cigarette and exhaled. Just before entering her office parking lot she flicked the cigarette out the window and pushed the buttons that made the windows go back up.

Jean showed a man a badge she had hanging from a lanyard. He nodded. No one said anything. She walked into an elevator with three other people. Jean pressed "2". One of the other people sighed. One snorted passive aggressively. One did not react. The elevator went up to four.

Jean left the elevator and walked into the office where she worked. The office had the thinnest blue carpet, white walls, and awful lighting that made noise all day long. She walked directly to the cube farm and took her place inside her cubicle without anyone noticing or saying hello. On the tag board behind Jean's computer was one picture of Patty wearing a hat and a glove, holding a ball. Patty had braces in the picture. There was a blue stick-it note next to Patty's picture and on the note were written these words: Hello, my name is _____, this call may be recorded for instructional purposes. Thank you for calling State of Health and how may I assist you today?

This concludes the list of items on Jean's tag board.

After one hour of surfing the World Wide Web, Jean went outside and smoked two cigarettes. She showed the same man her badge again and he nodded the same way.

At noon Jean pulled a Tupperware out of her bag. Pizza. Oh shit. Jean powerwalked into the bathroom and vomited into the toilet as quietly as possible. She sucked water from the sink faucet and spit it into the sink basin. She rolled out a few paper towels and dampened them and rubbed them over her teeth. She spit into the sink basin again and went out for a cigarette.

Badge. Man. Elevator. Cubicle.

At one O'clock, Jean received her first phone call of the day.

"Hello, my name is Jean, this call may be recorded for instructional purposes. . . . Thank you for calling State of Health and how may I assist you today?"

"Hi, yeah, ummm, yes. I'm on the State of Health website, and, ummm, I'm trying to sign up for Medicaid?"

"Okay."

"I can't get passed the first section, where I'm registering as a user."

"Okay, I'd be happy to help you out with this problem. Where do you live, sir?"

"Hamilton Hill."

"I thought so."

"Hey, what's that supposed to mean? It's temporary. I'm working part-time. I really thought I'd be a professor by now. That's the only reason I didn't sign up earlier."

"Well, we all have dreams, right?"

"Dreams? Jeez, I mean...I have a doctorate and published works."

"That's additional income."

"What?"

"Publications. You need to list those as additional income. You'll see that on page three of the application. Where it says: Additional Income."

"All right."

"Listen, sir, I didn't mean to offend you. The only reason I said I thought so is because there's a current glitch in our computer system that only recognizes Hamilton Hill when it's typed as one word. That's why it keeps telling you the town is invalid."

"Ohhhhhh."

"Is there anything else I can assist you with today, sir?"

"Hold on a min . . . it. I'm just gonna type it in now."

". . ."

"It worked!"

"Is there anything else I can assist you with today, sir?"

"Nope, I think I've got it now, thanks."

"All right. Well thank you for calling State of Health and have a wonderful afternoon."

Jean felt exhausted after assisting the caller and decided to go home. Pulling up to the curb she noticed that the red roadster no longer leaned against the side of the house. The tri-fold table had also vanished from the front yard. And that stupid birdhouse no longer hung from the tree.

Jean smoked a cigarette on the porch and smiled, pleased that her rent-free nuisance of a tenant had finally vacated the premises.

Jean became extremely disappointed when she noticed

all the scratching sounds coming from inside her apartment. It sounded like scrambling, like commotion.

"What now," Jean mumbled to herself, stabbing another cigarette into the poor porch.

Squirrels run amok. From the miniscule foyer, Jean spotted the rockin' domicile turned over on her bed. Feed spilled out of all four holes—from the steal your face to the ZOSO to the tongue and lip design. The squirrels ran around in circles on the bed, fighting with each other and gnawing and gyrating. A trio rushed for her pizza-filled purse. The little claws scratched horribly. As Jean ran for the door, she caught a glimpse of the *entire* bag of feed spilled over in the kitchen. Leonard Smock, that mother . . . fucking . . . bastard.

Jean smelled fresh marijuana smoke coming from the upstairs bay window. She trudged up the stairs ready for round two. And there she discovered her daughter, Patty, reclined and smoking drugs on Leonard's old couch, watching Leonard's old television. This disappointed Jean very much.

"Patty . . . what are you doing?"

"*DRUGS*," Patty said, without turning around.

Jean stood there looking at the back of Patty's head for too long.

She couldn't come up with one kind, useful thing to say. Not even sorry.

She went back down the stairs and opened all the doors and windows in her apartment and walked a few blocks to the bar.

Jean came back from the bar and most of the squirrels were gone except for two bloated, particularly greedy squirrels, more napping than gnawing on Jean's furniture.

She shooed them away with a broom and then used the broom to sweep up the rest of the feed.

Jean shut all the windows and doors and went to bed.

On Tuesday Jean drove to work, showed her badge, took the elevator, walked to her cubicle, looked at the Internet, took three phone calls, ate a Lean Pocket of cheddar cheese and broccoli for lunch, took one more phone call, smoked two cigarettes, looked at the Internet, drove home, drank three cocktails and went to bed.

On Wednesday, just before sunrise, loud music interrupted Jean's sleep. She woke up scared and surprised and mouthed a mixture of the words "what" and "who" that sounded like "*UhWhah,*" then yawned. She stretched her arms up and saw pit hairs germinating, some had sprouted. She put her arms back down. She cursed her daughter for playing that loud hippie crap. It also sounded like there was a man up there with Patty. Patty was either moaning or singing. Jean leaned on her side and opened a drawer in her nightstand and pulled out her vibrator and used it on herself, then went back to sleep for a while.

When Jean woke up again it was raining outside. She put on a raincoat and grabbed her umbrella by the front door. She smoked three cigarettes under the umbrella while at work. Also while at work, she took a total of five phone calls and ate Combos (Pizzeria Pretzel) for lunch. She washed the Combos down with lemon-lime soda.

On Thursday Jean spent the entire day at work searching the Internet for possible tenants. She made an ad and put it on a website: Hamilton Hill, 1BR apt. Clean. No Pets. No Smoking. No Music. Laundry in basement.

She trickily set the rent very high so that she could

seem like a kind landlady lowering it in potential rent negotiations. If the tenants accepted the listed rent, then Jean would be a happy and rich landlady.

The emails started flying into Jean's inbox, almost four emails between 9:30 and noon. Jean skipped lunch to reply to the emails. While Jean replied to the three emails her phone rang and she didn't answer it.

She let it again go unanswered during a second ringing period.

A supervisor in a necktie leaned into Jean's cubicle and said, "Why aren't you answering your calls, Jean?"

"I'm taking tomorrow off." Jean replied.

"Why?"

"My tenant moved out and I have to show the place."

"Can't you do it over the weekend?"

"I made the appointments for tomorrow. I have sick time."

"You aren't sick."

"I was sick on Monday but I came in anyway."

"Fine," the supervisor left disappointed.

While at work, Jean arranged a total of three appointments via email. She did answer two phone calls after lunch, both from residents of Hamilton Hill and both about the registering as a user section. Jean took a one-cigarette break between the two calls. Before she left work, Jean also emailed some friends to come over to her house and have a party. Wisely, Jean did not schedule any appointments before one o'clock on Friday. One of the friends Jean emailed was her special friend.

The party started on Jean's front porch around seven. A magnificent purple and orange sunset dipped behind the pointed rooftops of Hamilton Hill. Gentle senior citizens walked on the sidewalk and looked at the party suspiciously. There were six people at the party, all drunk on margarita drinks. At first, the margarita drinks were blended and slushy—when the party people went ARGLE FARGLE GOBARGLE-BARGLE, the slush plopped onto the porch and melted in place, further scarring the home's forlorn appendage.

When the sun did set, the party moved inside and quit the blender. They stumbled and smoked and poured margarita on rocks. They gesticulated wildly, raging veins protruded from rivers of sweat flowing along foreheads, every impassioned soliloquy designed to change the tides of time, but ultimately, contributed nothing more than added amounts of margarita spilled on the floor.

Throughout the party Jean whispered into the ear of her special friend, "Don't leave," or, "Don't go home."

When all the ARGLE FARGLE GOBARGLE-BARGLEing got old, some people yawned and asked Jean if that hippie guy upstairs could come down and play some of that fine, fine music.

"He *sucks*," Jean replied.

"He's pretty good, Jean," someone said.

"Yeah, he really is. I've seen him and the drummer out playing, they're pretty good," mostly everyone nodded their head to show agreement.

"Well . . . he moved out. And Patty moved in, for now. Got some people coming to see the place tomorrow," Jean said, "but not until one," Jean added, while making eye contact with her special friend.

Jean's special friend stared back at her and didn't make any noise. His eyes made him look sleepy. He had thick lips that Jean found sexy. Onetime, Jean said to him, "Put those pouty lips in my muff," and he did. His clothes were sad: baggy jean shorts to his knees and a white t-shirt, brand new black flip-flops flapping against his heels. Jean liked how tan he got in the summer. He worked with his shirt off and had sandpaper hands and smelled like cigarettes and dumpster leak. His name was Paul.

Paul looked at Jean, basically with only one eye open, like his head might crash onto the dining room table.

Jean mouthed these words to him: "Don't go home."

Paul, ever so slightly, nodded his head.

Once it became clear that the strange hippie wasn't coming down to play, everyone except for Paul went home.

Jean didn't waste any time. She straddled Paul right in the dining room and licked the sweat off his neck, she smooched all up to his ear and huffed sexy cigarette breath deep into Paul's earhole. Paul still had a margarita on the rocks in his hand and he took a sip while Jean dry-humped him. The sip made Paul feel like a very cool customer. Jean could feel Paul getting aroused. Jean thought it might make Paul really like her if she started giving him a blowjob right there in the kitchen while he still had his margarita on the rocks. But when Jean lifted her arms to tie her hair in a ponytail, so it wouldn't get in the way during the blowjob, Paul saw the stringy underarm hair coming at his eyes and became ill.

Paul tried to be polite and hold it back and cover his mouth, but this merely forced the upheaval to divert course and come spraying from Paul's nostrils—all down his shirt and upon his knee-length jean shorts. Paul mumbled a combination of the words "oh" "god" and "sorry" into his palm to make "Ohhgzurry."

"What is it, Paul?" Jean asked desperately, "Is something wrong?"

Paul shoved Jean off his lap and back against the table, spilling one pitcher of margarita, then sprinted for the bathroom with his flip-flops flapping.

"Lift the seat!" Jean yelled after him.

Paul lifted the seat and went, "*CAWWWW* . . . *CAWWWW* . . . *CAWWWW*," into the toilet bowl.

Paul flushed the toilet and stood up without lowering the seat. He wiped his pouty lips with the back of his tan hand and made a tough guy noise. When Paul flapped back into the kitchen Jean asked, "Paul, is it me? Did I do something wrong?"

Paul gave her no reply and left. Jean went to bed disappointed and passed out quickly.

Jean woke up Friday morning around 2 a.m. after her body had metabolized the margarita drinks. She went to the bathroom and peed and sucked some water from the sink faucet. Jean lay in bed staring at her ceiling trying to figure out if she'd had a dream, any dream at all, it really felt like there'd been *something*, but she couldn't remember. In the absolute silence Jean became all too aware of the blank canvas staring back at her, so she thought about the previous evening and her party and Paul. She tried to piece together everything that happened. She wondered things like, 'So what?' and 'Who cares'? Her mind flickered only flashes, insignificant images, a whole batch of soundless still-lifes adding up to zero.

She just lay there waiting.

Watching the ceiling and waiting.

Light entered the room and the early birds got up and Jean waited.

Simply waiting.
Waiting for nothing and for sleep.
She dreamed of a silent tenant.

Fall

Leonard Smock pushed that rosewood roadster through entire piles of leaves. A sickening wake of dead tree-petals spewed from the back tire all into the air. Pedestrians in the distance feared a mini-tornado approaching. Leonard's headphones were stationed on full blast.

The Rollin' L's completed their final rehearsal last night. Both members had arranged a week of vacation with their respective employers in order to devote their entire being to the critical first week of shows. Hopefully this badass reemergence would lead to some lucrative weekend gigs. And Smock secretly hoped that the additional income would be enough to move him and Bobby Dog out of LaTroy's apartment into somewhere nice. Smock double-secretly hoped that his new music would get *noticed*. That someone, somehow, might finally believe in his work—someone who really mattered. And then they would record an album. And then it would sell like crazy. And then people would love them and then him and LaTroy and Bobby Dog would go on the road and then they'd bring Patty out for guest spots and then. . .

Leonard's body filled to the brim with these hopes and dreams; in his mind they were only goals. It was upon these tremendous wings of pure inspiration that Leonard pedaled so swiftly to the first venue—a pub called O'Really's.

A large red man swept cigarettes out front. The end of his broom matched his mustache. Peering down his mark at the sidewalk, the peeling patterns of his quite bald head were consistent with that of the outdoor party animal. Telling by his sweeping technique, it could be assumed he did nothing with much urgency, save for the drinking.

The large red man was struck by Leonard Smock's determined arrival. A great wind followed the cyclist. Leonard did sense the red man's annoyance when wind blew the cigarettes back all over the place and a few leaves did creep into the scene as well.

"We don't open for another half hour," said the sweeper.

"Dude . . . *Bruce*, you don't remember me?"

"Take off that helmet."

Bruce watched intently as Smock removed his helmet to reveal the long, black ponytail. The barman exclaimed, "HO-LEE SHIT. Leonard *fuckin'* Smock, well god damn! *Look* atcha . . . GOD DAMN, man!"

Leonard smiled and nodded that he was good and Bruce brought him in tight for a powerful and nearly painful hug. Bruce smelled like vodka with tomato juice.

"Look at dem gray hairs on ya, Lenny."

"At least I *have* hair."

"Ya look like my fuckin' granny," and this brought forth a laugh that Leonard had not forgotten. Hacking and full barreled. Double barreled really, Bruce put his big paws on his stomach and rolled back, jutting the gut forward like Lenny should stick a coin in it out of respect for the joke.

"Well, *you* look like tomato juice and vodka," Smock retorted.

"And I been drinkin' jus' that since I woke up. What are you doing here already?"

"Sound check."

"Sound what?"

"You know. Check the levels."

"The levels? Listen, Lenny, this ain't a big deal or nothin'."

"Naw, I mean . . . I know," Leonard watched the leaves and cigarettes blowing around his sneakers, "I just want it to sound good."

"Who cares how it sounds when no one's listenin'?"

"They'll be listening."

"It's Monday, Lenny. There ain't gonna be hardly anyone in here."

"Okay."

"Look at this in here though . . . that pretty girl came down last night and drew you a promotional sign on my chalkboard. Was just gonna set it out after I finished sweeping."

The two men stared at the chalkboard art: A fat joint, lit, smoking. The smoke curled from the lit end to form exquisite psychedelic lettering, "The Rollin' L's. ReRollin' It. TONIGHT-7 p.m." Surrounding the creative and informative tidbit were pictures of music notes and tiny pink and purple marijuana leafs.

"She's really somethin'," Bruce mentioned.

"She's like, seventeen, man."

"Aye. She's got a seventeen-year-old ass on her."

"I think you could be arrested for that comment."

"I've been arrested for worse." Bruce lurched back and hacked and stuck his belly forward for another coin. Leonard said he'd see the big red man tonight and hopped back on his bicycle.

The L's took the stage at seven sharp. Actually, they just stood in the back corner and took the place of three tables that they'd moved into the basement. Bruce got rid of his cool little stage a while back because no one came out for music anymore. He put a billiards table in its place.

Three men sat at the bar sniffing ales. To see the performance, they'd either have to turn around two hundred and seventy degrees or have an owl's neck. Leonard tuned his guitar and it did screech. The man on the end turned around two hundred and seventy degrees and shrugged his shoulders dramatically, then said something from the corner of his mouth without hardly moving his jaw. Then he turned back and gripped his ale with both hands. His shoulders slumped low with his nose nearly brushing the rim of the glass. He looked up at the television again, suspiciously, like it might jump down and attempt to steal his ale.

LaTroy hit his drums really hard and specks of dust fell from the ceiling. Leonard Smock, dressed in converse sneakers, black jeans, black v-neck t-shirt, and black leather jacket, came in with a soaring intro. Words can't take the place of this music. It was like, the coolest, okay?

Patty showed up during Leonard's first solo, which

rocked.

All three men turned two hundred and seventy degrees the other way to stare at Patty. They said more stuff from the corner of their mouths without really moving their jaws.

Bruce interrupted them, "Hey, *fuckos* . . . she's seventeen."

Patty hardly noticed them because she smoked a J on the way over and was already way into the music. She stared at Leonard's hands shredding the guitar neck. The men with the ales became jealous.

Just after eight o'clock a bunch of people arrived at O'Really's looking ready to party. They ordered drinks and pointed at The Rollin' L's and nodded their heads a bit.

Someone yelled, "*FREEBIRD.*"

Smock answered with gnarly blues licks.

Someone else said, "Freebird," loudly. Other people laughed.

After two more songs even more people showed up and the entire pub smelled like chicken wing sauce. Bruce left the bar and approached the band.

"I'm gonna have to ask you guys to pack it up," Bruce said.

"They're just startin' to show up, man," LaTroy responded.

"They're here for ten cent wings. I do ten cent wings for Monday Night Football."

"What?" asked Leonard.

"They wanna watch the game with the sound on, Lenny."

"What sound?"

"You know, the commentary for the game. The, uh,

announcers."

Smock looked at Bruce with disappointment on his face, promoting the opinion that Bruce was a sellout. Leonard watched Bruce go back behind the bar and assure the wing eaters that the music was over. Serious male voices boomed down from all the surrounding speakers. The sound quality was crisp and outrageous. The athletes could be heard breathing during breaks in the commentary. One announcer noted that, "There's a war going on in Detroit *tonight*," and the color commentator agreed by saying, "You bet, Al, this one's as big as they come." The wing eaters looked at each other and nodded their heads. They devoured wings in a way that confirmed they weren't worth a quarter—fingers fumbling about the wing-filled baskets without ever removing their excited eyes from the screen. They plucked without bias, baring their overbites and chomping down with unnecessary aggression, turning their necks and chewing as sauce slid along wrists and chins. Sometimes they'd take only one bite of a wing, plop it down as though it were finished, pick up another and do the same. Sometimes, over-sauced wings would slip from their fingers and fall to the floor. They'd order more while gnawing the last. They'd order more by using sign language and body language—snapping the saucy fingers at Bruce or the cute server running back and forth from the frialator. Before long, crumpled napkins bespeckled the bar's surface. The napkins were pawed with even less consideration than the wings. They went over mouths and up noses and onto the bar, hungry men flung them down like generous tips, showing their gratitude with an outpouring of mess. Every time one of the athletes scored they went fucking crazy.

All things considered, the L's played a pretty hot show and were excited as the tour progressed further downtown for a happy hour gig at an uber popular chain restaurant. The restaurant manager greeted them at the door, clapping her hands for several bussers to unload the band's gear out of LaTroy's car and set it up over there. Certainly, the band had just smoked down a nice joint. The uber popular chain restaurant lighting offended their sensitive eyes. The floor was a wicked mixture of blue, orange, green and yellow tiles. A puzzling potpourri of posters lined the walls. Leonard watched the employees march all around the restaurant, moving at what seemed like turbo speed—dropping apps everywhere, they looked wired or wound. When they arrived at a table, they leaned down to hear better and smiled beyond happiness and nodded their heads yes to everything. After finishing whatever business at the table, the smile vanished and they reported back to the kitchen as quickly and efficiently as possible.

The manager sipped a massive coffee milkshake and asked the band, "Are you guys high right now?"

The band shook their heads no, and said, "No."

"Yeah, well, okay, whatever—it doesn't matter," replied the manager. The bussers finished setting up the band's equipment in no time flat and returned to the kitchen to bring out unlimited nachos and salsa for every person that walked through the door. The manager finally introduced herself as, "Caitlin, okay? Just . . . shout my name through the mic if you need something."

"Cool," replied the band.

"Try not to play it too loud, okay?"

The band didn't know how to reply.

Suddenly, Caitlin hopped into an empty booth and stood on the table.

LaTroy and Leonard looked at each other, frightened.

A powerful clapping had commenced in the distance. It grew louder. It was coming closer. It went clap-clap, clap-clap, clap-clap.

A child seated only two booths from the band screeched and covered her cheeks with her hands.

Caitlin cupped her hands over her mouth: "ATTENTION, ATTENTION. WE GOT A BIRTHDAY IN DA HOUUUUUUUUUUUSE!"

A great conga line of restaurant staff entered the barroom. The leader carried a plate of chocolate volcano with flaming candle eruption. Those following behind clapped a beat to this song:

Happy Happy Birthday,
From the restaurant crew.
We wish it was our birthday,
So we could party too.

At the end everyone yelled "*Woohooooo,*" with varying degrees of passion.

Caitlin hopped down from the table and leaned into the booth and with an unbelievable smile said, "Happy Birthday, Josephine!"

The restaurant crew marched quickly back to the kitchen.

Caitlin turned to the band, "So, anyway, like I said, we have some other things happening so try not to play it too loud."

"Cool," replied the band.

The show started at 4 p.m. LaTroy hit his drums really

hard and specks of dust fell from the ceiling. By the time Leonard Smock shredded his third chord people at the bar started doing insane shit—especially the bartender, who announced: "It's Tuesday, it's four o'clock . . . and you know what that means." It meant 2-for-1 drinks and the bar flair duel.

The first man in line asked for, "Dos margaritas, por favor," and rubbed his momentarily empty palms together as a physical display of extreme excitement. Whether his excitement pertained to the drinks or to the show or to the overwhelmingly awesome combination was impossible to know.

The bartender wore a logo shirt with several pins and a nametag: "Ricky." One of his pins had a yellow smiley face labeled: "Hot Ricky." Ricky looked and performed more like a ballerina than a bartender—he did have a gorgeous smooth face, perfect skin, and stunning white teeth that he never put away. As a fact, he worked as a bartender, but if he were wheeling a shopping cart around one would have to assume church-going virgin or catalogue model for affordably priced clothing.

"Dos margaritas," he confirmed, holding up the peace sign, smiling—he even bounced his eyebrows like, "You're not even ready for this."

First, Ricky grabbed a pint glass. He threw it around his back, over his shoulder, caught it and smiled. People clapped. He bounced it off the inside of his elbow, caught it with his hand, threw it in the air, caught it behind his back, threw it back over his back catching it with the same hand with which he threw it, smiled and placed the glass on the bar. Clapping mixed with a few oohs and aahs.

Next, Ricky grabbed the cocktail shaker and showed it

to the people watching him. Out of nowhere, ice cubes started flying from across the bar. It was Bobby. He knew Ricky had pulled out his cocktail shaker. Ricky snatched the cubes thrown in the air without looking. Before the cubes could even finish clinking at the bottom of the shaker Ricky flung the cocktail shaker almost as high as the ceiling and he didn't just fling it—he flung-spun it. The ice cubes never fell out. Ricky caught the spinning cocktail shaker with ease. He tossed two more cubes into the air at different heights and did back-to-back pirouettes with his body—snagging one cube per spin, the lower cube first, of course. After the pirouette movement Ricky grabbed *three* ice cubes from his cooler, said, "Aiyo," and casually flung them over his shoulder at Bobby, who captured them in his cocktail shaker. Ricky placed the cocktail shaker next to the pint glass. The tandem maneuver received much applause and an increasing number of oohs and aahs.

Finally, Ricky grabbed the sour mix, orange juice, and bottle of Jose Cuervo's tequila. He instructed the mounting crowd in front of him to stand back as he flung the plastic bottle of tequila at least seven feet into the air. The patrons' eyes followed it and from many mouths came the words "oh" and "my." By the time all three bottles were flipping through the air, the band realized they were hired to provide the soundtrack for the bar flair duel—they were *not* the main attraction.

Ricky's shoulders and elbows and hands moved with incredible fluidity. He looked like an octopus in outer space. He went behind the back, over the shoulder, he even bounced the sour mix off the floor and caught it and kept on juggling. As the routine progressed, Ricky's dimples deepened. Oohs and aahs filled the barroom. He tossed the bottles so smoothly and with such variety that patrons began to wonder if he hadn't grown a third arm. Just before the profound wonderment turned into fear, as if he had a sixth sense, Ricky cut the routine and poured all three bottles into the cocktail shaker. He shook the shaker over his right shoulder and said, "Chachacha." He shook the shaker over his left shoulder and said, "Chachacha." His heels clicked the black rubber mat each time.

Ricky poured the drink and bowed and said, "Voila."

Ricky turned around to get a pint glass for the second margarita. He threw it around his back, over his shoulder, caught it, and smiled. He bounced it off the inside of his elbow, caught it with his hand, threw it in the air, caught it behind his back, threw it back over his back catching it with the same hand with which he threw it, smiled, and placed the glass on the bar.

The first man in line finished his margarita in the time it took Ricky to retrieve the second pint glass.

Both men stared at the two empty pint glasses on the bar.

And then they looked at each other.

The first man in line said, "Dos . . . *mas*."

Not knowing how to verbally reply, Ricky grabbed his cocktail shaker and commenced a fresh routine.

The people waiting in line for their chance at 2-for-1 drinks began to shuffle their feet and look at each other and grumble without moving their jaws.

Ricky poured a second margarita and the first man in line drained it on the spot and said, "Dos . . . mas."

A man from the middle part of the line yelled, "Order a fuckin' beer and see what he does."

Then someone corrected him, "You mean *dos* . . .

cervezas."

But the first man in line was steadfast—he wouldn't give Ricky a chance to complete the order. He polished off eleven margaritas before he fell down and got ejected from the bar. On his way out the door he stopped and stared at the band with wretched drunkenness in his eyes. He seemed confounded by the L's complex movements. He pointed at them and said nothing and teetered. He pointed again. He had something on his mind, but he couldn't quite come up with it. You could see it working its way through his system. Like a toddler, he sounded, "Eff," and then, "Fuh," followed by, "Fuh," again, before he slurred the word, "Fuhhreeburt." He stumbled slightly forward with the effort, righted himself, and looked for a reaction from the band. After receiving none he tried once more, "*Fuhhreeburt.*" Finally, the man threw an empty pack of cigarettes at LaTroy and left.

Walking out with two gift certificates (redeemable at any time) for half off endless appetizers, the band agreed that their performance had been on point.

The Rollin' L's arrived at The Wine Bar, early in The Evening, as instructed. After the show at the uber popular chain restaurant, both Leonard and LaTroy had returned to the apartment and went straight to bed. They woke up and did not smoke anything. They put button-up shirts on their bodies that they tucked into pants and then laced fancy shoes on their feet and spoke nervously about the important people that dine at The Wine Bar.

The owner of The Wine Bar instructed Leonard that he should only bring his acoustic guitar. She instructed LaTroy to bring only his most pleasant set of drums. She told the band that wine and food were the real stars and that they (the band) were there to compliment the overall ambience.

And so, the ambient addition bumbled through the spotless glass front door of The Wine Bar with cumbersome equipment, colliding into a coat rack and umbrella rack, then jostling the maître d' stand. Mostly everyone dining in The Wine Bar turned around to evaluate the nature of the unwelcome cacophony. The owner of The Wine Bar scurried over and nearly whispered her introduction, "*Hi . . .* I'm Melissa Stevens . . . Sommelier and owner of The Wine Bar." She leaned in and kissed Leonard Smock on his left cheek and then leaned back, and then leaned in again and kissed his right cheek and quietly said, "Welcome." Then she moved over toward LaTroy, paused too long and leaned quickly in and kissed LaTroy on his left cheek and then leaned back and then leaned in again and barely pecked his right cheek and said, "Welcome."

Melissa Stevens stepped back to judge the band in its entirety. Silently she studied the band's footwear and overall formalwear while the band continued to be burdened by its gear. An exquisitely tanned gentleman in a navy sports jacket, trousers, bare ankles, and loafers came up behind Melissa and said, "You *must* be the band." Smiling with breathtaking whiteness, he displayed four fingers for the band—his stance implied that the band should not shake but examine and admire the fingers for noteworthy softness and moisture. Leonard was first up to caress the fingers of the impressively tan, white-toothed man. The man wasn't shy about showing his fingers. After about seven seconds it occurred to Leonard that the man would not pull away but possibly allow Leonard to endlessly admire the soft feel of these fingers. LaTroy watched the so-called shake with great trepidation as it surpassed eleven seconds . . . twelve seconds . . . thirteen . . . when finally, the man said, "*Hi*, I'm Dr. Stevens, Melissa's father and owner of The Wine Bar."

In his absolute sobriety, Smock didn't quite know what to do so replied, "*Hi*, Leonard Smock, um, I play guitar," and then adjusted the giant acoustic guitar case in his other hand.

Now Dr. Stevens turned his whole body to face LaTroy. He held the fingers out for LaTroy and said, "Dr. Stevens." LaTroy took the beautiful tan and soft fingers inside his giant palm and gently guided them up and down through the air. Dr. Stevens' fingers felt safe and looked cozy inside LaTroy's palm. Dr. Stevens tilted his head back and whispered, "Very nice to meet you," even though LaTroy had not introduced himself.

Suddenly, a large and sloppy man dressed in all white waddled toward the group. The thick, inner tube of skin that lined his belly peeked out from under his coat every other step. Without turning around, the Stevenses looked at each other, shoulders slumping noticeably. "This must be the band," the man said, in a loud voice.

"Yes, Chef, this is the band," replied Melissa, in a much quieter, instructive tone, meant to inform the Chef of the appropriate voice level.

"Oh . . . *shit*," the Chef whispered. "Big fan, I'm a big fan . . . I used to come to a bunch of your guys' shows back in high school." The Chef put his spatula in his left hand and grabbed Leonard's hand and nearly crushed it, "This is awesome. Graham Berry, huge fan . . . *huge*."

"Graham is our Executive Chef," Dr. Stevens noted.

"Hey man, thanks, I'm LaTroy," said LaTroy, now shaking with the Chef.

"Our patrons look hungry, Chef," Melissa cut in, suggestively, suggesting that Graham Berry return to the kitchen.

Graham Berry returned to the kitchen.

"Amazing what talent and creativity comes from that creature," noted Dr. Stevens, watching the Chef waddle away.

Melissa told the band to setup by the enormous picture window that overlooked a busy main drag. A symphony of smelling, sipping, and sometimes even spitting surrounded the band—the patrons ingested their wine through every known orifice. Grapes: exotic, exotically produced, shipped from exotic locales—and poured here, carefully, then contemplated with eyes, nose, lips, tongue—cheek innards aroused. The many sets of moist fingers pinched wine stems sexually, the off hand poised fashionably in the air, aloft, threatening, before striking down to stab the charcuterie that lay helpless on the table.

"*Hello . . .*" Leonard whispered into the mic, "we are *Thee*, Rolling, L's."

"Is this a Spanish band?" he heard someone ask.

LaTroy whisked a single drum stationed between his knees.

Leonard finger-plucked the gentlest note on the planet.

The soft-lit den of vests and necklaces and neckties and suits and scarves took particular interest in LaTroy, constantly turning to look, sneaking glances then quickly lowering their eyes before he could see. But he did see. And he wasn't high at all, so he started to feel really weird. And then he wondered if maybe they weren't looking at him but out the picture window behind him. He tried to stare at the drum while he played. But he could sense a great many glances in his periphery. An ear here, a nose there, shoulders shaped in his direction, then snapping away.

Lamb meatballs rolled out of the kitchen.

Graham Berry called, "Meatballs *up*." He hit a little bell too loudly.

A woman wrapped in a wool shawl scrunched her shoulders up to her ears.

Graham Berry appeared in the main room again, he showed the bell and mouthed the word, "Sorry," to the band.

The band nodded, "That's okay," to Graham Berry, who replied with a thumbs up before also mouthing, "Sorry," to the Stevenses who stared at him with serious anger. The Stevenses replied with a synchronized head movement meant to guide Graham Berry back into the kitchen.

Graham Berry returned to the kitchen.

The main dining area now took the form of a galaxy comprised of lamb planets. These planets whirred around the sun for only a short time before getting sucked into the deadly gravity of toothy black holes—once great conversations had devolved into animalistic grunts of satisfaction. The band played gently ahead. Their pitiful outfits and general shabbiness added a necessary grounding element to the otherwise supernal ambience— sparkling chandeliers danced in the air and spilled blanket-soft light upon the hand-scraped wood floor, which did twinkle and mirror the lusty culinary energy beaming from clients' eyes that grew even wider as lamb racks were deployed from the kitchen, still steaming.

Patrons rubbed their empty palms together and couldn't help but sniff the air. The lamb ribs pointed at the chandeliers and were convenient for holding. Executive Chef Graham Berry created a ravishing arrangement of turnips, carrots, artichokes, and watercress to compliment the meat. Also, each dish did feature a hazardous slash of mint pesto.

Once the racks had been considerably munched, the Chef waddled from the kitchen. He dipped generously to speak and shook many hands and did kiss some cheeks. Before leaving each and every table, the Chef pressed his palms together in front of his face and bowed his forehead onto his fingertips two or three times per table.

A teenage girl at the table nearest the band asked the Chef to pose for a few digital photographs. She took one of the Chef just standing there, a la carte. She took one of the Chef just standing there while holding the rack of lamb that he made. She gave the equipment to her mother and stood next to the Chef and put her hand on her hip with fine elbow flair and said, "Okay," and her mother dutifully pushed the button. A flash went off. The woman in the wool shawl blinked severely. The girl never wanted the flash and went and grabbed the equipment from her mother and adjusted the equipment and returned to the Chef, who she'd left standing there. She put the elbow out and smiled the exact same smile and said, "Okay," and this time they got it.

"Get one of us with this band," she said.

The Rollin' L's were god damn right in the middle of playing a terribly appropriate song by Simon & Garfunkel that had possibly caused one of the patrons to slip into a nap state.

Graham Berry mumbled, "I don't know," as the girl grabbed the plate and the Chef and eclipsed the band. The mother got up from her seat, shuffled around the outside of the table and moved in front of her daughter and Graham Berry. The Rollin' L's were too sober to believe what was happening. And before they knew it both Stevenses were in the frame: Melissa and Dr.

The under 21 teenage girl wanted to do one in which she was also holding a wine glass. She wanted to do one with her mother in it too.

She turned and looked at the band.

The band stared back at her.

"Do you have a request?" LaTroy asked.

"Yes," she said, blinking.

"Ladies and gentlemen, we have our first request of the evening," Leonard whispered into the mic.

"Will you take our *pic*-tuuuuure, please," the teenage girl politely asked.

Leonard and LaTroy looked at each other. Debating, in the open space between their minds, *who . . . exactly . . .* was going to stand for this.

Leonard argued that he was the leader of the band and had booked these gigs and written the lyrics and should not have to also be part-time photographer.

LaTroy argued that fuck these people and he'd been perpetually glanced at and who cares if you booked the gigs you live in my damn apartment and I've been taking care of your dog.

Leonard handed the d45 to LaTroy.

The girl gave Leonard the equipment and showed him where to push.

Dr. Stevens handed the girl a glass of wine and joked, "Don't tell your mother."

So, from left to right: teenage girl, mother, Chef, Dr. Stevens, Melissa Stevens.

Background (not pictured): LaTroy, percussion.

Before Leonard Smock could even say, "Say cheese," the teenage girl's mother put her hand up to signal the universal signal for wait.

Something was happening to her, this mother. Not quite an aching, but an urgency. She put her hand on Executive Chef Graham Berry's sturdy shoulder to brace herself, whilst holding her other hand out to prevent Leonard Smock from doing his duty. The teenage girl asked her mother, "What is it?" but her mother could only look down, shaking her head not wildly but casually. She signaled, "Give me one sec," to her daughter. On the far right of the frame the Stevenses waved tandem farewells to patrons exiting The Wine Bar—oblivious to the urgent thing working its way through this mother's system. She could feel it mounting, moving from her stomach up into her heart. Her eyelashes fluttered playfully over fresh moisture in her eyes. She tightened her grip on the Executive Chef's shoulder. She used her other hand to support the considerable arching happening in her lower back. Her face pointed at the ceiling, scintillating chandelier light flashed into her eyes between blinks. Every fantastic flicker recalled the shimmering scenes from her diamond life. She seemed possessed by the ambience, unable to control her physical movements. Her lean stomach extended so far forward that she looked ready to float horizontally upon an invisible featherbed. Her nostrils gyrated as the urgent thing worked into her throat. Her face now formed an absolute parallel with the ceiling.

"Mom, what *is* it?"

"No . . . " she whispered back.

"Just . . . "

"Uhh-ahh-wait . . . " she moaned.

The nostrils pointed out at the patrons like black, empty, owl eyes and vacuumed air. Her mouth wrenched open, "Mahh," she said, her lips and purple tongue vibrated, also urgently inhaling. And in this air arrived a necessary reminder. Normal breathing no longer satisfied this mother. She'd gotten bored—even sipping the earthy wine while forking the lamb meatballs and fingering and nibbling upon the lamb ribs below the breathtaking chandelier lighting couldn't do it. She needed this reminder—a reminder that breathing is an ultimate luxury.

Her mouth opened so wide it hurt her jaw. Phlegm strings, thick with wine and lamb, measured the distance between her lips, "Yahhhhhhhhhhhhhhhhhhhh," she said, her eyes totally closed,"Yawwwwwwwwwwwwwwwwnn nnnnnnnnnnnnnnnnnnnnnnnnnnn."

It took a few moments for everyone to come to terms with the jaw-dropping impressiveness of the breath.

"Okay," said the mother, modestly, "let's take it."

The daughter held her wine in an understated fashion and put her other arm around her mother, who had one arm around her daughter and one arm around half of the Chef's body. Both the mother and Dr. Stevens had to bend their knees to bear the weight of Graham Berry's powerful arms. Both the mother and Dr. Stevens worried that grease from the Chef's forearms might rub off on their clothing. Dr. Stevens' right arm hung awkwardly in the air behind the Chef's lower back and his face twisted with disgust and his other arm went over his daughter's dainty shoulder. Melissa Stevens put her arm around her father's waist and prayed that it would be over soon.

Leonard Smock pushed the equipment and captured the moment: Dinner in Paradise.

The people in the photograph thanked each other for everything and quickly scattered. The band quietly went to work packing up its gear. They sulked soberly and exchanged knowing glances with people looking through the picture window, fantasizing. It'd gotten cold out there. Jacketed folks moved briskly beneath skeletal tree limbs. Their lips were purple from the harsh wind, thin and chapped and terrible. They just filed past like gentle lemmings, totally unaware that plates of Persian-spiced lamb shanks were now being served right next to them.

"I don't even know if I have *room* for this," someone mentioned, staring at the Persian-spiced shank.

The band lingered by the picture window with its gear all packed, just waiting, waiting for someone to come over and pay them, or thank them, or feed them, or tell them to leave. The band was having trouble functioning in the unfamiliar social setting, in an unfamiliar mental state.

Leonard and LaTroy looked at each other and debated their options in the air between their foreheads.

They could: Unpack and go on playing. Technically, no one had told them to stop. Sit down at the table vacated by the mother and daughter. Perhaps someone would reflexively serve them lamb shanks. At least they wouldn't just be standing there like two buffoons. LaTroy's eyes said, "Maybe we should just get the hell out of here, man," and Leonard's eyes agreed.

But as the band clunked its way for the door, the maître d' stopped them, said, "Melissa wants to speak to you," and pointed, "in her office."

The band nearly suffocated as it entered the office—there were so many flowers, big white lilies on the desk and on the floor under the desk and on the second level of desk above the main desk. Purple tulips lined the rear wall, enough to conceal the floor. It wasn't impossible to imagine that the floor had been ripped up and replaced with soil. An automatic overnight sprinkler system installed in the ceiling seemed essential.

The band lingered in the doorway, confused, afraid of disturbing the unexpected meadow.

"*Hi* . . . um, guys? You can come in now." Melissa's head popped out from behind a massive bouquet of white lilies, her skin glowing in dynamic contrast, her face like a radiant autumn rose beaming from the sea of white.

"That was really great."

"Oh, thanks," replied the band.

"Seriously . . . you were like, perfect, we could just barely hear you."

"Cool."

"So . . . I can't exactly afford to pay you, but I mean, I think you got some great exposure. And I got you this. It's from all of us."

"What is it?" LaTroy asked.

"It's an Old-World red . . . bouquet of cherry with a touch of earth taste, hints of violet, notes of graphite and plum on the nose . . . you know, a real toasty finish."

The band stared at the bottle, quizzically.

Melissa Stevens giggled at the band, "Not big wine

drinkers I take it?"

"No, not really," replied the band.

"Maybe you'll be more interested in this," she handed a business card to Leonard, "Colton Jones. He gave me that before he left and said you should call his office if you guys have anything coming up."

"What did he say?"

"That's what he said."

"That's it?"

"Yup."

"Holy shit."

"Call him," Melissa said.

"We will," replied the band.

Then Melissa said that they should celebrate and so she uncorked the Old-World red right there. She told LaTroy to close the door and pulled two glasses from behind a main desk bouquet of lilies. The room fell silent with the door closed and the sound of wine splashing into the glasses felt soothing, setting a fresh note to this new ambience.

The band tried to drink slowly but they'd grown sick of sobriety. Melissa drank straight from the bottle, perhaps because she only had two glasses, but maybe because she wanted to show the band her rock 'n' roll side.

Feeling he had a few glances to cash in, LaTroy examined the way Melissa's lips pouted around the wine bottle and the hollow noise of release. He watched her eyelids dip as she poured the warm, aged liquid into her throat. Melissa's rosy cheeks became even rosier. She watched as LaTroy stuck his nostrils deep into the wine glass and searched for hints of violet and plum. As he sniffed, he looked at Melissa, who admired his powerful nose.

LaTroy took a sip and said, "Mmmmmmm," in his most velvet voice. He did not reposition his gaze.

"You like it?" Melissa asked.

"Yeah," LaTroy said, "I like it."

LaTroy took a step toward Melissa and said, "Why don't you go bring the car around, Leonard."

LaTroy reached into his pocket, took out his car keys and slapped them into Leonard's palm without ever repositioning his gaze. The unflinching gaze informed Leonard there wasn't any room in the air for debate. The confident slapping of the keys signified LaTroy's faith in the unlicensed driver, it said, "You can do this, Leonard. You are an adult. You can drive a car. You *have to* drive a car, right now."

Smock grabbed his leather jacket from the coat check employee and put it on. He removed his all-black aviator sunglasses from the pocket and put those on, inside. He took Colton Jones's business card and put it where the sunglasses were. He removed it, looked at it one more time, thought, "Halleluiah," then pocketed it for good. He flashed the peace sign at Graham Berry on his way out the door. Leonard stood in place and let the street people admire his look. He wanted to exude an aura, he lowered his glasses a touch . . . sparked a J right in the fucking street, man. Now waddaya think about that? Badass. Smoke streamed out his nostrils and steam seeped ghoulishly from his roasting dome. The leaf-crisp autumn eve could not cool him. He walked to LaTroy's car with the gait of a man about to do . . . something. Or of a man who just did something. Even, in certain strides, a man who could possibly do anything—things, so far beyond driving a car, it was not . . . even . . . funny. He started the car, lowered the window, raised the volume of the stereo and the sunglasses of his face. "It's just a shot away . . . it's just a shot away," blared from LaTroy's speakers, blessing the street people. Leonard put on the signal that signaled right turn and then made a right turn. The right turn signal shut off automatically, indicating Leonard had completed the right turn. Leonard lowered the window all the way and ashed dramatically upon the street. He took a nice long pull and exhaled everywhere. LaTroy came down The Wine Bar steps with his drum. Melissa Stevens came down The Wine Bar steps with no drum. Both of them hopped into the back seat—Melissa, in heels, elegantly. LaTroy: excitedly. Inside the car it became clear that LaTroy had been using his drum cleverly, to conceal a spirited erection, what from exactly—can only be hypothesized. Leonard handed the joint to LaTroy who said, "Ladies first," as any gentleman would. Melissa took two, expert-level puffs and passed to LaTroy. The drummer's heart skipped a beat—she smoked with majestic nonchalance, the entire car smelled like flowers, her auburn hair glistened in LaTroy's face as she moved onto his lap and hand-delivered the joint to the driver of this vehicle, Leonard Smock, who had his hands busy at nine and three, so allowed Melissa Stevens to hold the joint for him. She whispered in his ear, "I hear this is your first time driving a car." Smock nodded his head yes. Melissa had the joint between her fore and middle fingers, with her thumb resting on Lenny's cheek and her palm under his chin. Her left hand moved from the driver's headrest to caress Smock's ponytail, palming its length, like milking it. She did not remove her lips from his ear, he could sense her breathing in his eardrum, "I also hear . . . you two . . . are roommates," she said. Smock nodded his head yes and she licked at his ear just a little and said, "Fascinating."

Leonard hammered the accelerator on his way past the town mill. The dark windows blended to form one black canvas. Cute smooching sounds pecked rhythmically from the back seat, counting down the moments to arrival.

"Is this your place?" Melissa asked, looking up from the sidewalk.

"Yeah," LaTroy answered, "you like it?"

"Yes," she said, "I like it. I've never been to Hamilton Hill before."

"It's cool . . . real cool," said Leonard, pushing his shades.

Smock, still holding the keys, led everyone into LaTroy's apartment, which smelled like burning incense and had an unmistakable theme of leopards and leather. The percussionist had also installed a highly sensitive lighting system that he set at dim. To show off this sensitivity, he first raised the brightness far too high, as if by mistake, *then* lowered it to dim.

"Ohhhhh, that's fancy," Melissa said.

"You like it?" LaTroy asked.

"Yeah . . . I like it," Melissa answered.

". . . Yeah?"

". . . Yeah."

The lights were quite dim. Leonard Smock removed the red rubber band from his hair, unleashing the full mane. Melissa sat on LaTroy's big, black, leather couch and flipped off her heels to show she planned on staying. LaTroy stood above Melissa, who tickled his crotch with her toes. The drummer took her other foot and put it into his mouth and said, "Mmmmm."

"Ahhh," Melissa replied, lasciviously.

The crotch tickling turned into a full-blown crotch massage. She pushed into him with the pad of her foot, noting LaTroy's exquisite length as she pressed up . . . and down. Smock giggled and rolled a J, stared at Colton Jones's business card, set on a rock record, then moved to the couch. He watched his drummer kissing and licking the heel and midsection of Melissa's foot, his nose situated between her toes, gathering hints of earth taste. Smock handed the fresh joint to the Sommelier and licked her neck then moved to the ear. The guitar virtuoso slid his hand over Melissa's breasts, pausing briefly, then palmed the inside of her right thigh while still licking her right ear, shoving the tongue right in, nibbling the lobe, whispering, "Does that feel good?"

"*Yesss*," Melissa moaned, passing the joint to LaTroy. Now the Sommelier employed her newly free hand to measure what the guitar player had to offer. She unbuckled his belt. Smock put his head back against the leather couch and ran his fingers through his hair, moaning the word, "Yes." Rock music played from LaTroy's speakers and smashed into the walls. Leonard closed his eyes and envisioned screaming fans jumping up and down with their hands in the air, the stage vibrating beneath him, burning hot, wet energy—his whole fucking world about to explode. LaTroy laid down a steady beat from behind—clap-clap-clap-clap, clap-clap-clap-clap, and Smock took the front as always, the lyricist, more glory with less work, but certainly no more important than the trusty drummer, consistently back there pounding away, taking his joy from the pleasure of others, two individual artists coming together to form a greater whole, jazz, skin, sweat, lips, sweet, hot, rock . . . rock . . . rock . . . rock. . . .

The band rolled over and looked at each other. They were in LaTroy's room. They were in LaTroy's bed. The sun was up. There was no Sommelier between them. In the vacant space left by the Sommelier, the band debated this fresh predicament. Smock's eyes wondered if he'd been dreaming. LaTroy's nose answered that he hadn't—a fragrance of lilies lingered. The floral notes had Smock smiling. He looked deep into LaTroy's eyes and said, "Last night was the best night of my life."

"Yeah . . ." LaTroy replied, whimsically.

The band chilled in bed a while longer, blinking at the ceiling, sharing and even relishing the silent aftermath, thinking all things rock 'n' roll. Leonard listened to his drummer drift in and out of sleep, breathing heavily and rousing briefly, rolling from shoulder to shoulder.

"You gonna call that dude?" LaTroy mumbled into his pillow.

"Yeah."

"*Nice.*"

Ring.

Ring.

Ring.

"Def Records, this is Celine."

"Hello?"

"Uh-*yeah*, hello?"

"Ummm, hi. Yeah. This is, uh, Leonard Smock."

"Hi. Right. What can I do for you Mr. Smock?"

"Well, I was told to call Colton Jones about a show my band is playing tomorrow. He left his card?"

"Is this the xylophone quartet?"

"What?"

"Are you in Quad X?"

"No."

"Hmmmm . . . *oh*, the ponytail?"

"What?"

"You have a ponytail? And the black drummer—that one?"

"Yeah, uhh, well yeah. The Rollin' L's."

"There's just the two of you, correct?"

"Right."

"Is this the black guy or the ponytail guy?"

"I'm on guitar. . . . I, umm, sing."

"The ponytail guy."

"Yeah . . . "

"Cool, right, okay, Colton wanted me to find out where your next show is. Your next *electric* show, he said. He said he wants to see you on electric. He said that specifically. He said he wants to see the drummer with more than one drum."

"Can I talk to him?"

"Oh, haha, no . . . no, he doesn't talk on the phone. Says it's terrible for his ears."

"Wow."

"I know. Cool, right?"

"We're playing at Lone's tomorrow night."

"Electric?"

"Oh yeah."

"What time?"

"We go on at eleven."

"Okayyy . . ." computer keys chomping, "The Rollin' L's, at Lone's, at eleven."

"Right."

"All right then."

"Do you know if Mr. Jones is gonna come to our show?"

"Mr. Jones is very, very, very, *very* busy."

"Wow, that *is* busy."

"Super-busy."

"At eleven, on a Friday?"

"I'm pretty sure he'll be there."

"Seriously?"

"Seriously."

"Holy shit."

"Good luck, ponytail guy."

Smock hung up the phone softly and dramatically. LaTroy had heard the tail end of the conversation. He stood in the area between kitchen and bedroom, looking at his lead guitarist, holding up the biggest joint ever rolled, poised in the air between them like a question mark. Leonard answered, "Yes . . . he's coming. Yes. Colton *fucking* Jones is coming to our show, man."

The band smoked down the entire joint, getting high as a kite, as a motherfucker, as a motherfucking kite.

Leonard's thoughts were like: This is it. This. Is. My. Moment.

He immediately devised the most incredible, inspired, and inspiring set list anyone had ever devised. He cancelled their Thursday show, telling the venue, "We have to practice."

And the venue said, "No problem."

And Leonard said, "I promise, we'll make it up to you. I promise."

And the venue said, "Okay. No big deal, man. Take it easy."

Leonard showed the incredible set list to LaTroy, who agreed that the set had maybe the most perfect combination of old stuff, new stuff, and covers that he'd ever seen.

The incredible set list even featured a few Patty songs, as they were known. Patty came over to LaTroy's to rehearse and not one goddamn person thought to ask how Jean was getting along.

Patty looked beautiful. She looked like sunlight. She gave the band energy. Leonard knew they'd need her to hold the attention of the mostly male, college-age crowd at Lone's. They tried a new cover. LaTroy rocked out this like, funky sweet disco beat, with Smock picking notes that made Patty's knees shoot forward one at a time. Her cute butt had the guitarist's eyes moving back and forth like a ping-pong match. Her ponytail bounced wildly in the air as she sang.

I look up to the little bird that glides across the sky,
He sings the clearest melody it makes me want to cry,
It makes me want to sit right down and cry-cry-cry.

I walk along the city streets
So dark with rage and fear
And I . . . I wish that I could be that bird
And fly away from here
I wish I had the wings to fly away from here.

LaTroy smashed the cymbals on cue and Patty took off dancing, jumping three sixty from her toes while in orbit around the mic stand. One of her arms went up with each bounce, the arms and the bounce kept time with the beat and speedy disco rhythm . . . Patty took the mic in her hand again and roared . . . it seemed impossible that such powerful noise could come from this creature, or sound so sweet. . . .

BUT...MY-MY I FEEL SO LOW
MY-MY
WHERE DO I GO?
MY-MY
WHAT DO I KNOW?
MY-MY
WE REAP WHAT WE SOW.

They always said that you knew best,
But this little bird's fallen out of that nest now.
I've got a feeling that it might have been blessed,
So I've got to put these wings to the test. . . .

After that fine, fine music faded, ascending to the ether, replaced by silence, the band sighed a collective comedown. They'd been to a new place. All felt it. Unnamable, unspeakable, indefinable, the unique and mostly uninhabitable realm of near perfect verses—visible in the pronounced fluctuations of breathing.

Patty turned and looked at the band and the band looked at her. They hugged each other with their eyes. They whispered orgasmic nonsensicals to each other inside the imaginary hug. The melodies made them horny. But not horny, like, for sex—horny to play and be saved. They were horny for peace, horny for love, horny for politeness, horny for kindness, horny for charity, horny for rhythm and horny for blues. They felt a horniness they wanted to share—a sweet, pure horniness, a dramatic and giving horniness, a gentle, smiling horniness. They wanted to intoxicate crowds with their playing and bring everyone to the horny place.

And that night Leonard Smock lay on LaTroy's couch and waited.

Unable to sleep, he just waited.

Staring at the ceiling and waiting.

Waiting for his big moment.

Waiting for his vengeance.

Waiting to prove he's not a loser.

Waiting to flip all those looks of doubt and pity into eyes of admiration.

Waiting . . . to *show* . . . everyone. . . .

He dreamed of everything.

He dreamed the biggest, most perfect dream ever and woke up ready.

He told LaTroy to meet him at the venue.

He put on his big . . . red . . . headphones.

He turned the volume up all the way.

He mounted the rosewood roadster.

A thick headwind slapped Leonard's leather jacket. Cold, raw gusts burned his eyes and brought water. And through this mist he watched the people walking the sidewalks with twisted faces, squishing their bodies together, striding desperately, puffing hot breath into frozen fingers, jamming hands deep into pockets and sipping hot cocoa like an antidote.

Smock turned back to the road. The music had him going. The rosewood roadster sparkled under the graying sky and sliced through traffic like a switchblade, "Who is this bastard? Who is this bastard? Who is this bastard?" auto-enthusiasts inquired, mocking the flowing, flapping ponytail, then forgetting the mad cyclist the instant he went out of sight.

Oh shit. Leonard was confronted with a line of people standing outside, chest to back, waiting to get into Lone's. Lone's lounge. Lone's lounge and tavern. Lone's club and pub. A massive space with a massive stage and always stacked to capacity. A college bar with college-age people inside. This is *the* demographic, the trendsetters, the most important people in the world.

Smock parked the rosewood roadster in the alley and entered through the kitchen—deafening noise, immediate and uniform. Can something extremely loud be considered white noise so long as it's unchanging? The sound of humans yelling unified to form one perpetual screaming. No one stood alone—shoulders smashing shoulders, pelvis pressing pelvis after pelvis waiting to reach the bar. There were males, considered men, with shiny hair and trimmed beards and vertically striped shirts—waiting to reach the bar. And other men, with slick hair and trimmed beards and vertically striped shirts—waiting to reach the bar. There were men, with shiny hair and very trimmed beards already at the bar standing next to men with slick hair and very trimmed beards. Some of the men at the bar had vertically striped shirts with dark colored stripes. Some of the men at the bar had vertically striped shirts with bright colored stripes. Certain others had flannel shirts. A long line of right elbows flared out to the side, the weekend formation, a planned pattern, shooting black licorice liquor straight to the liver. High five. Laughing. Smiling. Yelling ear to ear. Pointing portable telephones at-their-own faces to memorialize each unique moment. Gorgeous shot girls tended to the impatient pelvises. Tilt the neck, stare at the ceiling, open the mouth wide, and get fed.

"Ladies and gentlemen . . . The Rollin' L's."

No one turned to look. Or maybe they did but the band couldn't tell. Or maybe they wanted to but couldn't. Smock stared at the sea of people, nervous they might be criticizing his hairstyle. Without music the collective drone sounded like the loudest "OWWWWWWWWW," of all time. In the moments before the band started rocking someone screamed, "Take your shirt off," presumably at Patty, and "You SUCK," presumably at the entire band.

The professional band ignored the yelling. LaTroy smashed his drums and shook dust from the massive air conditioners struggling to keep perspiration off all the hot bodies. Leonard jumped in with his wicked licks. Patty looked like something else—like a real star. Sexy black boots over black sheer leggings going up to her frilly jean skirt below a showy black v-neck t-shirt. They were staring even before she started singing.

A different group of men took a turn at the bar. They had stylish hair and perfectly trimmed beards with vertically striped shirts, earth tone in color. They put their elbows out and pinched the little cups and poured. They took bottles of beer away with them and were replaced by guys with sophisticated hair and long, rough beards hanging crustily upon flannel shirts colored in various arrangements of blue, red, white, and black. They did some licorice and were replaced by these dudes with sleek hair and beards—trimmed tightly. But before they could order, a crowd of bigger dudes who looked freezing finally made it inside. The bigger dudes had shitty haircuts and beards that were completely shaved. They wore exclusively solid, pastel colored shirts, unbuttoned to display varying degrees of chest hair. The bigger dudes were angry about being forced to wait in a line and were probably also angry about other stuff too. They used their big shoulders to shove through all the smaller people and then wedged their way between the guys with sleek hair and tightly trimmed beards still attempting to order. The biggest of the bigger dudes yelled, "Ten shots uh Yay-ger," to no particular bartender while focusing on his reflection in the mirror behind the bar.

"Wait yer fuckin' turn, man," a guy with sweet hair shouted.

"What?" asked the biggest dude.

The biggest dude turned around and looked down to meet the eyes of the guy with the sweet haircut. The guy with the sweet haircut cracked a slick smile and told the biggest dude, "Nice haircut, dude." The friends of the guy with a sweet haircut all laughed at the biggest dude's shitty haircut.

"What'd you say?" asked the biggest dude, who did step away from the bar. He touched his chest to the chest of the guy with the sweet haircut, Ryder. But Ryder didn't say what he said. Instead, he pressed his chest back against the chest of the biggest dude, Blake. One of Ryder's friends called out to Blake, "Do you know who that is?" Blake's nose touched the tip of Ryder's nose. Each man stepped in unison from one foot to the other. Their faces shifted back and forth, like trying to examine each other's ears. They stuck out their chins and ground their teeth severely. One of Blake's friends called out to Ryder, "You don't even know who yer fucking with, man." Ryder nudged his forehead against Blake's forehead. Blake nudged his forehead back against Ryder's forehead. All surrounding parties watched intently. Blake looked Ryder in the eyes and asked, "Do you know who I am?" through gritted teeth. Blake also asked, "D'ya know who yer fuckin' with?" Ryder pushed his chest as hard as he could into Blake's chest and answered: "Yeah, bitch. You're the pussy with the *shitty* haircut." And with the last syllable of, "haircut," Ryder deployed his most powerful shove, which sent Blake stumbling back into his nest of friends. Both parties shouted: "ARGLE-FARGLE-GOBARGLE-BARGLE," and charged. Female voices called out for peace and love as glasses and bottles crashed and splashed upon the floor.

From the band's vantage it appeared that the rock 'n' roll had induced a celebratory mosh pit. But the wave of wretched aggression quickly spread outward from the epicenter—everyone jumping and shoving, tearing at threads, formerly fine hairstyles approaching unknown regions of unkempt.

Sweet, sweet Patty covered her mic and said, "Lenny, we have to *do something.*"

Smock knew it. He covered his mic and said, "I know."

And before anyone could discuss a plan for peace or tell it to LaTroy, Leonard Smock struck those most familiar notes, "OHHHHHHH, GODDDDDDD, PLEEEEEEEASE." They cried out from his guitar, begging like church bells on Easter Sunday. And Patty cried out too—with all her soul and all her power and all the bottled-up frustration of an impoverished upbringing.

If I leave here tomorrow, would you still remember me?

For I must be traveling on now, 'cause there's too many places I've got to see.

But still the anger spread. They couldn't hear. Or didn't want to. Or didn't care. Patty saw everyone shoving towards the center, veins swelling, fuming foreheads of red. The freakish intensity of the room threatened the stage. The band needed to hurry the song, to get to the rock 'n' roll; to get to the familiar part. Patty felt Leonard's guitar speeding up, ready for takeoff.

Bye, bye, baby, it's been a sweet love, yeahhh, though this feeling I can't change.

But please don't take it so badly, 'cause lord knows I'm to blame.

But if I stayed here with you, girl, things just couldn't be the same.

'Cause I'm as free as a bird now, and this bird you'll never change.

Ohhhh-ew, ohhhh-ew, ohhhh-ew, ohhhh-ew, ohhhh . . .

And this bird you cannot change.
And this bird you cannot change.

Leonard Smock's guitar snapped into powerful action.

LOOOOOOOORD KNOWS I CAN'T CHANGE.
LOOORD HELP ME, I CAN'T CHAAA-EEE-AAA-EEE-AAA-EEE-AAA-EEE-AAA-EEE-AAA-EEE-AAA-EEE-AAANGE.

Patty's chest *heaved* as she poured out her heart. A couple of guys with sweet haircuts standing by the stage looked up and said, "Freebird. Oh, shit."

LOOOOOORD I CAN'T CHANGE.
WON'T YA FLYYYYY, HIIIIIIGH, FREE-BIRD, YEAHHHHH. . . .

Smock soared. He closed his eyes and faced the ceiling. The phrase, "You wanna see me smoke this electric," flashed through the middle of his mind. The soles on his black converse sneakers wore out the floor. His shoulders and arms and elbows and fingers and knees all moved as one wheeling unit signified and timed by the ponytail that went in wild circles like a grandfather clock on the edge of apocalypse.

All across the massive venue elbows and bottles flew through the air. People pouring on people, demonic howls of fury erupted from the dance floor and polluted the music.

Patty closed her eyes. She stretched her arms out as far as they'd go and spun around the stage faster . . . and faster, and fasterandfasterandfasterandfaster. . . .

With every spin she asked for accelerated playing and was answered. LaTroy hit the cymbals again and again and again and again to punctuate every step of Leonard's rise.

The band begged for the crowd to get horny. They pleaded with sweat. They dreamed of one magical harmonious utopian experience where the crowd and the band form a singular mind melded with joy. And the people celebrate the playing and get lost. And they stare at the stage and sway. And they forget to worry. And they forget to get pissed.

The band's pleas for peace and horniness were answered by sirens. Red and blue lights slashed through the venue. A parade of men marched in wearing the same blue uniform with skintight haircuts and *mustaches*. They unholstered black bats and started smashing people. They wielded chemical spray bottles and sprayed people. All kinds of people were rolling around on the ground holding their faces and heads in unique ways. The men with mustaches kept saying the situation had been neutralized.

The band quit. Music gave way to chaos and fear and sadness.

Leonard Smock put his guitar down and walked off the stage. He moved calmly through the hysteria. The uncuffed clawed at their faces. Those who could still speak begged for another chance.

Smock ignored everyone in the kitchen asking, "What's going on?" "What happened?" "Que Pasa?" He instead grabbed his knapsack and put on his forest green wool cap and his fire hydrant headphones. But when Leonard Smock reentered the alley the rosewood roadster wasn't there. He stormed back into the kitchen and asked everyone, "Where's my bike?"

"What?" everyone answered, stunned.

"Did any of you move my bicycle?"

"No."

"Did you hear anyone outside?"

"It was there last time I went out to smoke," said the sous chef.

"When was that?"

"Not long, fifteen, twenty minutes ago . . . right when the cops started showing up."

"Okay. Thanks, man."

Smock sprinted down the alley toward the cop cars and professional personnel still parked in front of Lone's. The men with mustaches were shoving people into wagons, stacking them tight, telling 'em to shut the hell up. A pretty, red fire truck parked on the other side of the street even though there was no threat of fire—although two or three ambulances did arrive out of necessity.

Drawn to the flashing lights and loud noises, every resident within a five-block radius arrived to examine the scene—they pointed and traded hypotheses from the periphery. Smock shifted politely through this initial obstacle, saying, "Excuse me . . . excuse me . . . sorry, excuse me," as he made his way to the front.

"Uhh, *excuse* me," Leonard said, firmly, "I think someone stole my bicycle."

The officers did not respond.

"*Sir* . . . excuse me, *sir*?"

"Back up, son," said an officer with a mustache, not looking at Leonard, but holding his hand out like a shield, "this is a crime scene."

"No, I mean, what? Hey, uh, officer, someone stole my bike."

"Back up, please." The officer hardly turned around. He stuck each of his thumbs through belt loops. He sniffed the cold air. He rocked back on his heels and may have been whistling, though the sirens overpowered him.

"I'm here to report a *CRIME!*"

The officer rolled his neck to the side and spoke from the corner of his mouth into a black box, "Ten-four, the situation has been neutralized. Over and out."

"Hey man," Leonard said, pulling on the cop's shoulder.

The cop spun around and unholstered his bat.

"*Hey* . . . whoa-whoa-whoa," said Smock, putting his hands up.

"What the hell are you doing, son?" the officer asked, holding the bat aloft in a very threatening fashion.

"Hey, relax . . . listen. Please, I'm sorry. I'm just trying to re—"

"Don't you tell me to relax," the officer replied.

"I'm sorry. Please just listen, someone stole my bicycle. I've been *robbed, okay*?"

The officer took a step closer to Leonard, still holding his bat, and asked, "You wanna take a ride downtown or something?"

"I just want to get my bike back."

"What'd you say to me?"

Stray whiskers from the officer's mustache tickled Leonard's eyelashes. Brumes of coffee breath, visible in the freezing air, flowed into Smock's nostrils.

"Sorry, officer . . . it's just . . . my bicycle. . . ." Leonard recoiled from the breath.

"Do we have a problem?"

"No, sir, *we* don't. But whoever stole my bicycle. . . ."

"I think you better get outta here if you know what's good for ya."

"What?" Smock asked.

"You wanna take a ride downtown?"

"To file a report about my stolen bicycle?"

"You gettin' smart with me, son?"

"*Shit*, man . . . can you please just *listen* for one second?"

The officer said, "That's it," then grabbed a fistful of leather jacket and pulled Leonard toward his cruiser.

"Officer *wait . . . please.*"

The cop spun around and looked at Patty, standing in the cold in her v-neck t-shirt. He looked at her face and studied every inch of her slowly down to the black boots and then up again every inch back to her face. He did not respond but continued to stare, holding the leather.

"Officer Todd, don't you remember me?" she smiled. "Jean's daughter."

"Very *good*," Patty said, "Don't you remember when you came over to my house?"

"Yes . . . uhhhhhhhh, yeah, *Patty*, yeah, uhhh, I sure do."

"Why don't you let Lenny go."

Officer Todd released the prisoner, "Okay, sure Patty. Sorry, Patty. I didn't know he was a friend of yours."

The two songbirds beat it the hell out of there. They walked up the street and turned the block and walked some more. Smock removed his coat and gave it to Patty and rubbed her arms and shoulders up and down for warmth. They walked until the sound of sirens faded to nothing. They walked until the flashing lights disappeared from the sky. They took comfort in the absence of sound—their hearts and minds slowed, soothed by silence.

A few fugitive leaves tiptoed across the sidewalk. The season's first snowfall drifted from the sky—nameless, faceless, alleged individuals, falling at the same rate with one chance to dazzle the crowd before melting into nothing. And yet for the songbirds, the familiar flakes rose from the moment. In these pearly dots they recognized one of time's trademarks. As the sky blessed them their minds raced to recall a pleasurable history of snowy scenes, whittled to nothing but vague flashes by the passage of time—their actual lives, like the faint recollection of dreams in the morning.

And the songbirds rambled on, headed for the hill.

Smock inspected the sky.

Patty held her tongue out for snow.

They walked silently, arm in arm, until they reached

the mill where Leonard stopped and stared. Just staring. He walked over, picked up a rock and fired it at the vacant building and waited. It was too dark to follow the path of the rock—nothing but bricks. He moved closer and grabbed a bigger rock and threw it harder. He stumbled as a large section of bricks smashed apart and crumbled on the ground. He scrambled to collect three more rocks and made a feeble grunt as he threw the first . . . and the second . . . as Leonard reared back to throw the third, he was shocked by the shriek and clatter of massive shattering glass. He fell down and watched as a flock of forty blackbirds flew from the roof, their wings flapping the applause of a great ovation, rising to the sky, blending into the night with dreams and all the world's music.

About Atmosphere Press

Atmosphere Press is an independent, full-service publisher for excellent books in all genres and for all audiences. Learn more about what we do at atmospherepress.com.

We encourage you to check out some of Atmosphere's latest releases, which are available at Amazon.com and via order from your local bookstore:

Tales of Little Egypt, a historical novel by James Gilbert

For a Better Life, a novel by Julia Reid Galosy

The Hidden Life, a novel by Robert Castle

Big Beasts, a novel by Patrick Scott

Alvarado, a novel by John W. Horton III

Nothing to Get Nostalgic About, a novel by Eddie Brophy

GROW: A Jack and Lake Creek Book, a novel by Chris S McGee

Home is Not This Body, a novel by Karahn Washington

Whose Mary Kate, a novel by Jane Leclere Doyle

Stuck and Drunk in Shadyside, young adult fiction by M. Byerly

These Things Happen, a novel by Chris Caldwell

Vanity: Murder in the Name of Sin, a novel by Rhiannon Garrard

Blood of the True Believer, a novel by Brandann R. Hill-Mann

About the Author

Bobby Williams is an avid tennis player and philanthropist to the delivery service individuals of Southern New Jersey. He is a listener of music and a gentleman in town. He longs to see your smile. He is also the author of the novel *Two is for You.*

CPSIA information can be obtained
at www.ICGtesting.com
Printed in the USA
BVHW081635050521
606419BV00004B/784